I0654254

# DEATH OF A WANNABE

*The Frank May Chronicles*

## Lawrence Friedman

A QP Mystery

QP Books
New Orleans, Louisiana

# DEATH OF A WANNABE
*The Frank May Chronicles*

Copyright © 2011 by Lawrence Friedman. All rights reserved. This book or parts of it may not be reproduced, copied, or transmitted (except as permitted by sections 107 and 108 of the U.S. Copyright Law and except by reviewers for the public press), by any means including voice recordings and the copying of its digital form, without the written permission of the publisher.

A QP Mystery, published in 2011 by QP Books.

QUID PRO, LLC
5860 Citrus Blvd., Suite D-101
New Orleans, Louisiana 70123
*www.qpbooks.com*

ISBN: 1610270959 (pbk)
ISBN-13: 9781610270953 (pbk)
ISBN-13: 9781610270939 (Kindle)
ISBN-13: 9781610270946 (ePub)

This is a work of fiction. Names, characters, incidents, locales, and characterizations either are a product of the author's imagination or are used fictitiously. Any resemblance to actual names, persons (living or dead), places, or events is entirely coincidental.

Printed in the United States of America.

## Publisher's Cataloging-in-Publication

Friedman, Lawrence.

Death of a wannabe / Lawrence Friedman.

p. cm.

Series: *The Frank May Chronicles* (#3)

ISBN: 9781610270953

1. Lawyers—California—Fiction. 2. San Mateo (Cal.)—Fiction. 3. May, Frank (Fictitious character)—Fiction. I. Friedman, Lawrence. II. Title. III. Series.

PS3557.F811N34 2011

814.'33—dc 22

2011017756

*for Leah, Jane, Amy, Sarah,*
*David, Lucy, and Irene*

# DEATH
# OF A
# WANNABE

# 1

I could start this story at the beginning; but you see, I didn't
know it was the beginning. I mean, I didn't know what was
going to happen. I didn't know that my client, whose name was
Barney Bell, was about to become mixed up in a murder. So
maybe the best way to begin is with that awful night when the
phone rang, and rang, and rang. It was 4 a.m., and I was fast
asleep (of course). Somehow, there's no sound so shrill as a
telephone, ringing in the middle of the night, when you're
sound asleep. Anyway, when the phone rings, at that ungodly
hour, you can't help but suspect the worst. You reach for the
phone, and you're nervous: what could this be all about?

Celia—that's my wife—she woke up, too. Naturally. She
sat bolt upright in bed. "Oh God," she said, "it must be
mother." That was my reaction too. Celia's mother was 82, she
had a heart condition, and she lived in Cleveland, Ohio, which
is thousands of miles away from where we live. She almost
never called, unless disaster struck. She was from the old
generation, when long-distance meant something special. Long-
distance was only for emergencies.

So I was a bit apprehensive (as well as sleepy), when I
picked up the phone. But it wasn't my mother-in-law at all, or
Celia's sister-in-law, who also lived in Cleveland; or anybody at
all from the greater Cleveland metropolitan area. In fact, it was
Barney Bell.

"Frank," he said. "It's me, Barney. I'm in a jam."

"At this hour, Barney? What kind of a jam?"

"Well...it's serious, Frank."

I said: "It better be, Barney. For God's sake, it's 4 a.m."

He said: "I don't know how to say this. It's about Blanche.
She's.... Well, she's dead."

Blanche was his wife. I felt immediately guilty and embarrassed. I said: "Oh my God. This is terrible. Barney. You poor

guy. What happened....? I mean, was there...an accident?"

"Well...no...not exactly," he said. "Frank, you won't believe this. Somebody killed her."

"Killed her? What? I mean, how? And why, Barney?"

"This statuette...."

"Statuette? Barney, what are you talking about?"

"You know. A bronze thing. Bronze, yeah. Kind of...well, not big. That's what I mean. Somebody bashed her head in. I don't know who...or anything, Frank. Only: it was just awful. I...found her. Anyway.... She's dead."

I gasped or grunted or made some other noise, whatever noise you make when somebody tells you this sort of thing over the phone, I don't remember exactly what. Meanwhile, Celia was sitting up, absolutely frantic. "What is it, Frank?"

"Hold on, Barney," I said. I cupped my hand over the receiver, and I whispered to her, no, it wasn't mother, everything was OK, it was just a client. "A client, Frank?" she said, "A client? At this hour?"

I said yes, a client, and whispered not to worry, go back to sleep, it's OK, I'll handle it, words to that effect.

Celia said: "What kind of clients call you at 4 a.m.?"

An excellent question. I didn't have a heart to tell her, the kind of clients whose wives just had their heads smashed in; I just said, I'd explain later on; and told her to go back to sleep.

Barney said: "Frank, are you there?"

I stumbled out of bed with the cordless phone and went into another room. Celia sighed and turned over in bed. It was chilly in the house, at that hour. I was shivering. I didn't know what to say. "Barney, this is really awful."

"Yeah. Worst thing ever happened to me, Frank."

"Tell me about it, Barney."

"We're...in this house.... Travis' house; we were house-sitting, it's a long story...."

"Travis...?"

"Travis Hinchcombe. I told you about him; he's this zillionaire, and anyway, we've been here, in his house, maybe a week. Travis, he's...on a trip somewhere; and we were supposed to be there, look after it, you know? Blanche and I... we...were in different parts of the house, you know? Anyway, the way I see it, somebody must have broken in...and, well, killed her...."

"A robber you mean?"

"Who knows? Her purse isn't gone, I don't know.... Maybe he was scared off.... But...Frank, this is the really terrible thing, they think it was me...."

"They.... Who's they, Barney? The police?"

"Yeah.... The police, Frank."

"They think you killed your wife?"

"Well, they didn't actually *say* so, but that's what they think, Frank, I know it."

"Why do they think so, Barney?"

He said: "It's complicated. Look: Can you come here? I'm still at the house, Travis' house, and I really need a lawyer."

"But not me, Barney."

"Why not, Frank, you're a lawyer. In fact, you're *my* lawyer."

"I am, Barney," I said, "But you have to understand. Lawyers are specialized. Like doctors, you know? You need your appendix out, you don't go to an eye doctor. Me, I don't do criminal work. I never do. I don't touch that stuff. I don't know anything about it. It's...something, well, you need a real expert."

"Frank, can you get me one?"

"At this hour?" That was my first reaction. But maybe the hour wasn't a problem. For the people who defend criminals, I mean. They must get calls in the middle of the night, all the time. The middle of the night is when most people get into trouble, if they're going to get into trouble at all. Me, I never get calls from clients in the middle of the night. I do wills and trusts, some tax work, I do the paper work for small businesses; nobody calls you at 4 a.m. with a tax problem, trust me on this.

"I guess it can wait," he said. "Until morning. I just.... I guess—well, they went away, they won't arrest me tonight. I'm going to try to sleep, Frank. I got me a pill, a sleeping pill. Can I call you tomorrow, Frank, I've got to talk to somebody."

"Sure, Barney. And I'll help. I know somebody really good. A criminal lawyer. His name is Nolan Thom."

"Can you give me his number? I need somebody, real bad."

"Sure, Barney, hold on." I rummaged around, in the little

book we keep phone numbers in, and I actually found the number. I gave it to him. "Give him a call."

"Thanks, Frank," he said. "I feel lousy.... Like my head is coming off."

"Listen," I said, "I'm glad you have something, a sleeping pill, something so you can get some rest, Barney. I mean, are you OK? You got somebody with you?"

"No, Frank...just me, that's all. My sister, Susan, she was staying here, but she's gone, she left; there was just the two of us in the house, me and Blanche."

And Blanche was dead of course. I said, "Yeah, Barney. You call that number. Then, well, try to lie down and get some sleep. And, Barney, I'm really so sorry. About Blanche.... I know how terrible this must be.... You poor guy...."

He said "yeah" and something else, basically inaudible. It occurred to me then, that Barney certainly sounded distraught, but he didn't sound particularly *sorry*. About Blanche, I mean. He was upset, terrifically upset, but what was he upset about? Getting arrested, mostly; at least that's the way I heard it. Suspicion of murder. His new status as a widower did not seem to be causing that much distress. I can't explain why I thought so. A feeling, a vibration. Somehow, I just wasn't hearing grief.

But then, it was a shaky marriage. Very shaky. I knew that already.

As I drifted off to sleep—it wasn't easy—I kept thinking, poor Blanche. I knew Blanche. The late Blanche. She had been a client, like Barney. Not that I liked her. Actually, I didn't like her. But she was young, and very vigorous, and very much alive. To think of her, dead, murdered. It was truly awful, truly.

Poor Blanche. And poor Barney. What a mess, I thought. I was glad I could refer him to somebody, glad I gave him Nolan Thom's number. Nolan was one of the best. Skilled and experienced. Barney would turn the matter over to Nolan, and then I could wash my hands of the whole miserable affair.

That was easier said than done. Lady Macbeth had trouble washing her hands of her troubles, and so did I. But that's the rest of the story.

# 2

I'm writing this account, first, because I think it's extremely interesting; and second, because I'd like to get the record straight, about the things that happened, about Blanche's death, and what came after it—the way the whole thing turned out. In the end...well, I was surprised; even stunned. And particularly about my own role in the affair. My role in bringing it to a close. In actually *solving* it, for God's sake. But at the time, as I told Barney, I really didn't want to get involved. I never want to get involved, in something like that. It's not my style. But somehow, despite myself, it happens.

Let me give you some background. First, about me. My name is Frank May. I'm a lawyer. Member of the bar of California. Age: 44. Married—you've already met Celia. We have a nice, bourgeois marriage. We've been together 19 years. I have two teen-aged daughters. They are what they are. I love them, but sometimes they test me and Celia quite sorely. I could tell you more about them, but I won't. They don't play a part in this drama. Celia has a role, but a very minor one. I'm the one with a big part, the one telling the story. That makes me, I suppose, the "detective," in the sense of, say, Sam Spade. But please don't expect anything like Sam Spade. Don't expect seductive women coming into the office. Don't expect a lot of sexual adventures. If you do, you'll be sadly disappointed.

And don't expect violence—people waylaying me in dark alleys. For one thing, I stay away from dark alleys. For another.... Well, it just doesn't happen.

I'm in the general practice of law. I never ever take a criminal case; that's what I told Barney, and it was absolutely true. I've never handled a criminal case. I wouldn't know how to do it, frankly. Criminal law, it's a specialty, like patent law, or mergers and acquisitions. I don't do any of those things. But I especially don't do criminal law. You have to have experience. I don't have that experience. And I don't want the experience. The clients are, to be blunt about it, the absolute scum of the earth. I don't want to sound narrow minded, or, God forbid, like some sort of law-and-order Republican, but truth is truth. The clients are either dimwitted smalltime crooks who put on ski masks and rob people, or sell cocaine to high school kids; or else they're Mafia types; or major drug kingpins, or inside traders, or whatever. In any case, nobody you want to deal with, or have over for dinner.

I know that these people need lawyers. It's the American way, fair trial, and all of that. I'm glad that some people have the stomach for that kind of case. I'm grateful to those people. I'm glad, too, that there are proctologists in the world, and people who work in hospices, and scientists who study vulture vomit, or the physiology of worms, and so on, but it doesn't have to be me.

Not that all of my clients are nice people. Most of them are. Some of them are colossal pains in the ass. On the whole, I like my clients, either because they're decent, or because they're interesting. They can be greedy, annoying maybe; but they're never *dangerous*. They don't commit crimes of violence. At least I don't think so. You never know. But for most of them, it's pretty darn unlikely.

I have a kind of curse on me, though.... Or maybe it's just bad luck; or coincidence. For some reason, my clients, my nice clients, my business clients, my clients with wills and trusts and ordinary corporate affairs and house mortgages and tax returns and houses in the suburbs.... Somehow, they have this ungodly tendency to get involved in a murder or two. Either they're the victim, which is too bad, because then I lose them as a client; or, more often, they're accused of murder, or tangled in it in some way or other. I don't know why this happens to me. It's my karma, or whatever. Maybe it's just carelessness. Maybe a really good lawyer would keep his clients alive; or at least alive until they had gotten rich enough to make their estates worthwhile; maybe a truly good lawyer would so arrange it, that no clients are ever arrested for murder.

This account—you've surely already guessed this—is about one of those affairs, those coincidences. Specifically about Blanche, a client, who came to a sudden and violent end; and another client, her husband, Barney Bell, who was under deep suspicion of killing her. I know the police sometimes do fix their beady eyes on somebody who is perfectly innocent. Which was Barney. At least I was convinced of it. Trouble was, I have to admit, Barney certainly looked guilty, or at least extremely suspicious. You'll hear more about this, as I go along.

Anyway, as I said, I'm in the general practice of law. I have a small office, in San Mateo. That's a kind of suburb of San Francisco, down the peninsula south of the city. If you know the San Francisco Bay area, you'll understand. If you don't it won't mean anything to you.

I'm a solo practitioner, which means I have no partners and no staff. I share a receptionist and some space with two other solo practitioners. The receptionist does word processing; and there's another woman who comes in part-time and helps with the work. One of the other lawyers does divorces and that sort of thing, rich peoples' divorces, I hasten to add. The other guy is like me—he's in the general practice of law. None of us are big and powerful. The divorce lawyer is rich, I think. The rest of us make a living.

My office is in the downtown section of San Mateo. It's a nice building, well kept up, and it's got the usual mix of tenants: orthodontists, lawyers, small businesses. The businesses come and go. Especially the startup companies. They open up offices, give themselves names like the Xyloquex Corporation, God knows what they do; and then six months later they're gone. Whether they ever make any money, I have no idea. What they do is wholly mysterious to me.

Unlike the Xyloquex Corporation, the orthodontists stay. They have a steady business. And so do I. I've been in this office fifteen years. I'm as steady and long-term as the orthodontists.

But all this is background. Now let me tell you about Barney. He was a new client, a fresh client, and I'm always glad to see fresh clients. In a few years, I'm going to have to pay college tuition, for my daughters. They never seem to study, and they seem to display little or no interest in careers, the future, or anything else except the music they listen to (if you can call it music), and boys; but they'll get through high school somehow and go to college for lack of anything better to do. I've been putting money away, but tuition at colleges has become totally astronomical. So any new client is extremely welcome.

His name, he told me, was Barney Bell. He was about 30, I would say. He was thin, wiry, medium height; and not bad looking in a sort of washed-out way. He had very regular features. His hair was pale brown, or dark blond, whatever you want to call it, and he sported a tiny blond moustache. The hair looked styled, if you know what I mean. The moustache was carefully trimmed. His eyes were very blue, watery blue, the kind of blue you associate with real honest-to-goodness Wasps. Not that he was a Wasp. He wasn't born Barney Bell. He was born with some sort of name like Zizzowicz, or something even worse. I think the Barney part may have been authentic. If so, I thought, it was an odd name for a thirtysomething.

"Barney Bell is my stage name," he said. "I had it legally changed."

I personally have the name I was born with. My birth certificate says Frank May. Not Francis, but Frank. Plain Frank. Punchy and short. Maybe if I was born a Zizzowicz I'd feel like changing my name. Barney certainly did.

Barney was an actor, he told me. I have had very few actor-clients—he was only the second one, I believe. Actors are either very rich and successful, in which case they have fancy "entertainment lawyers" with offices in Los Angeles; or else they are poor and unsuccessful, and work as waiters in seafood restaurants, and in this case they don't have a lawyer at all. Barney Bell, according to his own account, fell into neither of these two extremes. He had an occasional gig, as he put it—a commercial here and there. And a few movie roles. "I was in *Sunday Killers*," he said. "Did you see it?" I had to confess I hadn't. He seemed very disappointed. "I'll rent it," I said. "What part do you play?"

"There's a scene in a laundromat. You'll recognize me."

I did indeed rent the movie, which was one of the worst I've ever seen; and I've seen some bad ones in my day. It was one of those movies with car chases and bullets and explosions and people shooting huge, automatic gun-like things and bombs going off and bodies all over the place. A thriller; very popular with young males, I suppose. I graduated from the young male category years ago. Anyway, the movie was something about drugs, gangs, and the CIA. The plot was hard to figure out exactly. The CIA was...well, never mind. There was this scene in the laundromat, where the hero is running away from some evil people who are chasing him for some reason or other. The hero was somebody like Matt Damon, but not Matt Damon; I don't remember who it was, actually. Anyway, Barney walks in to the laundromat with a load of wash. He's wearing a white t-shirt, and has tattoos on both arms. I have to admit, he looked pretty good. There's a young woman doing her wash, and he says, "Hi, honey," to her. She ignores him. He says it again. Then the hero comes running in, panting, desperate; he's somebody famous from television, but I had never seen that particular show, though my kids knew who he was; he was somebody "hot," as they put it, and they made oohing noises when they saw him on the screen.

Anyway, he comes in, and he grabs Barney; he's gasping for breath, and has this wild look in his eye, which is understandable, because a gaggle of really awful people are after him, with enough hardware to blow up Manhattan and the surrounding counties. "What the hell do you think you're doing?" says Barney. "Don't move a muscle," says the hero, panting. Barney stands there, sort of confused. All of a sudden this whole crowd of villains comes storming in, with Uzis or whatever they have, and the bullets start flying, and the hero leaps over the laundry machines, and the women are screaming, and the bullets spray all over the machines, and water and laundry come pouring out, and the hero shoots two of the bad guys, from behind a bank of washing machines, and then he throws a bunch of wet sheets at then, and runs out the back. Barney meanwhile is panic-stricken, and says "shit," and he's crouching in a corner, near the dryers. One of the bad guys—a very bad guy, too, with a black jacket, and scars all over his face—pulls the trigger, and leaves Barney in a puddle of blood on the floor. Completely dead. That was the extent of his role.

"How'd you like it?" he asked me, when I told him I had seen it.

"Fabulous," I said.

"That was a great scene," he said. "And I had real lines to say. Real dialog."

Barney had an agent, he told me. Not a top agent

naturally, not one of those big shot agents who represent the stars; but an agent nonetheless. I'm a little in awe of people who have agents, even when, as in Barney's case, the agent doesn't seem to do much for them. Barney obviously liked to say "my agent"; he was always saying my agent this and my agent that.

Barney at the moment had no need for an entertainment lawyer, he said, by which he meant of course the big firms in Los Angeles who handle stars, write up fancy contracts, dicker with TV companies, arrange endorsements for toothpaste, beer and athletic shoes and that sort of thing. If Barney needed one of those, he could get one I suppose. "But you wouldn't believe what they charge, man, they're robbers." Anyway, Barney had come to see me on a much more mundane matter: an estate. His aunt's estate. His aunt had died, and left him some money. "That was Aunt Martha," he said. "She was quite a character."

I pretended to be interested in Aunt Martha.

"She loved the fact that I was an actor. Aunt Martha was crazy about movies, television, anything. She went to all the movies, you know, she went to the early show, because it's so cheap, or if she couldn't make it, she went as a senior. It's half price. She really loved to save money, Aunt Martha. She was a widow, no children. I was her favorite nephew. Barney, she said, I saw you on television. On that dog food commercial. It was the biggest thrill of her life. She used to tell all the neighbors, my nephew, he was on a dog food commercial. She even went out and bought a ten pound bag of that dog food, and she said to the guy where she bought it, I'm buying this because of that great commercial. Frank, she didn't even *have* a dog. She threw the bag of dog food away. And for Aunt Martha to throw away something she paid good money for, I tell you, that was something."

"Really," I said.

I was having trouble seeing the relevance of Aunt Martha and her attitude toward dogs, dog food, and commercials. But Barney liked to talk. And talk. And talk. Well, Barney was a client; and he had a right to talk. Whether he realized it or not, he was likely to end up paying dearly for his conversations. If I charged him an hourly rate, that dog food story was, shall we say, worth about $100; or even more.

He went on talking: "She was much older than my mother, Aunt Martha was. She was really a half sister of mom's. They never got along, my mother and Aunt Martha; but, hey, nobody got along with my mother. Anyway, it didn't matter much to Aunt Martha, she didn't hold it against me. I was her pet, you know? And she lived here. I mean in the Bay area. She had an apartment in Daly City. My mother—did I tell you this? She lives in Fresno. God-forsaken place, let me tell you. She dumped my father years ago. Then he died. Married my stepfather. A real jerk, that guy. Now she's in some sort of home, God help us."

I let the flow of words wash over me. Barney was not a star, and probably never would be. But he had that gift of total self-absorption which is, I guess, part of show business.

"When I got to know Aunt Martha," he said, "actually, it wasn't that many years ago, it was when I first moved out here to the coast; to me, well, she was always this really old lady. She had her points, you know what I mean, as old ladies go. Dyed her hair though. Looked real fake. And she had a boy-friend. Or partner, whatever you want to call it. I can't imagine Aunt Martha having sex, but maybe that's just prejudice, you know? I mean, they have Viagra now and stuff like that. She was living with this guy, oh, it must have been ten years. I guess she was 70 something when she started in with him. He was no kid, either. He's 70 something now; she was 85 when she passed away. Anyway, they actually got married, a few years ago. Millard Hinchcombe was his name. Is his name. He's still alive. She met him at a senior citizen thing. I know the whole family. His son is Travis Hinchcombe. You know him?"

"Not really."

"You never heard of him?"

"No. Is he somebody famous?"

"Wow, I'll say. He's a frigging billionaire. Made billions and zillions, before he was thirty; some kind of computer thing. Then he sold the company, in the nick of time, you know? Before the whole market situation went bust. Some big company bought it, I don't know, Microsoft or Intel or somebody. He walked away with a real pile of dough. People said, a billion dollars. Maybe more. Honest to God."

Where on earth was all this leading?

Barney must have been reading my mind. He said: "You're saying to yourself, so what? Why is this guy telling me his whole life story? OK. Fair enough. Aunt Martha, she was married, I told you that. But her husband, Millard Hinchcombe, he's not exactly living on his social security. I mean, Travis isn't the most generous guy, but blood is thicker than water, you know? The old man is taken care of. He's got everything. Stocks and bonds, annuities, whatever. Some kind of trust fund. He sits back and the checks roll in, it's not a bad life. So Aunt Martha, well, she figured, I don't have to leave him anything, do I? I'll leave my money to my dear nephew Barney, the actor, the guy on the dog food commercial. And that's exactly what she did. So I'm an heir. A frigging heir, can you imagine?"

"You're her closest relative?"

"I'm close, and I'm a relative."

"I mean, are there other relatives?" I asked. "I take it, she didn't have any children."

"Nope."

"Are there other nephews and nieces? Or are you the only one?"

He said, "Hey, there are heaps of them. There was Uncle John and Uncle Sid, and then my mother, the half-sister. Uncle John and Uncle Sid, they've been dead for years, but they had kids and grandkids. She just didn't care for any of them. First of all, most of them live in New Jersey. That's a fate worse than death, if you ask me. I ought to know, I was born in New Jersey. Second of all, there was some kind of argument or something, between Aunt Martha and the two brothers, don't ask me what, probably nobody even remembers, but when they were alive, she wasn't going to give them a penny, and when they died, she said the same goes for their kids and grandkids. Anyway, who the hell are they? I'm the one that did the dog food commercial, hey, I was in tight with Aunt Martha. Well, I have a sister here, Susan; but Aunt Martha, well, she couldn't stand Susan. Can't say as I blame her. If you met Susan, you'd know why. She's a frigging phony. So.... Aunt Martha, well, I was the one. I mean, she could have left it to charity, but she didn't believe in charity. So I'm getting the money."

"Who was her lawyer?"

"Nobody. She did the thing herself. She had this.... What do you call it, a hologram or something."

"Holograph," I said. "That's the word. A handwritten will."

"Yeah. That's it. She didn't believe in lawyers. Hey, don't get insulted. That was Aunt Martha. Parasites, she called them. Bloodsuckers. Didn't like doctors either, but to her, lawyers were the worst. She had nothing to do with them. Wasn't crazy about accountants either. Had a dentist, though. Believe me, Aunt Martha had very definite opinions. About everything. I always played along. I always said, yes Aunt Martha, no Aunt Martha. I mean, who cares? Just make an old lady happy, that was my philosophy. Maybe that's why she loved me. And she loved me being an actor, you know? She used to say, my nephew, he's in Hollywood. And I played up to her; hey, why not?"

I nodded my head. "Anyway," he went on, "She loved me, she always said, Barney, you're the best. Then she died. Kind of sudden. Came down, would you believe it, with chicken pox. It's really serious in grownups, did you know that? Turned into pneumonia, and first thing you know, she was dead. Well, she was 85, I told you that, what do you expect? She died, and they cremated her, she wanted to be cremated, she always said that, cremate me, but none of that scattering the ashes shit, just plain cremation; and then, well, Millard found this paper, in a sealed envelope. Her will."

"Really."

"It said: last will, on the envelope. It was in a drawer. Place where she kept her papers and stuff. So he opened the envelope, and inside, there was this piece of paper, with the date on it, and it was all in her handwriting, one page, and she said, she was leaving nothing to Millard, because, well, she did love him, and he was a good man, but he didn't need her money, and she was cutting out the rest of her relatives 'for reasons that they are very well aware of' as she put it; and she gave a little bit of this and that to some friends; and all the rest, to my beloved nephew Barney. Me! And I'm the executor, too, can you believe it? Me, an executor. I don't even know what that means."

"It's the person who handles the estate," I said.

"Some guys told me, I better see a lawyer," he said.

"They were right," I said; and I then launched into an explanation, in simple language—I'm good at this—telling Barney exactly what an executor does and how he does it. Barney nodded his head, but it was plain the words were going in one ear and out the other. Barney was not good at focusing. I could see that already. I could also anticipate trouble. Executorship is serious business. I was afraid Barney was going to be the kind of executor who paid absolutely no attention to the sensible things his lawyer told him.

I made a mental note to ride herd on Barney. I would make sure he did the right thing. Barney might be—let's be honest—something of a dim bulb; but I could tell already that there was really no malice in him. Just an ordinary guy; even likeable, despite everything. I firmly believed in my mental picture of Barney, even when, as you will see, just about everybody thought him guilty of murder.

At least I understood (at last) why he was consulting a lawyer. He had to have somebody to help him manage the estate, give him legal advice, fill out the forms, make sure the i's were dotted and the t's crossed. I was happy to do it. It meant a nice fee.

"An executor, can you beat that? Barney Bell, an executor. I like the sound of that. And I'm the heir too. Hey, maybe I killed the old lady."

That startled me. It must have been obvious, from my face. He laughed.

"Hey, I'm not serious," he said. "I mean, I saw a show on TV, you know, year ago, maybe more. I was watching it, it was a mystery thing, a series, about this detective, and he has a cat, and the cat helps him solve the crimes, that was the gimmick; and my agent thought I might get a part on one of the shows; I didn't, by the way...anyway, there was this old lady, and she died of pneumonia. That's what they said. But in fact, they murdered her, with poison. Made it look like a natural death. To inherit the money, of course."

"Who murdered her?"

"I don't remember. The people she left her money to. Or some of them. You know how those shows are. They throw you off the track, then you find out, it's somebody you never suspected. But Aunt Martha...I guess I'd be the prime suspect, no?"

"Prime suspect?"

"The heir. The guy who gets the money. That's suspicious, isn't it?"

It wasn't, really; until he mentioned murdering her.

"Except that your aunt wasn't murdered," I said.

"That's what *I* say," Barney said. "But naturally, I'd say that, wouldn't I? And how do we know? She was cremated, I told you that; well, that's suspicious, isn't it? She's nothing but a bunch of ashes, in some kind of jar or something; nothing to dig up and examine, the coroner or whoever does that. No trace of the poison."

"What poison?"

"The poison I gave her. In her tonic. I read a script once, I was hoping to get a part, and this old lady, before she went to bed, she took a tonic. I'm not sure what a tonic is. It's not Gatorade, that's for sure. Or maybe it was a glass of warm milk. That was a different script. Anyway, there was poison in it. In the tonic, or the milk. Rat poison, you know? Kills them dead. The old lady, not the rats."

He had a way of playing with his mustache, I noticed. He would stroke it gently, first on one side, then on the other. It was a little, narrow moustache, pale and insignificant. But he obviously liked it. I noticed, too, that he was wearing a wedding ring.

"So," he said. "Now you heard the story of my life. And Aunt Martha's life. And...you know why I need a lawyer. It's this estate business."

"Absolutely," I said.

"So.... I'd like to hire you. You do this sort of thing, right?"

"Of course. It's my business. Could I ask, who recommended me to you? I'm just curious. People don't just walk in off the street."

"Oh sure. It was this guy I know. Sam something. Owns two tanning salons. I've been going to one of them, it's in San Carlos. I don't like to look all white and pasty, it's not good for my business. I got friendly with him, Sam. Used to talk to him. Nice guy. Around your age. He recommended you."

I knew who he meant. One of my small-business clients. Sam was the son of Russian or Polish immigrants. He was a fairly troublesome client, demanding, suspicious, an all-around pain in the ass, as a matter of fact. He was on his third wife, and he was constantly in trouble over his divorces, his tax bills, and various other items. All of which was bad for him and good for me. I really can't vouch for his personality or his integrity. But he was a client. I'm not in a position to be fussy. And now he had brought me another client.

"Sure, Sam," I said. "Sam Tannenbaum. Fine fellow. He's been my client for years. Anyway, Barney.... Let's talk a little more about your duties, OK? First of all, do you happen to know...or have a guess...about the size? Of the estate? How much did she leave you?"

"No idea. Uncle Hinchcombe, he'd know. Not that much; couple hundred thousand. But to me, wow, it's a frigging fortune."

To him, it might have been a frigging fortune; but to me it was something of a letdown. I was hoping it was millions. Fees are based on the size of the estate.

I asked him what was in the estate, what the assets were "Hey, I don't really know. Do I have to get into that stuff? I thought, they'll just give me a check. Hey, wait, I'm the executor. I'm the one that gives the checks."

"You don't know what the assets are? In the estate? The one you're supposed to manage?"

"Not exactly. Millard knows."

I made a mental note to talk to Millard.

"There's another thing," he said. "I guess I need a will now, myself. That's what people tell me. I never had one.... Hey, what's the use, if you don't have any money? But now...suppose something happened to me, where would the money go?"

"Do you want to talk about this now?"

"Sure," he said. "Why not?"

I have a checklist of things I ask people, when they're about to do a will, or thinking about it; by now, I know it by heart. I asked him, did he have any assets, besides what would come from Aunt Martha. "Hey,' he said, "my handsome face, that's my biggest asset. And my talent. But that's about the size of it."

I had serious doubts what those assets were worth; but I kept these thought to myself. I steered the conversation around to the topic of how he would dispose of the money from Aunt

Martha. "Do you have a family?" I asked.

"What do you mean, kids? No. I don't have kids. I'm married though. I guess I'm supposed to leave stuff to my wife."

"Well, people usually do. 'Supposed to' isn't quite right. In most states, you have to leave a share to the wife, but...."

"But only if we're still married, right?"

That struck me as an odd thing to say. "Why do you say that, Barney? Are you...you and your wife.... I mean, uh, your relationship...."

"It's touch and go," he said. "We have issues."

I knew better than to ask, what issues. Later, after she was brutally murdered, and Barney was deeply implicated, I was sorry I hadn't dug more deeply into this particular subject. But at the time, of course, I saw no need to. I thought it best to stay clear of sensitive areas. Unless Barney volunteered to talk about it, which he apparently did not. I started exploring various contingencies. "So, let's suppose.... OK, let's suppose you're not married anymore, you're divorced, or, for example, supposing your wife was dead...."

"She's healthy as a horse."

"Right. And I hope she stays that way. But things can happen. Accidents, you know. We have to bring this up."

"Why?"

"Well, if you don't leave money to your wife, then who to?"

"I dunno. Maybe my sister Suzie."

"Your sister. OK."

"I could leave it to my mother; but I don't want to. Wouldn't do her any good. She's in Fresno, like I told you; but she's in some kind of place for people like her. She's lost it totally. Doesn't know whether it's Tuesday or Wednesday. Alzheimer's or something like that. If they found out there was money, they'd just grab it. I mean the people that run the place. Anyway, it's in Fresno," he added, as if this was an important consideration.

I kept my mouth shut and waited for him to continue. He veered off the subject again: "I never got along with her anyway. Shit, now she doesn't even recognize me. I went down there once, Fresno. It was summer, it was so hot you could fry an egg on the sidewalk, as the saying goes. Actually you could. They tried that once, would you believe it?"

"Tried what?"

"Frying an egg. Or maybe it was Phoenix. The heat in Phoenix, I mean, it could kill you. Anyway, my mom, in Fresno, she was sitting there drooling, honest to God. I said, hi mom, I bought you some flowers. Actually, I picked them in somebody's yard, but what's the difference? She looked at me, with that, like, blank stare. Didn't know me from Adam. I couldn't wait to get out of there."

"So...your sister," I said, trying to get him back on track. "You prefer your sister."

He said, "I don't 'prefer' her; tell you the truth, I can't stand her. We don't get along."

So far, there was nobody, as far as I could tell, that he got along with. I suppose he had "issues" with all of them. Oh yes, there was Aunt Martha. That relationship had been issue-free. But Aunt Martha was dead.

He must have been reading my mind: "Hey, I know what you're thinking, what kind of a guy is this? His wife, his mother, his sister.... He's on the outs with everybody.... You know, I'm actually easy. I'm really an easy guy. You just don't know these people. I got friends, buddies, we get along fine. You should meet my friend Charley. I've got *lots* of friends. But these three women.... If you knew them, knew how they operated, well, you'd be on my side, believe me."

I didn't wait to hear how they had operated. Frankly, I didn't care. I said: "OK, I'm summing things up. You want to leave everything to your wife. But, if you're divorced, let's say, or she's dead, then you're going to leave your estate to your sister, Susan. That's pretty straightforward...no problem writing it up. By the way, your wife, what's her name?"

"Oh, right. Her name. She calls herself Blanche Baleine. That's not her real name. Her real name is Frances Elfenbein, but that's no name for an actress, even an actress as lousy as Blanche is. Do you have to use her real name, you know, the one on the birth certificate? She never had it legally changed. Everybody calls her Blanche, though. Like the woman in that play, *A Streetcar Named Desire*, Blanche something she was. That's my wife. Blanche. Call her Frances, she'll bite your head off."

I thought: she's no better at picking stage names than her husband is, if he picked Barney. Frances sounds nice. Blanche would evoke, to a casting director, a senior citizen, not a woman of 30; or maybe the woman in *Streetcar.*

"It's OK to call her Blanche," I said. "It's the name she goes by. Blanche.... What did you say her last name was?"

"Baleine. I'll spell it. People always get it wrong. B-A-L-E-I-N-E."

I said, "Baleine. It sounds French."

"French, Italian, I don't know. Something like that. It's some literature thing, something she got out of a book. She's tickled pink with the name. You're supposed to know what it's all about, I mean, the reference. Myself, I haven't got a clue. I don't give a damn, frankly. It's out of some novel she read in college. I think. I asked her once, what did it mean; she just laughed and said, you're an idiot, Barney, you wouldn't get it."

I was beginning to understand what Barney meant by "issues."

"She's always calling me an idiot," he went on. "Two years of some community college, and she thinks she's Albert Einstein. I quit after high school, trying to get into show business. She never lets me forget it, no college. She's always putting me down."

I said nothing, of course. It wasn't hard to see why Blanche might think Barney was, shall we say, something less than a rocket scientist.

But she married the guy, after all. She couldn't have had any illusions about his brain power. I asked: "She's also an actress? I mean Blanche."

"A wannabe. Like me. She doesn't even have an agent right now. She gets a few calls, but not many. We're both in this rotten business. Waiting for a break. It's a crap shoot. But I figure, success could be knocking on the door. Any day. You just need...a chance. It happens to people: why not me? Other than luck, what does Brad Pitt have, that I don't have?"

I thought of a short list of things, but I kept it to myself.

He went on, "You get the idea, we're not getting along too well, me and Blanche. So...suppose we break up. I'd need a new will, won't I?"

"Well.... It's complicated. But basically, yes. Maybe you don't want to rush into this. Maybe you'd rather wait and see."

"Wait for what?"

"For, uh, well, your marital situation to clear up. One way or another."

He said. "Fat chance. I don't know. I keep thinking.... Oh, never mind. For now, how about we do it this way?"

I said: "Fine. You're the boss."

He said, "I could wait, though. I don't really need this now, right? I'm healthy, I'm like an ox. I take care of my body, you know, we have to, show business I mean. I work out, go to the gym, lift weights, watch the old calories. But who knows? I could be in an accident, could be squashed by a truck, could be killed by a terrorist bomb, whatever."

I said: "You're too young to die."

"I could be murdered," he said.

I said: "Murdered? What put that idea into your head?" I hated to hear the word. "Look, Barney. Nobody like you gets murdered. People who get murdered, they're gang members, they're drug pushers. That's not you."

"You're right. Hey, I've done my share, you know? Smoked dope. But I'm clean now. I'm no gang member. No tattoos, I don't go for that shit. I'm Mr. Respectable, believe me. But actually...." And he leaned forward. "What would say, if I told you, I got some death threats? Honest to God death threats."

"Death threats?"

"I kid you not. Death threats. Regular death threats. It's because of this show I was on...television show."

"What show?"

"Complete shit. The Tony Crass show, you ever seen it?"

The name rang a distant bell. I had heard of it, vaguely. Maybe from an article in the newspaper. I'm not really a fan of television. I think television curdles the brain. It turns people into zombies. I actually read books, which I think sets me off from 99% of the population. I love to read, I'm a voracious reader. OK, it's not Wittgenstein that I'm reading, or Kant's *Critique of Pure Reason*; or *Finnegan's Wake*. But it's not Gothic romances either, or books about the six people you meet in heaven.

Celia and I are not really television people. But when we're very tired at night, I have to admit, it's easy to turn on the set and let your mind turn to soft oatmeal. Of course, the comercials get on our nerves. Sometimes we watch public television. It's occasionally interesting. Not programs about advances in dentistry; or "exciting new independent filmmakers of the greater Bay area." But things like *Masterpiece Theater*, watching all those beautiful English castles and so on. The acting is fabulous; and they have those great accents. Or we watch Sherlock Holmes. Or programs about the life of the cheetah, that sort of thing.

But Tony Crass? I more or less knew what that was, from an article I read once in the *San Francisco Chronicle*. Some kind of talk show. Or reality show. But I never actually saw it.

Barney was clearly disappointed. He expected me to know instantly all about it. He said: "Hey, everybody watches it. Everybody. It's number one, well, at least in that time slot. It's shit, as I said. Totally. But a gig is a gig. They have these theme programs, you know? It's what they call shock schlock. Tony comes on, and the audience, they just love him, they're cheering, shouting, all that stuff. So he announces the theme: Guys who screw their best friends' wives, or things like that; grown men who wear diapers, you know, something sensational. Anyway, he gets a bunch of people together, and half the time they start screaming at each other, punching, hitting each other, cursing, half the words get bleeped out, and the chicks are pulling each other's hair out, and the guys are fighting, and then some beefy guy breaks it up; the audiences love it, they eat it up, they're hungry for more. Garbage, of course; but, hey, garbage sells, that's the sad truth."

"And you went on this program?"

"Damn right. I mean, it's as fake as a three dollar bill. I got paid, it was a job. The night I was on, the theme was: men who sleep with their mother-in-laws."

"You mean mothers-in-law."

"Whatever."

"You don't sleep with your mother-in-law, Barney, do you?"

I didn't really think he did. Perhaps the two of them, too, had "issues."

"Frank, don't be ridiculous. Me? Of course not. My actual mother-in-law, she's an old bag, she's got moles, she weighs a ton, she hates me, I can't even look at her without wanting to barf, let alone screw her. It was all a fake, like I said. This old lady, on the program, the one I was supposed to be sleeping with, she was an actress too...."

"Let me get this straight. You're acting, you claim to be somebody who sleeps with his mother-in-law...."

"Exactly. The audience doesn't know I'm an actor.... Well, maybe they suspect I am, but what difference does it make?"

"And she's there too: the mother-in-law, I mean, the actress?"

"Right. And so was Blanche. My wife."

"Your actual wife?"

"My actual wife. I mean, she was acting too. We need the work, the exposure, you know? The whole thing was a total gas. Supposedly, on this show, Blanche is supposed to be my wife, and she has no idea I was sleeping with this old bag, and she finds out on the show; it's this big revelation thing, and then she starts screaming at me, and the old lady, the actress, she starts wailing and weeping, and wringing her hands, you know, and the audience goes crazy, people were jumping up, cursing me, and saying, how could you do that, you scumbag, you creep, you're got this beautiful wife, and you go for this old lady, and I say, oh but I love her, and I put my arm around the old woman, and the audience goes, yuck, and Blanche, she starts hitting me with her purse, and her fists, and calling me names, and all that: it was wild. Tony loved it. There was another couple, after the commercial, same theme; but they weren't nearly as good—they were the real thing, the guy, he was a complete dork, and he was really sleeping with his mother-in-law, some 50 year old floozy with dyed hair, and, frankly, they just weren't believable. I mean, a good actor beats a real person any day. The real people, they get freaked out on TV, or they clam up, they just don't know what to do. It's better to use professionals, actors, people like me, we know what to do, we can handle the situation, if you follow my drift."

"And...this program.... What does it have to do with, well, these threats?"

"I mean, I've been getting hate mail. Goes to the program,

of course. Addressed to Terry Bonseur. That was my name on the program. But they show it to me. People calling me scum, and all that. You deserve to die, one of these letters said. People like you, you're ruining this country, you pervert. I mean, they don't know my real name, but what if they find out? There's some real loonies out there."

"I wouldn't worry," I said. "They won't find out."

"You sure? I mean, they could hire a private detective and stuff."

I reassured him. He was as safe as a baby in its mother's arms. Nobody was going to kill him.

Naturally, I wanted Barney to stay healthy and alive. But I did have this secret thought—it was unworthy of me—that if somebody compiled a list of the most valuable members of society, the ones we needed the most, top candidates to be hustled into bomb-proof shelters, in case of atomic attack, poor Barney would be far down the list.

It's a sad fact of human nature that most people are a bit lacking in self-awareness. I'm sure Barney thought, as he went on and on, that he was making a terrific impression. Actors have to play different roles; but I was sure we were seeing the real-live, actual Barney.

Truth be told, I have to be something of an actor myself. Lawyers are like that. You have to play up to the clients. If a client realizes you consider him a complete unmitigated jerk, or if he realizes you think he is pretty dumb, which is what I thought of Barney—well, let's say it isn't good for business.

I have clients that I do get to like, I even meet the families, we go to dinner together, sometimes Celia and I even make a small dinner party, and we invite selected clients. Barney I thought was never going to make my A list. Still, a client is a client. I need the business. And, I didn't really dislike him. In fact, I kind-of liked him. There was a sort of innocence about him, a naiveté. He seemed to be stumbling through life, a foolish, fairly futile, but basically harmless guy.

All this was running through my mind. Barney was not going to be a major client. But he was worth my time, so long as I could get to manage Aunt Martha's estate. We talked a little more about her will and his, I explained a few things, and then Barney took his leave.

Of course, I had no idea then what the future would bring. That Barney would play a role in a drama of sudden death. That he would the prime suspect in a murder case. And that this would all happen quite soon.

Life is full of surprises. But you know that already.

# 3

I realize that I'm telling this story somewhat out of order. I'm using a bit of a flashback technique. You already know that Blanche is dead. You know that Barney called me in the middle of the night, to tell me that somebody killed Blanche—bashed in her head with a bronze statuette. Blanche hasn't made an appearance yet, in this story, except as a hearsay corpse.

Barney's phone call: well, that's not an everyday occurrence. Fortunately. It didn't surprise me, though, that the police suspected Barney. They always suspect the husband, don't they? And who else could it be? I gathered that, basically, the two of them, Barney and Blanche, were, as far as anybody knows, all alone in the house. At that point, I didn't have the whole story. It was clear that Barney was in terrible trouble. And needed help.

I put him in touch with Nolan Thom, a guy I know—not well, though—who is an absolutely first rate criminal lawyer. If anybody could help him, it would be Nolan. Nolan has a terrific reputation; and he tends to get a lot of very high-profile cases. There was this man, in Mountain View, whose wife died under mysterious circumstances. Cracked her head open, in the bathroom, blood all over the place, awful scene. She was a high school teacher; very popular; taught the journalism class, ran the school newspaper. To me, the casual newspaper reader—I didn't follow the case that closely—the husband seemed guilty as hell. Something about bloody sneakers in his car; or fingerprints, I forget what. There was a trial; and Nolan got him off.

Of course, Nolan doesn't come cheap. You want the best, you have to pay for it. Nolan was likely to eat up the $200,000 from Aunt Martha's estate in short order, or at least take a man-sized bite out of it. And I couldn't help thinking, selfishly, that Barney would be useless as a client when the money ran out. Then again, he'd be useless to me on Death Row, too. In either case, his utility was shrinking by the minute. But he was a human being, wasn't he? And, even though he seemed like a fairly dim bulb, still, in his vain, bumbling way, he appealed to me, as I said; like a little puppy dog. And I simply couldn't picture him as this savage killer, bashing in his wife's head with a heavy bronze statuette. I couldn't imagine Barney in such a rage as to commit this bloody murder.

Meanwhile, I had plenty of work to do for my regular clients, I'm happy to say. I had a particularly nasty and difficult trust to draft. This client, Phil Bush, owned a big restaurant in San Carlos. It was basic, diner-style food, cheap and tasty, always crowded; and Phil made heaps of money. The guy had been married four times, and had six legitimate children, plus one more born out of wedlock, courtesy of one of his more succulent waitresses. He also had an old mother, a daughter-in-law he didn't speak to, an alcoholic son, and various other complications. His estate plan, if you can call it that, was so involute I felt I needed a supercomputer to work out all the angles. Anyway, I spent much of the morning on this thankless job, tinkering with this clause and that.

During a coffee break, on an impulse, I called Nolan Thom. "Hey Nolan," I said, "how's it going?"

"Oh, comme ci comme ça. You know."

"How about lunch?"

I never expected him to be free; but in fact he was. "You're in luck," he said, "Just had a cancellation." We agreed to meet at one of my favorite Chinese restaurants, the Crystal Dragon, on El Camino Real, in San Mateo. It's a quiet place with booths, and it's never crowded. Sometimes we're the only people there. I've never understood how they make a living, but apparently they do. Maybe they sell rare Chinese herbs on the side, ground rhinoceros horn or the like. Lucrative but illegal.

Nolan weighs well over 250 pounds. He's about 50, he's slightly bald, and his shirt is always not quite tucked into his pants; he generally wears a business suit, but it's always rumpled. He looks as if he slept in it. Maybe this is deliberate, part of his image. He's one of those lawyers who's larger than life in every way. But he's not a trickster. It's all solid work, careful use of evidence, and great arguments, things that impress a jury. He's careful, he's intelligent. But he does try to project something to the jury, he wants to hold their attention; he's got a forceful voice, and a vivid personality. Criminal lawyers tend to be like that. They ooze personality. They have to. They have to be able to attract an audience. They want publicity. It's a way to get clients. They don't have people or businesses on retainer. I mean, how often does the average client murder somebody? You need some constant way to get fresh blood (so to speak). You need a reputation. You need a dash of flamboyance. You need to get your name in the paper. These, by the way, are among the many reasons I avoid criminal law like the plague. I have a very small stock of personality, and I'm saving it for a rainy day.

We gossiped about this lawyer and that one, then we ordered our food. Nolan said he'd like the lunch special. I ordered vegetables. At this period in my life, Celia was nagging me, insisting I had to lose weight. She was worried about diabetes, I think. In truth I *was* getting a paunch. I didn't want to end up like Nolan. Hence the vegetables.

After the waiter took our order, we got around to the subject of Barney.

"Man, he's in real trouble," Nolan said. "*Real* trouble."

I nodded my head in agreement. I said: "Your clients are always in trouble. They wouldn't need you if they weren't."

"Very true."

"Has he been arrested?"

"Not yet. But it's coming. I don't know when."

"Can you do anything for him?" I asked.

"I'm going to try. I think I'll see if I can get him to plead guilty, to *something*. Maybe involuntary manslaughter. Maybe it was an accident, that kind of thing. Or she fell and hit her head. Worst case, second degree stuff. They had a fight, and he lost his temper. The prosecution is going to try for murder in the first degree, but that's ridiculous. There isn't any evidence. I'm sure I can beat them on that."

"You said, a guilty plea?" I was a bit bewildered. Barney told me he was completely innocent.

"He's got to cooperate, of course. I mean, it's his decision."

"Nolan, he told me he didn't do it."

"Well, do you believe him?"

"I guess I do. You've met him, Nolan. He's not exactly the

ace in the deck, if you know what I mean; and he talks a lot. He has his faults, Nolan, but to kill somebody? To me it seems completely out of the question."

"Oh, you'd be surprised, Frank. I've represented people who, well you wouldn't believe it. You know, mousy guys, little guys, CPA's, guys with horn-rim glasses. You think my clients, the ones that are accused of murder—you think they all look like the guys in the gangster movies? Well, they don't. Not my clients. I get people who *always* seem unlikely. The likely ones, the gangsters, I don't get them. And I don't get the dumb kids from the ghetto who stick a knife in somebody because he dissed their mother. These kids can't afford me."

"But honestly, Nolan...this guy.... It just doesn't seem likely."

Nolan shrugged his shoulders. A plate of Chinese food arrived, and Nolan attacked it vigorously with a fork. I use chopsticks, myself. He said: "Look, I shouldn't be saying these things, Frank. You know that. He says, he didn't do it. Great. It's not my job to prove he did, you know what I mean? But, between you and me: *somebody* killed this woman. It wasn't Jack the Ripper. And she sure didn't bash her own head in with this heavy bronze thing. Let's look at the facts. Barney was there. He was in the house. And he had a motive. Sort of. He admits, they had a terrific fight that night."

I knew that. Barney had told me that himself. We'll get to this later. Meanwhile I said: "So they had a fight. That's a motive? Don't you ever have a fight with Vicky?"

Vicky was his wife. Ten years younger, and about a hundred and fifty pounds lighter. A woman with a lot of pizzazz. Feisty. She has a law degree, but she doesn't practice. They have six children. Nolan said: "Sure. We fight all the time, me and Vicky. That's not the point. Vicky isn't dead. She's alive. Blanche is dead. So we have to ask, why? Then we look into things. And lo and behold, it turns out, this dead women, she had a fight with her husband. That very night. People get mad, they do stupid things. Like killing their wife."

"Still, Nolan...."

"And the main thing is this: there was nobody else in the house. The front door was locked. He doesn't deny that. When the ambulance came, he had to open the door and let them in.

There's no signs that anybody broke in, no windows opened, nothing. And the statuette...it's got his fingerprints on it.... Just his."

"His fingerprints? What does he say?"

"Oh, he's got a story," Nolan said. "Not such a bad one, either. He says, when he found her like that, her head bashed in, bleeding and all that; and the statuette was lying next to her, he picked it up. He wasn't thinking of fingerprints. It was a natural reaction, he says. OK, maybe. I might do the same thing myself. But the fact remains, it's just his fingerprints. Now somebody else could have killed her, and wiped off the prints. Sure: still, it's just speculation. The fingerprint thing would sound pretty damning to a jury. Juries, they watch TV, they're crazy about fingerprints. They think they know all about them."

"The door was locked?"

"So it seems. Windows, too. No sign of anybody else in the house. Just Barney and Blanche."

I said: "Maybe somebody had a key."

"Who, for instance?"

"I don't know, Nolan. Maybe Travis, the guy who owned the house. He's got a key."

"Sure he does. But he was out of town."

"He could have given it to somebody."

"He could of. But did he? Again, this is all speculation. Look: I'm not the prosecution. I didn't ask Barney, did you do it? That's not my job. I'm just talking to you, Frank, very quietly. You were his lawyer. Now, if we stick to the facts, the known facts, they don't look too good for old Barney. I'm going to do my best. I've got some ideas. But it's an uphill battle, Frank. I'd be a lot happier if he'd plead guilty to something. Anything. I don't care what."

Nolan ate with great gusto. Usually, I do too; but I felt depressed. I picked at the vegetables. Normally, I'm not one of those people who can't eat when they get depressed. Quite the contrary. When I'm unhappy, I positively pour food down my throat, obsessively. Only not vegetables, but rich, greasy, heavy, satisfying food. "How about dessert?" I asked Nolan. But he had to get back to his office.

I went to an ice cream store. I had two scoops of chocolate ice cream, hot fudge on top, and sprinkled with copious quantities of nuts. Afterwards, I hated myself. And it was all Barney's fault.

Poor Barney. Was it possible he actually did it? Killed Blanche? Smashed her head in? Somehow it didn't compute.

I went for a walk. I felt I needed the exercise. I got back to the office late, sighed, and labored once more over the trust.

# 4

That conversation, of course, took place after the murder. Now I'm backtracking again. As you recall, I had had this meeting with Barney Bell. We talked about drawing up a will. I drafted the document quite quickly. After all, it was no big deal. Basically, I used a form, and adjusted it to his situation. Then I called him, told him the will was ready, and would he like to come in and sign it. "Sure thing," he said, and we set a time.

He was a little late, but nothing serious. We got down to business right away. I showed him the actual will, all nicely prepared on the word processor, and printed out neatly. It was six pages long. "It's just the way you wanted it," I said. He picked it up and looked at it. He had a way of squinting when he read a document, as if he was trying to decipher tough words. Maybe he was. I'm sure he had no idea what a lot of it meant. At times, he had a puzzled look on his face. "A lot of this stuff is technical," I said. "Don't worry about it."

"I guess," he said, "it's the fine print, right?"

"Sort of."

"A lot of legal terms, right?"

"Naturally. But the real stuff, it's just the way you wanted it." I explained what I had done, and why, slowly and carefully; and he nodded his head.

I had an idea he wasn't listening to a thing I said.

He said: "So, what do I do now? Do I sign this thing? And then it's all legal?"

"Well, we have to have witnesses," I said. "If you're ready, if it's OK, and you want to sign it, I can call in some guys, some witnesses, they'll be here in a minute."

For witnesses, I usually use young associates from a law firm on the floor right above me. It's a boutique firm that deals mostly with shopping centers. There's a lot of money in shopping centers. For the lawyers, anyway. One of the partners, Dan

Groves, is a friend of mine, went to school with me. Shopping centers have been very good to him. He drives a Mercedes, goes to very expensive Caribbean islands once a year, has nice rugs on the floor and modern art hanging on the walls in his office. He has two partners, and six or seven young lawyers ("associates"), who work for him. I don't begrudge him any of his perks. My impression is, he works a lot harder than I do. The young associates certainly do. They want to be partners, and they know it's a long shot. Anyway, when I alert Dan, when I tell him, send me witnesses for a will, he ships down three of these long-suffering associates.

But Barney wasn't sure he was ready. At first he said nothing. He turned the document over and over, and leafed through the pages three more times, as if there was something new there for him to see. Frankly, he was trying my patience. For a simple will like his, I don't charge much money; and I can't afford to spend a lot of time on it either.

"You think I'm doing the right thing?"

"In what way, Barney?"

"I mean, leaving money to Blanche...."

"It's your call," I said. "We went over that already."

"Yeah. We did. I know. But...well, things are deteriorating, if you know what I mean. Who knows what's going to happen. Frank, we're not getting along too good. I don't know, maybe she's going to dump me."

"Well," I said, "I just wrote what you told me. It's up to you."

He said, "Take last night. We had this big fight. She thinks I've been a lousy husband, you know? Maybe I have been. She's no bargain as a wife, believe you me. I mean, she's... tough to get along with. Me, I'm easy."

"I guess Blanche doesn't think so," I said.

"I guess not. Hey, it was crazy, getting involved with her, you know? I ask myself, why the hell did we ever do it, I mean, get married. Must have been, we were drunk. You know, she has a great figure, when I saw her the first time, I said wow. Maybe that was the trouble. She was in this agent's office, and I started talking to her, you know? We knew each other a couple of weeks, that's all. I mean, maybe I turned her on, I'm not bad-looking, and I'm an actor and stuff; and she was pretty sexy.

Hey, I'm a guy, I take it when and where I can get it. Maybe we were drunk. I guess I said that already. It's not like we didn't know each other at all. I mean, it was only two weeks, but we had a ball. I mean, we really clicked. I think she was getting pretty high on something, around that time. Now she's clean as a whistle. Anyway, we were in L.A., we were going out together, seeing each other, having sex, partying, and this particular night, we were laughing and carrying on, and we had this rented car. Make a long story short, we drove to Las Vegas, checked into a hotel, on the strip, and we were having fun there too, like it was one long party, playing the slot machines, staying up all night. Sex, too. I don't have to draw you a picture."

I had, of course, no need for a picture. I'm an adult.

"Anyway, they have these wedding chapels there.... It's nothing special, getting married in Vegas. It's like buying a pack of cigarettes, you know? Anyway, we did it. The next day I said to myself, what got into us? But, you know, I thought well, this isn't so bad, she's pretty classy, and I wasn't exactly going to throw her out of bed. I kind of liked the idea, you know, a married man, and a good-looking wife like Blanche. But I guess, she, Blanche, she wasn't so thrilled with the idea."

I nodded my head. He was off on a monolog again.

He said: "Yeah, when she realized, we really were married, I think it freaked her out. So far, we stuck it out. But it's touch and go."

I sighed.

"I guess we do have stuff in common," he said, "me and Blanche. I'm an actor, she's an actor, you know? There's not much business, though. That's why we do things like Tony Crass. In fact, she had another gig, on his show, besides the one with me. That show was really something. You ever watch?"

"Not really...."

"He's always got a theme, you know? That week, it was, uh, babysitters who get it on with the dad, you know, the dad whose kids they're sitting. Blanche comes on as this little slut—she was dressed up like a teenager, Blanche can get away with it, she doesn't look her age, and she's prancing around on stage, making goo-goo eyes; and the guy tells his story, he says, he goes out with his wife, to a movie or something, and he comes back, and he says, here's the babysitting money, and I'll drive you home, and they make out like bandits in the car. Then it becomes a real thing with them; they're in love and all that shit; and the wife, she supposedly finds out about this right there on the program, for the first time, so now she knows what's going on; and she says, how dare you, you two, and wham, bam, they're all screaming at each other. Crazy."

"But...how could she be on this show twice?" I said. "Blanche I mean. I don't understand. She was on a program same time you were, right? Wouldn't people recognize her?"

"No; they wouldn't. A little makeup, dye your hair, change the hair style, and nobody has a clue.... They do it all the time. Hey, it's what actors do, you know? They play all these roles."

About this time, I started to get a little bit impatient. I wasn't really interested in his work history, or the Tony Crass show. I had other clients, who were coming in later on, and I had work to do before they got here. I tried to get back to the item on hand: "Now the will...."

"I just don't know."

"You're having second thoughts?" Great.

"Kind of. Maybe...instead of Blanche.... I could leave money to Suzie. She'd love to get her hands on some of the money. Boy, would she."

"Suzie?" I vaguely remembered a Suzie, in his last mono-log.

"She's my sister. My older sister. Two years older, but she always says, when we meet anybody, this is Barney, my older brother. She's a real loser, Suzie. If I left her any money, she'd spend it in a month. One frigging month, I swear."

"Some people are like that," I said, lamely.

"She can't stand me, that's the God's truth. But you know, she's been living with us. Off and on, anyway. She doesn't want to, but she has to. She's divorced, twice in fact, two losers in a row, she didn't get a dime out of either one; right now she hasn't got a job, she spent every penny she's got, she a mess. She's...irritating, talks with a phony accent, talks about high class topics, and she doesn't have a pot to pee in. I could kill her sometimes. I told her, Suzie, get a job and get the hell out of here, you're getting on our nerves."

"Jobs are hard to find," I said. "What does she do?"

"Mostly nothing," he said. "Her idea of a job is to sponge off somebody rich. She's got all these airs. You'd think she was God knows what. The job she really wants is to marry somebody with money, so she could buy fancy clothes, go to the opera or something, and sit on her ass the rest of the time. If she can't get a husband, she'd like a sugar daddy. That's the only job she wants. Actual work, it's not for Suzie."

"She sounds terrific."

"I'm not telling you the half of it. Meanwhile, she's sponging off *me*; and I don't like it. But she's says she's dating a doctor."

"That's encouraging," I said.

"This doctor, well, Blanche went to see him once or twice. Ross Tanager, that's his name. He's got a real nice practice. Suzie could never afford him. But she gets it for free. He gets it for free too, if you know what I mean."

I assured him I did.

As gently as I could, I also told him that I didn't have much time; I had other clients; if he wanted to take the will home and think about it, that was fine with me, he could decide exactly what he really wanted. If he wanted to do the whole thing over again, it was no big deal. I used all my patience and charm.

In the end, he signed the will. He said, "what the hell," and said he was ready to sign. I called Dave, the three witnesses came down, two guys and a woman, all dressed in dark and tasteful clothes. These people seem to blend into the woodwork. They seemed totally interchangeable. I know they're real people, with real personalities, real sex lives; some of them like chocolate ice cream and some like vanilla; in law school, they were bright, vivid, highly individual; they wore blue jeans and flipflops, they went to parties, they argued about politics. But in this unnatural habitat, the office, spending day after day on the legal affairs of shopping malls, they come to look like peas in a pod. On the outside, anyway. Doesn't matter. We went through the ceremony, Barney signed, the three witnesses signed, and the bloody deed was done. I kept the original. Barney took home a copy.

Two weeks later, Blanche was murdered. Her head smashed in. And Barney, as I said, was Suspect No. 1. What a world.

# 5

Up to that point—the point I just described—I had never met Blanche. All I had to go on, about Blanche, was what Barney had told me. As we all know, there are two sides to every story. I never thought I would get Blanche's side, or even meet her; but in fact it happened.

It was a few days after Barney executed his will. Blanche called me on the phone. She introduced herself, and said she wondered if it was possible to come and see me. "You did a will for my husband, Barney Bell."

"That's right."

She laughed—oddly. I hadn't said anything funny. "Well, if Barney has a will, I had better have one too, don't you think?"

"Why not, Miss...."

"Baleine. But you can call me Blanche."

I thought to myself, Barney's not a total loss: he brought me a client. I was a little apprehensive, I have to admit. Barney said, they weren't getting along. It was perfectly normal to do wills for both a husband and a wife—I do it all the time—but these two seemed to be teetering on the edge of a divorce, which is always a bit messy, and sometimes you're forced to choose sides.

Even then, it's not a problem, so long as they're still friendly. Which doesn't always happen. Our next door neighbors, the Gumps, got divorced; he moved out, into the arms of his secretary; she stayed behind with two small kids. Celia is friendly with her, asks her over for coffee, and tries to be helpful; but all Brenda Gump can talk about, night and day, is what a bastard her husband is, and how could he do this to her, and how the kids are suffering, and does he care, and so on. Then he, Jack, the bastard in question, decided he and I were still friends, and he calls me to have lunch, and even dropped in to the office one day. "Brenda and I aren't together anymore," he said. "But you and me, Frank, we can still be the same."

The fact is, it couldn't be the same. No, not with Brenda right next door, watching; and Celia pouring coffee for her, every once in a while in the evening; and our older daughter picking up spare change as a babysitter for poor Brenda, on the rare occasions when Brenda got to go out and "have a little fun for a change."

But you're not interested in Brenda and Jack. Or in Michele, the shameless hussy that broke up their marriage. You're more interested in Blanche.

We made an appointment for later in the week, and she showed up right on time.

She was a striking redhead, tall and slim, 30 or a year or two older. She had good features—she was basically attractive; and she had a terrific figure, just like Barney said. She looked like a woman who spent a lot of time making herself beautiful. The effort, I must say, paid off. She had the look of an actress, or what I imagine an actress must look like. She was elegantly dressed too. At least I thought so. Celia says I have no clothes sense at all. Celia, like a lot of women, can tell you what a dress must have cost, down to the last dollar, simply by looking at it. She can tell whether a necklace is really 24 carat gold from a distance of 50 yards.

Celia only buys clothes when they're on sale. Which happens quite frequently. But she has definite opinions about quality.

Blanche and I began with small talk, the weather, the problem she had parking—the usual things. Then she said, "I call myself Blanche. Blanche Baleine. That's my stage name; but I use it all the time. Credit cards, everything. Actually, my real name, the one I was born with, is Frances Elfenbein."

I nodded my head.

"I never had it legally changed," she said. "Neither did Barney. You know, Barney isn't his real name either, he had this stupid Polish name. Anyway, we both have the same initials now, BB. Cute, no? It would save money on monogrammed bedsheets, if we had monogrammed bedsheets, which we don't."

She gave a hoarse little laugh. She had a funny way of

laughing, with the edges of her mouth curling up. It was a full mouth, sensuous I thought, although I have no business thinking such thoughts. She had lipstick on, bright red, flame red I would say.

Of course, I already knew the name Barney wasn't authentic. It was a stage name, which (to me, anyway) evoked either a caveman, a bumbling southern deputy, or a purple dinosaur. At least her name had a certain dramatic irony. And it had two literary references—one to Blanche Dubois, in *A Streetcar Named Desire*, and the other, God help us, to *Moby Dick*.

She went on: "Barney told me about the will. He was quite excited about it. Sometimes he's like a small child, the oddest things really tickle him. Of course, there's the money, the money he inherited. That would tickle anybody. Anyway, I was thinking, possibly I need a will, too. It's a coincidence, but we—Barney and I—have a very similar situation. Everybody says, I should consult a lawyer. There's no lawyers in my family. I wasn't going to look in the yellow pages, was I? So, when Barney came to you.... I thought: well, here's a lawyer. Not that I trust Barney's judgment on this. Or anything. You could be a total washout as a lawyer. He got your name from some creep who runs a tanning salon, that's hardly the way to go about it. But I looked you up, on the web. You seemed at least respectable."

"I try."

"When we get down to it, I'll know, if you're any good. I don't know anything about law, but I can read character. I'm not easy to fool."

"I won't fool you. I don't fool my clients," I said.

She said: "I know I could go to one of those big firms. To be honest, I don't want to pay the kind of money they want. They charge a fortune in San Francisco, the downtown firms—that's what I hear. I don't need that. Anyway, I want something more private, more personal, more one-on-one. You know what I mean."

I said I knew what she meant.

She went on: "I have to ask, is there some reason you can't represent us both? What I mean is: do I need my own separate lawyer?"

"Well.... no, not at this stage...."

"What stage is this?"

I felt foolish. I had been thinking bad thoughts. "I mean," I said, "it's pretty standard, I make out a will for the wife, then for the husband, or for the husband, and then for the wife. It's the usual way, really. But...well, suppose you two broke up, and it was a question of, support payments, dividing the property, who gets the car, that sort of thing; then maybe two lawyers would be better."

She laughed. "If we broke up? Is that something you bring up with all your married clients?"

"Not if he's 85, she's 82, and they've been married 60 years...."

"And in our case? Barney and me?"

I was embarrassed. I muttered something about younger couples, the high divorce rate, and how a lawyer has to think of every contingency, and so on.

She seemed to enjoy my discomfiture. But then she said: "Listen. Don't be embarrassed. Barney can't keep his mouth shut. I'm sure you noticed that, I'm sure he talked about our marriage. Our wonderful marriage."

I said: "He made some comments, yes."

"That's Barney. I'm sure they weren't favorable. He went on and on, didn't he? About me, our marriage, I wouldn't be surprised if he talked about our sex life. That's Barney."

I didn't know quite what to say. I groped for words, but nothing came to mind. Finally I said something inane about how difficult it was sometimes for people to get along, marriage wasn't easy, and it takes time to adjust.

She laughed again. She had long fingers, and a way of fidgeting with them. She was rubbing the ring on the fourth finger, left hand. The wedding band. A plain gold band. Was that just a nervous habit, or was she making a statement?

She said: "You don't have to commiserate. It's a lousy marriage, but what else is new? Are there any good ones? Marriages, I mean. I don't know of any. Why do people get married altogether? You have to be crazy."

I just nodded my head. I try not to disagree with clients.

She said: "You don't have to comment. I'm just talking. Look: Barney and I, well, we're still together, if that's what you're wondering. We live in the same house. We eat at the same table. We sleep in the same bed. We even talk to each other, once in a while. It's not great, but for now, let's leave it at that."

This was hardly a ringing endorsement. In a way, it was none of my business. But if she was going to execute a will, her personal life was relevant, after all. "Should we talk about the will?" I said.

"Sure," she said. "My first question is, do I have to use my real name, the one on my birth certificate? As I told you, I never had my name officially changed. Do I have to write my will as Frances Elfenbein?"

"No; it's not necessary. It's up to you. If everybody calls you Blanche Baleine, then your name is Blanche Baleine, and that's that."

"Even though it's not my legal name?"

"It doesn't matter. I mean, not for this purpose. For a will."

She seemed pleased. I went on: "I have a checklist.... Things I have to ask. Family information, what you have, your assets, that sort of thing, who you want to leave your money to, any special terms and conditions."

She nodded her head. "I understand. Where do we begin?"

"Well, with your family situation. If that's relevant."

"Relevant?"

I said: "Sometimes it isn't. If you said, I want to leave everything to charity, then it's less relevant...."

"That'll be the day."

"OK. So tell me, what you have, who you want to leave it to, and so on."

She crossed her legs. "I'll start with my background. Do you want to take notes?"

She seemed to expect me to take notes, so I opened a desk drawer, took out a pad of lined yellow paper, picked up a ballpoint pen, wrote her name at the top of the page, and started doodling.

"I was born in Dayton, Ohio," she said. "I grew up in Los Angeles, though. I was six or seven years old when we moved. I've been here in California ever since. I'm registered to vote here. When I feel like it,. Right now, we've got an apartment, in Mountain View. Anyway, I'm a California resident."

"Uh huh," I said, writing some of this down.

"My father was in the restaurant business. He owned a restaurant, German restaurant. He was German. Elfenbein is a German name. He was born in Germany, came to the states when he was two or three. Married an American woman, my mother. She had a little money, from her grandmother. Anyway, he went into the restaurant business. In Los Angeles.... To tell you the truth, I can't stand German food. Some people seem to like it. All that sausage and cabbage and dumplings. It sits in your stomach like lead weights. I was vegan for a year."

One of my daughters had been vegan for two months. An absolute nightmare.

She went on: "When I wouldn't eat the food, my father was so mad he could spit nails. He took it personally. Oh, but he wasn't just mad at me. He was having a hard time. Everything was going wrong, in the family. My mother and father.... They did nothing but yell at each other.... She didn't like the food either, but that wasn't the issue. They just didn't like each other. Who knows why people don't get along."

"Right."

"The food *was* wretched, by the way. But anyway...the family was hell. God knows why they got married in the first place. They had nothing in common, I mean nothing. My mother had airs, she was a Presbyterian, kept talking about her ancestors, and he was a crude, fat vulgarian. Anyway, I was thirteen at the time, the time of the divorce, I was going through a phase, not just the vegan thing. My brother Max was eight. My father moved out. He just packed a suitcase and left. My mother.... Basically, she said, good riddance."

"You have a brother."

"One brother, yes. Max. As I said, he was eight when they split up. Max, he always blames the divorce, for everything.... Ruined his life, he said. He was a real handful as an adolescent. Drove my mother crazy. Truancy, shoplifting, smoking dope, the whole thing. Got some girl pregnant when he was 17. You know, the usual story."

The "usual story"? Is this what lay ahead for me—for my daughters—truancy, shoplifting, dope, and finally pregnancy?

"Father made a lot of money," she said, "on his restaurant, believe it or not. He had two branches, one in Long Beach, one in Pasadena. Lots of people ate there. There's no accounting for taste. People lined up to get in, God knows why. It was heart-burn city. Anyway, some big chain bought him out.... He was glad to retire, the restaurant business is murder, it's one of the toughest there is. He managed one of the restaurants for a while, then he quit. Two years ago, he died. Cancer of the liver."

"I'm awfully sorry."

"Don't be sorry. I hardly knew the man. I mean, Max and I went with mother, after the divorce. She got custody. Who knows if he even wanted us. We didn't see much of him after that. He never came around, never visited. Then he married some woman, maybe he had been fooling around with her, she worked in one of his restaurants. She dumped him after a year or two, ran off with a cab driver. Mother moved to San Jose and got a job. We saw our father, oh, maybe once a year. Max never saw him at all; he didn't want to. The feeling was mutual. I think he was disgusted, I mean, my father was disgusted; he thought his son was a juvenile delinquent. Which of course he was, at the time. Mother had to pay for an abortion, for this girl, the one he got pregnant. A real slut, by the way. Ugly, lots of acne, a typical high school tramp; but she was an easy lay, that's what attracted Max.

"Anyway: that was Max. A lot of water under the bridge, since then. I've kind of lost touch. Haven't seen him for years. He joined some kind of crazy cult, some sort of swami, a faker no doubt; they spend the whole day chanting and peeling potatoes. Well, at least it got him off drugs and alcohol. I think. He's got an actual job somewhere. Maybe this cult arranged it for him, the swami or somebody. He wrote me a letter, but he didn't give any more details. The point is, father thought Max was a total loser. A bum, a disgrace. And it didn't help when he joined this cult. That was just another disgusting thing, as far as my father was concerned. So.... there was just me, in a way. I wasn't even nice to him, my father, the few times I saw him. I thought he was an asshole. I used to just snarl and sulk. When he died, I didn't even go to the funeral. My mother said, I had to, but I refused. So...it was a big fat surprise when I found out that the old creep had, well, left me his money."

"I see. He had a will?"

"Yes. As I told you, my father married again, this woman who was some kind of cashier, maybe she was the bitch that broke up his marriage, but anyway, it didn't last. I said that, didn't I? He divorced her. Two marriages was enough. He never remarried. So he was single when he died. He had a brother, Dieter, my uncle, a bachelor, Dieter was older than my father. He had some kind of small business, lost his shirt, dad was supporting him. The will left the money to Dieter, my uncle, some sort of trust. Dieter gets the money, the income, as long as he lives. When he dies, the money comes to me. And it's almost a million dollars."

"And...Max...."

"Not a cent. Nothing. Mentioned his name in the will, said something nasty, like, I'm leaving you nothing, you know why, you're worthless, you disappointed me, etc.."

"Your brother.... Did he resent this? I mean, that you're going to get this money, and he isn't?"

"I haven't seen him, for years. I told you that. No communication, except for this one letter; but it had no return address. I don't even know if he's aware about his uncle, or the money. We don't know where Max lives, what his phone number is, nothing. Anyway, the money is going to be mine. It's a coincidence, it's like Barney's situation. His aunt didn't leave a penny to Suzie. That's his sister. She's furious, but she doesn't let on. She hates Barney like poison, she resents him, she's insanely jealous. Can you imagine, she's jealous of Barney? Now that's a joke. Anyway, she's trapped; she has nowhere to go. Of course, it's her own damn fault, she's screwed up her life; still, there she is."

I steered the conversation back to the subject at hand. "Your father's money. You say, you get it, after your uncle dies?"

"It says in the will, after he dies.... I have a letter here, from my father's lawyer...if I live six months after my uncle dies, then I get the money."

She showed me the letter. It was exactly as she said, couched in that thick, gooey jargon lawyers use. Lay people find this jargon exasperating. Myself, I find it exasperating, too. But in fact, it's very hard sometimes to say things in clear, simple English. Legal things, anyway. We've got to be accurate, and that's not as easy as you would think.

The relevant sentence in the letter was this: "You are to

receive the entire remainder, after the life estate, provided you survive your uncle for a period of six months from the time of his demise; and if not, then the estate passes to your issue *per stirpes*; and in default of any such issue surviving upon your death, then the remainder passes to the then living lawful heirs of the deceased uncle."

I said, "You understand this, don't you?"

"More or less."

"You get the money, if you live six months longer than your uncle. If not, then the money goes to your children. If you don't have any, then it goes to your father's closest relatives, whoever they might be."

"Max, I suppose," she said.

"Or other nieces and nephews?"

"There aren't any."

"Well, maybe it's all hypothetical," I said. "Meanwhile, how old is your uncle?"

"Old enough. And dead enough. He died last month. A rotten, fat old goat. He drank like a fish. Bad tempered; he and my father were two of a kind. Anyway, the clock is running," she said. "That's why...well, why I want to make out a will. Five months from now, the money comes to me. If I last that long," she said, and laughed. Ironic, when I look back on all this.

"Oh, you will," I said, "you're young and healthy, you're going to make it."

"Do I have to wait the five months? To make out the will? Right now, I don't have much of anything."

"No; you can do it now. In fact, it's a good idea," I said. "And there are no restrictions. Basically. You can leave money to whoever you want. Your mother, for example...."

"My mother? God forbid."

These people had such warm, loving families. "And.... Barney?"

"Lord. Do I have to?"

"Well, he's your husband. In fact, you don't really have to leave him anything.... Of course, he gets a share of the community property, if you understand what that is...."

"Oh, more or less. Other than that, I can cut him off without a penny?"

"Well, in the will...not exactly, but...and anyway, I don't

actually advise it...."

"Oh, you don't, do you? Well, why not?"

I swallowed hard. She had a certain sharpness to her tone. "It...it just breeds trouble. I mean, you two are still married."

"He doesn't need the money," she said. "He's getting this inheritance from that stupid old aunt. And, since he babbled all over the place, when he was sitting where I'm sitting now, about how we're not getting along, and what a rotten relationship we have, I should take him at his word, shouldn't I?"

"It's up to you," I said.

"Screw him. I don't owe him anything. I don't owe anybody anything. Maybe someday, when I have kids—not with Barney, don't get any ideas.... Right now, I'm trying to put together a career. That's what's uppermost in my mind. This money from my uncle, it's a big help, it's going to mean a lot to me, but I'm not sure what I want to do.... I know, when you come into money like this, you've got to make arrangements. I have a friend, he told me that...."

"A lawyer friend?"

"No, just a friend.... Anyway, this is what I was thinking: I'll leave Barney something, just so he doesn't get insulted. He doesn't deserve it; but what the hell. As for the rest.... I'll leave a little bit to charity. I'm not particularly charitable; but maybe something for retired actors, whatever. Or to save the whales. Who cares."

"And...the rest...why not your mother?"

"She doesn't need it.... She's got a pension, and she never spends money on anything. We don't get along. She let herself go to hell, she's fat, she doesn't do anything, she doesn't even get dressed half the time. This was a woman who used to be, well, proud of herself, her ancestors, that kind of thing. Now she sits at home, and watches soap operas. She clips coupons out of the newspaper, you know, get a free pizza. She's as stingy as they come, always looking for bargains. I just don't feel like dumping a pile of money in her lap. Anyway, when she died, what would happen to it? I shudder to think what she would do with it...."

"How old is she?"

"Very old. Seventy maybe."

"Is she...mentally OK?"

"Was she ever? But the answer is yes."

I swallowed hard. "Ms. Baleine...."

"Blanche."

"Blanche, it's your money, but...I have some experience. I think your mother, if you inherited all this money, and she's living in, uh, tight circumstances, and you didn't leave her some of your money, well she'd be hurt; this sort of thing causes trouble in families, believe me."

"I don't give a shit. I'll be dead." She said this in a cold, even heartless tone. Maybe too cold. She wanted to shock me. Suddenly it occurred to me that she was maybe acting a part. And I started to wonder, what impression was she trying to make? Was I seeing the real Blanche? Or Blanche in some sort of role? Did she just enjoy projecting this image, an image of cold realism?

Maybe I preferred Barney to Blanche, if I had to choose. He was dumb, he was vain, and he talked too much, but he lacked actual malice. Blanche—I wasn't so sure.

She seemed to read my mind. "You think I'm pretty awful, no? Cold. Hard. Unfeeling bitch, right?"

"I don't judge my clients."

"Of course you do."

"Maybe. But...what you choose to do, it's none of my business."

"You're right. It isn't your business. OK, I'll think it over. Maybe I'll leave her some money. My mother. Not a lot, but some."

"And your brother?"

"Nothing," she said. "I'm sure of that. I told you, he's in one of these cults, all of the money would go to the swami. No thanks."

"So," I said, "there's something for Barney, something for your mother—maybe—and the exact amounts or proportions, we'll talk about later; and then maybe something for charity. But the rest? You're talking a nice pile of money."

"Maybe. Tell you the truth, I'm not sure *what* I want to do."

I said: "If I'm going to draft a will, I have to have more to go on.""

She said: "I know that. I do have an idea. But I'd rather not say.... Suppose I tell you, such and such to Barney, and the rest, I'll give you a sealed envelope, it'll have a list in it, where I want the money to go, you'll attach that to the will."

I shook my head. "No way. A will is a will. A sealed envelope is nothing. You can't do that; it won't be legally valid. Here in California, the case-law...."

She interrupted me, obviously uninterested in California case-law. She said, "Forget it; I believe you. You're the lawyer. But...what you're saying is, I have to confide in you. Is there no way I can keep my secrets?"

"Well...everything you do say here is confidential, Blanche. And you don't have to tell me everything. Just the things that are relevant. To the will."

"And you won't tell Barney what I'm doing?"

"No; not if you don't want me to."

"I don't. I...I'm going to be brutally frank with you. I'm going to trust you. I heard, when you talk to a lawyer, it's like talking to a therapist. Or a doctor. It's strictly confidential. That's right, isn't it?"

"Absolutely," I said.

"You're married?" I nodded. "And you don't even tell your wife?"

I laughed. "She isn't interested. Usually. Believe me, most of what I do is deadly dull. And no, I don't tell her what I do."

She paused. "I was talking," she said, "about the money. The inheritance. But there's something else I want to talk about...."

In a way, I wasn't surprised. Nobody comes to see a lawyer about a will, until they know what they want to do with their money. Blanche seemed to have no idea what she wanted to do. But she was no fool; that was clear. She was a sharp, intelligent woman; maybe a ruthless one. The will was probably a pretext.

"I'm an ambitious person," she said. "I want to make something of myself. I've made a lot of mistakes in my life; I'll be frank about that. I'm an impulsive person. Listen: marrying Barney, that was impulsive, let me tell you. But I want to get somewhere. Acting, it's too chancy. I'd love to be a star. It's not going to happen. It's like winning the lottery. Barney thinks, his ship is going to come in. There isn't any ship. I know that. So I'm considering, well, a new career."

I said: "A new career? What sort?"

"Journalism. I've always been interested in journalism. I took some courses in journalism, at a community college. I'd love to be an investigative reporter. Print or TV, I'm not sure. Maybe TV. There's some money in it, but, more important, I want to be known. Famous. It's like being a star. I don't want to be stuck in this rut, struggling for a few scraps, a commercial, a bit part on some show. I want people to notice me. Is that awful? I want people to know who I am. In acting, you need luck, you need a lucky break.... I want to do something where I can make my own breaks, if you know what I mean."

I didn't know where this was headed, but I nodded agreement.

"I want to make a splash. You're making a face. You have a look of disapproval. It reminds me of my mother."

I said no, no, I didn't disapprove. "It's none of my business, Blanche. Lots of people want to be somebody. You know, the fifteen minutes of fame."

"I don't want fifteen minutes. I want a lifetime."

"Why not," I said, trying to smile.

She said, "I'm a woman with talent, and nerve; if I do say so myself. I'm *looking* for something, if you know what I mean. A chance to break out of the pack. I don't want to be...mediocre. Barney's mediocre. I don't want that. I want to try something different. I was even thinking of having a webcam in the apartment, people would pay, and they would get to watch me, in my natural habitat, see what I was doing. Me and Barney. They could watch us get dressed, eat, take showers, even watch us make out in the bedroom, I don't care. But...of course, Barney; he'd never do it. He couldn't. He'd freak out totally. Men have this performance thing, when it comes to sex. Not that he's such a star at it anyway; but if you had a camera there, he'd be completely impossible. Anyway, too many people are doing that webcam stuff already."

"Really."

"You didn't know? There's lots of them. But I have other ideas. Better ideas. Big things. Things that could make a real splash. I want to find out certain things, make people sit up and notice, things I could sell, to the tabloids, whatever. I have ideas. I'll have exclusive rights. It'll be worth money, but that's not the main point; the main thing is, it'll put my name out there."

"Ideas? What kind of ideas?"

"Well, it's still sort of unformed. I'll just give you a hint: I got the idea, when I was on the Tony Crass show. You know, Barney and I had a job on that show, did he tell you?"

I nodded yes.

"OK," she said, "so you know, more or less, what kind of show it is. You don't watch it, do you?"

"God forbid."

"I don't blame you. Pure junk. But millions of people do watch it, it's got ratings you wouldn't believe. Anyway...I want you to keep an eye on the program. Not right now, but next month. You're going to see something important.... You'll know it when you see it. And I've got another idea, for a different episode of the program. But let's not go into that. You watch. Watch the program, it won't kill you. You might even like it. And you'll understand, what I'm up to. More or less."

If I had known then, what I know now, I would have paid closer attention. I would have asked her for more details. Why was I supposed to watch this program? I thought she was mainly bragging; and I couldn't see what it had to do with me. I had, in fact, no intention of watching the Tony Crass show. Celia and I watch TV together, when we watch it at all; and she would absolutely veto the idea; that much was certain.

I didn't know it then, but the future really did have a big role in store for Blanche. It was a role she never expected. The role of a victim.

She said, "Anyway, there might be important things coming up...and...besides, I'm getting my uncle's money; so, I was thinking, I'd like to incorporate."

"Incorporate?"

"Are you deaf? That's what I said. You're a lawyer, aren't you? I want to incorporate. Form a corporation. That way you don't pay taxes. You make yourself a corporation, and then it's no taxes. A friend of mine told me that."

I hardly knew where to begin. "That's...not exactly true."

"What isn't true?"

"The part about the taxes.... Well, it's complicated. I don't know if you want to go into it, right now. You see, a corporation...."

She interrupted me: "Whatever. I don't need a canned lecture. Not at the moment, anyway. When the time comes, though, I'll need your advice.

I hate to admit it now, because she's dead, dead at a young age, tragically dead; but the more she talked, the more I felt sympathy for Barney; and, oddly enough, the more I *liked* him. She was an attractive woman, physically. But she was cold, unloving, hard. No man could be happy, living with Blanche Baleine. No wonder the two of them had "issues."

She said: "This is preliminary, I'm just setting things up. I assume you don't charge for the first session."

She assumed wrong. I charge for every session. I don't offer bargains, discounts, I don't give away frequent-flier miles. I'm trying to make a living. But in her case, I agreed, no charge for this session, partly to get rid of her, partly because I was sure I had no choice. Clearly, Blanche Baleine expected this "session" to be free. It was no use billing her; she had no intention of paying.

That was more or less the end of our encounter. She left, telling me she would think about the will, and that she would be in touch with me about the "corporation thing," as she put it. And she reminded me once again, to keep my eye on her show.

She never got in touch. Neither about the will, or the "corporation thing." I did watch the show, as you'll see. But this was after she was dead.

She got her fifteen minutes of fame, after all. In a way, a lifetime of fame. She got her name in the newspapers, along with inches and inches of coverage. But not the way she wanted it, but only because somebody smashed in her skull and left her dying on the floor.

# 6

Then came that night, the night Blanche was murdered, the night Barney called me on the phone. In the morning, when I woke up and dragged myself out of bed, after what little sleep I could manage, I felt sick to my stomach. I kept remembering my one meeting with Blanche. OK, I didn't like her. But to think of somebody you know, getting murdered, in a way that seemed quite brutal and senseless—it was nauseating, depressing.

In the bathroom, I looked in the mirror and thought I saw rings under my eyes. I took a shower and got dressed. I was feeling sorry for myself, so I ate a doughnut for breakfast instead of granola. I made a cup of coffee and drank it boiling hot. Celia was dressed already, and about to go to work. I didn't feel like talking about Blanche, or about the phone call; fortunately, she didn't ask.

It was 9 o'clock, long past my normal time to get going. I'm a morning person. I love to see the sun come up. I like the smell of the air in the morning. But this morning, I felt like I was made out of lead. Luckily, I had no appointments in the morning, so I could indulge myself.

I looked at the morning newspaper. The usual terrible news. I couldn't concentrate. I kept thinking of Blanche...and Barney. I called him as soon as the coffee began to revive me, when I could feel life stirring inside my protoplasm. Barney's phone rang and rang, and I was about to give up when he finally answered. Barney was, as you can imagine, in a miserable state. He said he couldn't talk, and could he get back to me later.

"Sure, Barney," I said. "But did you call the lawyer? Nolan Thom?"

He had.

"He's the best, Barney," I said. "You're in good hands."

"Yeah. I hope so. I sure need it."

I was telling the truth. Barney was in very good hands. But even good hands aren't always enough. Barney wasn't the type to do research; he wasn't likely to go through old newspapers and records, and check up on Nolan's batting average. If he had, he would be even more frightened. Even very good criminal lawyers can have a fairly low success rate. Lots of men and women who had excellent lawyers are now rotting away in San Quentin. Some of them are even on death row. Not even a legal genius can rescue a hopeless case.

One case I remember had a kind of vague resemblance to poor Barney's predicament. This husband, I forget his name, or what he did for a living, but he lived in a nice house in south Palo Alto, and he was accused of killing his wife, and dumping her body in the bay. Turned out he had a girlfriend; that didn't help him with the jury. He said he was miles away at the time she died ("accidentally"); but some very credible witnesses flatly contradicted his alibi. They found the body of the wife, floating in the bay, with a nice bullet in the brain. Nolan had just gotten an acquittal in another case of a murderous husband, I think I mentioned it, the blood-stained sneakers and all that. This time Nolan struck out. His work in this particular case (according to the experts) was simply brilliant. But not brilliant enough. The jury failed to appreciate his performance. They brought in a verdict of guilty. It took them a week to decide, which might have been in a way a tribute to Nolan. I doubt that the defendant was properly appreciative.

A good lawyer can't work magic.

I didn't actually speak to Nolan that morning; I called his office, but I never got him. All I got was a receptionist, a woman with a cheerfully professional voice; she asked me my name, said "one moment please;" and put me on hold. Then she came back and told me that he was unavailable, and would I check back later.

Barney called me again in mid-morning. "Frank," he said, "Can I come see you? Like now?"

I hesitated. "Well...."

"Look, man, I'm supposed to go down to the police station, but I put them off for a while. After lunch. I said to the guy, Jesus, I lost my wife, I'm all broken up, it's, like, a big shock, I just can't face things now, I got to pull myself together, and then there's all this shit about funerals, undertakers, all that stuff."

"Do you need help, Barney?"

"Help? With what?"

"The funeral and all that."

"Listen, I don't give a shit about the funeral. I hate funerals. They give me the creeps. Her mother's doing all that stuff. She can handle it. All that crap, those guys with their caskets, all they want is money. I told the old bag, I said, Blanche, she wanted to be cremated, but her mother, she's gotten religious or something, she said, no, she was going to get a Christian burial, can you believe it, and a real honest-to-God funeral. I said, OK, have it your way. Look: I'm in a funny position with Blanche's family, you know? I mean, they're thinking, maybe he killed her.... Jesus, have I got troubles, Frank. I've got to talk to you."

"You talked to Nolan, right?"

"Yeah...he'll go with me. To the station. He says, don't say anything.... OK.... But Frank, will you talk to me, man? Can I meet you for lunch?"

"Sure thing, Barney...."

Barney wanted some place very private, so we went to a rather pricey Italian restaurant, with soft leather booths, and very few customers, in downtown San Mateo. I was as hungry as a bear. I have a food weakness, and a special weakness for pasta. Italian cooking: now *there's* what I consider soul food.

Barney was a little late. I was on my third piece of bread, with olive oil. We ordered. I ended up with a ravishing ravioli. Stuffed with butternut squash.

Poor Barney wasn't the least bit hungry. I can imagine why. He picked at his food. I felt guilty, wolfing down my ravioli, drinking a glass of red wine, the works.

"How was your talk with Nolan? Did it go OK?" I asked.

"Yeah. I'm meeting him at two.... We'll have a chance to talk again, him and me, then it's the police.... This is going to cost me, right? An arm and a leg. These lawyers, they're bloodsuckers. I mean, not you Frank. Anyway, I've got to pay this guy, I know that. I'm in deep doodoo, Frank."

"You want to tell me about it?"

"Yeah. I have to tell *somebody*. I've got this friend, Charley

Morgan, maybe you'll meet him; but I couldn't reach him this morning.... Anyway, I want to tell you the whole story. From start to finish. God, it's a frigging nightmare. Frank, they think I killed Blanche. They're frigging positive. You know me, could I kill anybody? I'm a frigging coward."

"I know, Barney."

"*You* know, and I know; but *they* don't know."

"So what happened, Barney?"

"OK, it's like this. You know this guy Travis Hinchcombe. No, you don't know him, but I told you about him. He's this zillionaire. His dad was married to Aunt Martha. My aunt, the one that's dead, the one with the money. Well, Hinchcombe, now he's *really* got money, he's got apartments all over, London, New York, Paris, God knows where. But he lives in Atherton, big house in Atherton, you know where that is...."

"Sure." Atherton is a suburb, south of San Mateo; big homes, mansions mostly, leafy streets, very quiet, people with Mercedes sedans and Filipina maids.

"He's divorced, Travis, twice maybe, maybe more, I don't know, and he's always flying all over the world. Flies first class, that kind of thing. Business deals, who the hell knows? So he was going away, for a few weeks he said, going to Paris, and he asked me and Blanche to housesit for him."

"Housesit?"

"Yeah. Keep an eye on things."

"He doesn't have a housekeeper? He's so rich?"

"Yeah, he had one. A housekeeper. She walked out on him, or something; maybe he was balling her, who knows. I saw her once, she wasn't bad-looking, Chinese or something. Maybe Japanese, they all look the same."

They really don't. But I did not feel like preaching at the moment.

"Anyway, Travis called me and said, look, my housekeeper quit on me, I'm going away, I don't have time to get somebody, why don't you and Blanche stay in the house, keep an eye on things, use the pool, use the jacuzzi, help yourself to the liquor, how about it Barney. So I said, sure, if Blanche wants to, and naturally she did. Oh yes, there was Suzie, too. She insisted on coming along. My no-good sister. So there we were, the three of us, in this big house, swimming pool, tennis court, the works.

Then came yesterday....

"At first, I thought this is great. This is the life. Six bedrooms, seven, who can count them; four bathrooms, main bathroom's as big as my whole apartment. The house, it's this two-story thing, kind of colonial style, you know? Lot of land, acres and acres. There was supposed to be some kind of garden guy, supposed to come during the day, take care of things, the pool, and so on. Actually, he never showed up.... I was going to complain, actually, to Travis; the pool was getting a little disgusting, green stuff growing on it.... In fact, I did call Travis."

"I thought he was in Paris."

"You and me both. But, the day before the thing with Blanche, he called up, he said, I'm back in the country, here's a number, my cell phone. So.... about this pool thing, I thought, it's got green stuff in it.... Funny, it seemed so important yesterday, today, who gives a shit? The things you worry about.... Anyway, we were sleeping in this big room, it was *twice* as big as my apartment, for Christ's sake, had this humungous bed, with a kind of canopy, real sexy bed, and the bathroom, like I told you, gigantic, you could wash a horse in it, with all kinds of stuff, water spraying all over you if you wanted, and a bathtub you could step into, and things to clean your private parts, and a toilet that was heated, I swear, a high-tech toilet. A real kick. OK: but then, last night, we were in the bedroom, it was night time, nobody around...."

"Suzie?"

"She wasn't there. She left. Actually, I kicked her out. We had an argument. I don't know where she went. She'd been gone for a day, maybe she went to her boyfriend's house, this doctor guy. I'm always glad to get rid of her. So we were alone. The two of us. And...well, we had this tremendous fight, I mean, we used to fight a lot, Blanche and I, but this was worse than usual, she threw something at me, she was so mad."

"What was it all about?"

"I don't even remember, how it started. I mean, you're married, you know what I mean. You have these arguments. To start with, she was real pissed about something. Then I was in the mood for a little romance, you know how it is, she said she wasn't having any, not that night, and I said, well, what night, let me make an appointment, or something snotty; and she was snotty right back; and she brought up something else, who knows what, and then, you know, one thing leads to another, and it kind of escalates. She started calling me names, bastard, dirty shit, idiot, that sort of thing. I mean, Blanche can really pour it on. And I got mad, naturally—well, she was calling me all those names, and I started in, you bitch, you slut; what else could I do? I mean, tit for tat. And then she threw an ash tray at me, like I said, and she stormed out of the room."

"And then what?"

"Then nothing. She came back, in ten minutes or so, I was watching TV, she said, you can go to hell, something like that, she grabbed some clothes and said, I'm sleeping downstairs, and I said, I don't give a shit, I mean, we weren't exactly being polite to each other; and I said, get out why don't you, I'm watching this show. So she left. I told you, there's six bedrooms in the place, seven bedrooms, who knows how many, so she went to some other bedroom, downstairs. I guess. I watched TV for a while, then I went to bed."

"What time was that?"

"Maybe midnight. I fell right asleep. Me, I'm a good sleeper."

"Then what happened?"

"Well: in the middle of the night, maybe it was two o'clock, maybe later, I hear this terrific scream, it wakes me up, and another scream, a real scream, it was awful, first I think, this is something I'm dreaming, but then I'm up...so I pulled my pants on, and I ran downstairs, and there's this room, a kind of study, off the living room, and there she is, lying on the floor, and there's blood all over, and she's kind of gasping, and this statue thing, it's lying next to her, and she's going, help me, help me, and I could see, she was in bad shape, and I said, hang on Blanche, I mean, I was shaking like a leaf, I didn't know what to do, I don't like blood, I have to tell you; but I grabbed her purse and she had a little book inside of it, with phone numbers and all, and she was gasping and gurgling, it was awful, and the blood gushing out of her, and there was a phone in the room, and I found Ross Tanager's number, he's the doctor guy that Suzie dates, and I called him, and said, something's happened, an accident, Blanche is hurt, she's bleeding, can you get here. And he said, OK, I'll come as soon as I can, but meanwhile, call 911, call an ambulance, is she conscious? I said, sort of. He said, I'll be there, maybe ten minutes, but call 911, like I told you.... And I did, I mean, man, I was shaking all over, you know? Felt like puking. But I pulled myself together, I tried to stop the bleeding, but hell, I'm no doctor, I didn't know what to do, I was never even in the boy scouts, and meanwhile, as I said, I felt like puking, and she was making these awful noises, and her eyes were all funny, and the blood was all over the place...."

Poor guy. I could imagine the scene. What would I have done?

He went on: "And the ambulance came, pretty quick, and I opened the door for them, and then Ross came, maybe a minute or two later, but she was dying, Blanche, she couldn't talk, and she died before they could even get her into the ambulance. It was a frigging nightmare, Frank. The worst day of my life. And somebody called the police, maybe the paramedics, I can't remember, and they came and they did this whole crime scene shit, and I did finally puke. Thank God Ross was there, he was really cool, he helped me out."

"You say she was in a kind of study? Not in a bedroom?"

"No; it's like I told you, this room, off the living room. Bookcases, you know, bunch of bookcases, a desk, chairs. I don't know if she went to bed, she had her regular clothes on, when she ran out of the bedroom, she took a nightgown and stuff, but she wasn't wearing no nightgown, she was wearing the same clothes she had on, I mean, that was pretty weird, what was she doing all that time, why didn't she go to bed."

"Maybe she was too upset. You know, because of the fight."

"Blanche? Upset? Give me a break. No way. She wasn't that kind of woman, you know; I mean, she was tough as nails. I don't know what she was up to. Maybe she heard somebody prowling, something like that. Must have been. Yeah, a prowler, and...he got in somehow, and smashed in her head.... Me...you know, Frank, when you're in some kind of situation, like the one I was in, you don't know what you're doing, so I guess I did something stupid, I picked up the thing...."

"What thing?"

"The statue. Statuette. Whatever you call it. It had blood on it. I picked it up, and I looked at it, it was some kind of thing from Europe, Travis collects stuff, made out of bronze or whatever. I picked it up and then I put it right down. But, I mean, it's got my fingerprints...."

"And maybe somebody else's too, Barney," I said, trying to be helpful. "Not just yours. The other guy's too. So don't worry."

"I got to worry, Frank. I know I didn't kill her, but *somebody* did. She sure as hell didn't bash in her head by herself."

"Could it have been an accident, Barney?"

"I wish. I mean, that bronze thing, I noticed it before. It wasn't that big, but it was pretty noticeable, it was a naked lady, bending down, with a dog or something next to her. It was sitting on a table. It was heavy, too. Solid metal. People can fall down, and crack their head open, but that thing didn't walk off the table. I mean, I got to be realistic."

"So...and there was nobody in the house?"

"No. I mean, yeah, there had to be somebody. I told you, a prowler. Somebody broke into the house, Frank. That's the way I figure it. And Blanche, she saw him, and he got panicky, you know, those guys, the burglars, they're all high as a kite on some shit they take, they shoot up before they go out, and they don't even know what they're doing half the time."

"Was anything stolen?"

"The police say no. But I couldn't find her cell phone. She always had the thing in her purse. It wasn't there. I had to go through her purse, to find that address book, I dumped everything out on the table, that's where the purse was, I needed to get Ross' number; and I saw right away, no cell phone. I told the police about it, but they didn't seem too interested. I said, the guy took her cell phone. They said they'd check into it, but they didn't look like they were going to."

"What do you mean?"

"Frank, I don't know what's going on here.... Some guy called me, detective somebody or some police guy, and they said, Mr. Bell, you reported a missing cell phone, and I went, yes, I did, my wife's cell phone. He said, well, Mr. Bell, as far as we can tell, she didn't have a cell phone. I said, yes, she did, I saw it, she used it all the time. They said, what make was it, I said, I don't know, I never paid attention, some foreign thing; but they said, there is no record of any cell phone. I mean, am I going crazy or what?"

I didn't think he was going crazy. And why would he lie about the cell phone? It was very strange. A missing cell phone. Hercule Poirot would store this fact away, in his little gray cells, for use later on. Whether I could do the same was something I didn't know as yet. "No, you're not going crazy," I said. "They made a mistake, that's all."

"Could you...look into it, Frank?"

"Look into it?"

"It's a clue," he said, with a pathetic look on his face. "I give them a clue, and they don't take it. The guy took her cell phone. The police think I'm lying, so they don't give a crap about the cell phone. But...could you help me out here, Frank?"

"Barney, I'd love to help you; but I'm not a private detective. I have no idea how...or what I'd be supposed to be looking for, with the cell phone. Really, Barney."

"I need help, Frank."

"I know you do. But trust Nolan. He's the best there is."

"He's good, Frank; I know he's good. But he...well, he doesn't know me, really. And I'm in deep, deep shit. I kept saying, somebody broke in, look, they stole her cell phone, it's a prowler. But they don't believe me. They're all very polite. Mr. Bell, they're always calling me Mr. Bell. Well, one of them says Barney, but the rest.... Anyway, they go like this: Mr. Bell, how do you explain the fact that there are no signs anybody broke into the house. Door was locked, wasn't it? I guess it was, I said. I mean, I had to open it for the ambulance guys. So they said, what about the windows? They were closed were they not? I just shrugged my shoulders, I mean, I never ran around the house checking windows. Frankly, the house, it's air-conditioned, nobody opens the windows. So how did your burglar get in, Mr. Bell, they said to me. And I say, how the hell should I know?"

"And...besides this cell phone, nothing was stolen?"

"You mean in the house? Dunno. It's not my house."

"Her purse?"

"Looked the same to me," he said, "but hey, I can't be sure."

"Did somebody check? To see if stuff was stolen."

He said, mournfully, "they say, nothing was stolen. How the hell do they know? And they keep saying, nobody else in the house. Just you and Blanche. Or the deceased, they like to say, 'the deceased.' Suzie wasn't there. They know that. So I must have killed Blanche. That's what they think. They get these ideas in their heads, you know? I mean, I told them the truth, everything that happened that night. Maybe I should have kept my mouth shut. But I had to tell them, we were sleeping in different rooms, I was upstairs, she was downstairs. Oh, they say, and why was that? So I said, well, we sort of had a disagreement. Oh, they ask, what sort of disagreement. I said, you know, you're married, you have fights some time, it doesn't mean anything. Well, what was this fight all about? I said, this and that. I could see they were suspicious. They get that look on their face, there was two of them, and they started giving each other, you know, glances and shit. I was stupid, I told them about the ashtray. She threw an ashtray at me, I said, she was really pissed, and she went into another room.

"I thought I was being smart, God, how stupid can a guy be. I wanted to say: look, see, I wasn't even there when somebody bashed her head in. But they thought, aha, this is the guy. I could see what they were thinking. Oh, oh, she threw an ashtray at him, he got pissed, he ran after her and hit her on the head with that bronze thing."

I didn't know what to say. If I were a policeman, and didn't know Barney, I would feel the same way I suppose. He must be the one. When you exclude all the other possibilities, what are you left with? No burglar, nobody else in the house.... Only Barney. The husband. Cherchez the husband. Had a fight with his wife. Not getting along. Open and shut case.

But the difference was, I *did* know Barney. Or thought I did. Two sessions in my office; was that really a basis for deciding?

Still, I felt I had to be supportive. "Don't let it get you down, Barney," I said. "The whole idea, it's ridiculous. You couldn't kill anybody. I'm sure it's going to come out OK. The main thing is, you're innocent."

"Yeah, I'm innocent. Hey, Frank, I know it, and you know it. But *they* don't know it. You know those guys, they frame people. I mean, why should they run around busting their asses, when they can just stick it to me, right? They kept on saying to me, over and over, nobody broke in, Mr. Bell, there's no signs of that whatsoever, and nobody was in the house but you and Blanche, and now she's dead, how do you explain that? There was this guy, he gave me the creeps, asking all these questions in this quiet voice, as if he was such a sweetheart, only interested in helping me out, you know? And all the while, he's thinking, I've got this guy by the balls. Well, did somebody have a key, he asks me. I said, how do I know? It wasn't my house. Travis, Mr. Hinchcombe, he had a key, it's his house, isn't it? Well, says this guy, Mr. Hinchcombe, yes, he must have had the key; but he wasn't around now, was he? So...Barney—now they're calling me Barney, no more Mr. Bell, I'm going to ask you again, how do you explain this? I went, I don't know, that's what you guys are supposed to find out. That got them mad.... Frank, I'm scared. They're going to send me to the electric chair, I swear it."

They don't use an electric chair in California. It's a lethal injection. But I didn't think this was the right time to correct Barney on this point.

"Barney," I said, "you've got the best criminal lawyer in the business, well, at least the best in the Bay Area. It'll be OK." To be honest, I had the same question on my mind as the detectives: if there was nobody around, and nobody broke in.... But I didn't say this out loud. Instead, I said, "Barney, is there anything I can do? Can I help you, in any way?"

"Could you talk to Suzie, Frank. My sister.... We're on the outs.... I had this big fight with her, too.... I mean, when I say fight, you understand, not a real fight, physical stuff, no...it's all talk. I'm not that kind of guy, Frank, you know, somebody that smacks people, with me, it's all just yelling, it's just noise, Frank. I'm a wimp, I holler a lot, maybe, but Frank, honestly, I can't stand the sight of blood...."

"Your sister. What should I talk to her about?"

"Maybe she knows something. Blanche used to tell her things, sometimes. Call her up, Frank; do me a favor."

"Maybe you should call her yourself. I don't know her."

"I don't want to call her, Frank. Not now. She...she got on my nerves. As I told you, I kicked her out. I told her, she was freeloading, I was sick of it. Get a frigging job, I said, for a change. And...she started screaming at me. Called me names, I mean, she was yelling and yelling. These women, Frank, God bless them. Her and Blanche...bunch of ball-breakers, if you know what I mean....

"So I had enough, I said, get the hell out, Suzie, I don't want you here. I threw her suitcase across the room, I said, pack up and scram, in fifteen minutes, I don't want to see you here, you're out of here, Suzie. She was so mad she looked like she could kill me, I mean, I could have been the one with my head bashed in, you know what I'm saying? Anyway, I can't call her, I can't go crawling to her now. I want to know if Blanche told her something, they were all whispering and blabbing, a couple of days before this, you know, before I kicked her ass out of the house. I said, Blanche, what are you talking about, you and Suzie. The two of them, like they had some big secret. Blanche, well, she said, none of your Goddamn business. Can you call Suzie, Frank?"

"What's my excuse?"

"I don't know. You're my lawyer. You'll think of something. Look, Frank, I've got money, you know that; my aunt's money. I want to pay you."

"Barney, I like getting paid, believe me; but shouldn't you be working with Nolan? He's your lawyer. Criminal lawyer, I mean."

"Oh, he's great, he's terrific; but this is something you can do.... I can't ask him, he's busy with my case. And...I don't really know him yet...."

Reluctantly, I agreed. I didn't want to be dragged into this morass, but when somebody in trouble appeals to you, you have to agree. Barney said: "There's somebody else I want you to talk to. His name is Charley. Charley Morgan. That's not his name either, but never mind. He's a buddy of mine. He's been on the Tony Crass show too. I tell you, that was one great episode. He was supposed to be a gay scout leader, fell in love with a boy scout, 16 year old kid. Wow, that was dynamite. Charley's about as gay as I am, meaning zero, and if he's ever been a scout leader, I'm an Eskimo, but you know, a job is a job."

"Well, what about him?"

"He's...got a message for you. Don't ask me about it, he'll let you know...."

"Why can't you tell me now?"

He said nothing, but I could read the answer in his face: he didn't think this place was "secure." In his vivid imagination, the police were following him around with sensitive listening devices. "They can hear a pin drop," he told me. "I mean, it's like some kind of Communist country now, the way they spy on you." I assured him, this wasn't the case, there were no listening devices here, it was an Italian restaurant, it wasn't hooked up with wires; and I could have said, if they can hear a pin drop, won't they hear it when Charley Morgan gives me the message? But it wasn't worth an argument.

The waiter came and took away the plates. Barney had barely touched his food. I didn't dare bring up the subject of dessert. I was aching for some tiramisu, but I thought better of it. Here was a man facing a lethal injection, maybe; or at the very least, a long, long prison term; and I was sitting in front of him, lusting passionately after a rich Italian dessert. I was vaguely ashamed of myself. And Barney looked terrifically distraught.

"You know, Frank. I got only one hope. Only one," he said.

"What's that?"

"You got to find the guy who really did it."

"Me, Barney? Why not Nolan...."

"Shit, Frank, he's not Perry Mason. He's going to try to defend me.... He's going to do a lot of tricks, you know, fool the jury, whatever. It's what he does. It's a full-time job, I bet. But you...."

"Hey, Barney," I said, "I have a job too, you know. Anyway it's not my line of work. I never touch it. Criminal cases, I mean. If I could help you, I would. Really. But I'm not an investigator or anything like that. But let me ask you a question, Barney: why would somebody want to kill your wife? Can you think of a reason?"

"Kill Blanche? Shit, no. Why do people want to kill *anybody*? I mean, we're not that kind of people. It's not like in the movies, all those bullets flying around and stuff. Nobody wanted to kill Blanche. Nobody."

"But somebody *did*."

He stared glumly at the tablecloth. "Yeah: but who? That's why...like I told you, it's got to be some burglar, a kid, you know, some punk, I figure he broke in, he saw her, he got scared, and pow! He picked up that thing...."

His voice trailed off. He knew he was talking nonsense; but he was desperate. It was time to change the subject, at least slightly. I said: "You know, she came to see me, don't you?"

"Yeah. I did. She told me. About a will, right?"

"Right. But, there were other things, too. She said, she was going to do something big, going to be an investigative reporter. Did you know anything about that?"

He shook his head. "Never heard that stuff. Maybe she was making it up. You didn't know Blanche. She's dead, so I shouldn't badmouth her, you know, somebody bashed her head in, but hey, she was always going to do something big. Full of plans. Nothing ever panned out. Biggest thing *she* ever did was marry me; and that was some huge success, huh?"

I felt I was supposed to ignore that comment, and I did. I said: "She sounded serious. She said she was on to something. Do you have any idea what she was talking about? Maybe she was investigating something, she found something out, and that was why somebody felt, they had to kill her."

He shook his head. "She never said boo. I mean, even when she was talking to me, and wasn't yelling...."

"And she said something too about the program. The Tony Crass show. Do you know about that?"

"She had a gig. Yeah. She was going to be on one of his shows, something about a dentist. That's all I know about it."

"A dentist? What about a dentist?"

"I dunno. Just a dentist. She just mentioned it, like... casual."

I said: "She told me to watch it. Said it was important. What I'm thinking, Barney, is that...well, it might have something to do with what happened."

"That show? Tony Crass? I mean, it's just a show, it's a bunch of crap."

"Well, she was quite definite about it. She told me to watch the program, she said, I'd learn something. So.... I don't know, it could be important. She was excited about something, maybe she was blackmailing somebody, maybe she was going to expose some sort of racket. It's something we might want to follow up on."

"We? Follow up? Frank, you're not getting the picture. I'm going to be sitting in jail. Those frigging cops, they're going to cut my balls off. They're going to get me, I swear."

"How about Nolan?"

"What about Nolan?

"Maybe he could do it. Follow up, I mean."

"Nolan? He charges $500 an hour, I'll go broke at this rate; I can't afford to give him that kind of dough, here, Nolan, why don't you watch this program, and just put it on the bill. Hey, Frank, you do it; I'll pay you. I mean, you don't charge that kind of money."

He was right about that. In fact, I had made up my mind not to charge him anything, if he lost the case. It would be heartless to send a bill for professional services, to a man on death row.

He said, again: "You watch it, Frank. And, hey, ask Charley. He'll watch this show with you, the one that Blanche was supposed to be on, he knows all about this stuff, maybe he'll see something you don't see."

I agreed to this too.

He sank further into the seat. He looked so woeful and depressed. I skipped dessert. I could see the guy was suffering, I could see he felt totally lost. I called the waiter, got the check, and put down my credit card. Barney hardly even noticed. He was deep in thought. I said: "Listen, Barney, I'll watch the program, don't worry. And I'm not going to charge you. Look, I watch TV, like everybody else. It's not like it's part of my work. So I'll watch. There's probably nothing to it; but I'll give it a try."

He perked up a bit. "You really think...."

"I don't. Not really. But it's worth a try."

He grabbed my hand. I thought he was going to cry. "You're a real buddy, Frank," he said. "You're going to figure this out."

"Whoa, Barney. I'm not getting involved, you better get that through your skull. I'm going to do this thing for you, I'm going to watch this damn program; but I'm not going to play detective."

"OK, OK."

I said: "Look, Barney, maybe it had nothing to do with the program at all. That particular program, I mean. Maybe it was something about the show in general. She was maybe going to spill the beans, tell people the program was a fake...."

"It's not fake. I mean, not *all* fake."

"Well, it's part fake. That's what she was going to expose."

"Shit, everybody knows that...."

"You think? I doubt it," I said. "All those people out there, watching it; they believe in it, don't they?"

"Who the hell knows?" he said.

"And then there's the investigative reporter thing, if there's anything to it," I said. "Or maybe both things are the same."

He said nothing. He fiddled with the knife and fork. He had a hollow look in his eyes.

Poor guy. There were other theories, I suppose; but whatever they were, they were terrifically weak. Feeble. The husband theory, unfortunately, was the only one that seemed to fit the facts. It was the story everybody else believed.

Only I didn't believe it. Barney seemed so...helpless and dim. OK, killers are losers; and many of them are dim. But they're a different kind of loser, a different kind of dim, aren't they? They have tattoos and they pack guns and they're violent, and they swagger. They're not two-bit actors and movie wannabes with pale blue watery eyes like Barney.

We got up and left the restaurant. It was brilliant sunshine outside. Not a cloud in the sky. Pleasantly warm, dry heat, heat that nourished and energized, heat without humidity and mosquitoes. The hills in the distance seemed to be shimmering. It was a typical California day. Great to be alive, unless you were Barney Bell.

I put my arm around his shoulder and told him everything was going to work out alright. Then we walked out to our separate cars.

# 7

As I told you, I had no wish to get mixed up in the dreary affairs of Barney Bell. I did feel sorry for him; he seemed like a poor scared rabbit caught in a trap, waiting for the hunter to come and put him out of his misery. The least I could do, I thought, was to watch the stupid program he mentioned. Beyond that, nothing.

But I had made some promises and of course I would keep my word. I did my duty, and called his sister. Barney, before he left me, had given me a phone number. "Call this number," he said.

"It's your sister's place?"

"Man, she doesn't have a place. She was freeloading with us, and I kicked her out, remember? I think she's with her boyfriend, the doctor. It's his number. I got it from Blanche, actually...."

At the office, when things got slack, I punched in the numbers. A man's voice answered: "This is Dr. Ross Tanager."

"Uh, Mr. Tanager, this is Frank May. I...did some legal work for Barney Bell. I'm trying to reach his sister. Is she there?"

"No," he said, "I'm in a car, on my way to the Sunnyvale clinic. This is my cell phone. But I know where I can reach her. What is this about?

"I'd.... Well, I'd rather not say."

He paused for a moment, then he said. "OK. I'll give her your message. Where can she reach *you*?"

Reluctantly, I gave him my home number. It was late afternoon, and I planned to go home as soon as possible. Celia doesn't like me to get business calls at home. But she knows that it happens. Naturally, Suzie called during dinner. It was 7:30, and we were sitting down at the table, eating a freshly delivered pizza. Celia has long hours, just like I do, and she doesn't cook every night. I have absolutely no objection. I'm a modern husband. I can fend for myself; and I don't demand a lot. At least that's what I think.

Both my girls were home, which is unusual—they're teenagers, and like all teenagers, they much prefer the company of their friends to the company of their parents. I think they would have to admit that we're mammals, and even primates, but beyond that, they see no cultural kinship with us whatsoever.

In their minds, we are simply hopeless. You get used to this idea. If you have teenage children, you know what I mean.

They adore pizza, however.

The dinner was eaten in sullen silence, as usual. Celia and I asked questions, about how the day went, and so on, what happened in school; all we got in return were mumbled monosyllables, and an occasional audible word, usually "whatever." Eventually, we gave up and just talked to each other.

The phone rang. "Dinner time," I said, "ten to one it's another telemarketer." The last phone call had offered us a deal on accident insurance. I hung up immediately. Celia says I should at least pretend to listen. "They're just trying to make a living. Everybody hangs up the phone when they start in," she said, "I feel sorry for them." I appreciate the sentiment, but I don't share it. I have sympathy for stray cats, for war refugees, for people with loathsome diseases, or low IQ's; but not for telemarketers.

This time, though, it was no telemarketer. It was Suzie. She had a husky phone voice. There was also a kind of British accent. No doubt phony. After all, if Barney had been born a Zizzowicz. It follows that Suzie, too, must be a former Zizzowicz.

I told her I had spoken to her brother, and that he thought she could help him.

"Help him? How? He's got a lawyer. What else does he need?"

"I'd rather not talk about it over the phone. Can you come see me, in my office?"

She sounded reluctant. "Is this necessary? I'm awfully busy. I have so many things on my plate," she said. I said nothing. Silence is sometimes a powerful weapon. "Oh, all right," she said. "I suppose I owe it to Barney. But really, it's such an imposition."

"When would be convenient?"

She hemmed and hawed; and finally, we fixed a time— 3:30 the next afternoon. I told her how to get to my office. Then she hung up. I wondered how much she actually had "on her plate." According to Barney, she was unemployed.

She appeared, half an hour late, which was awkward, because I had a client scheduled at 4:00, and I certainly wasn't going to keep the client waiting—he, after all, was a cash customer, which Suzie most certainly was not. The client, who doesn't figure in this story, was a small businessman from Cupertino, who wanted to execute a living trust. He actually came five minutes early, and we were talking when Suzie arrived. I excused myself, and went into the outer office. She was sitting there, with a man, who I assumed (correctly) was Ross Tanager. "You're late," I said. She said: "I'm running behind schedule." The man gave her an incredulous look.

I said: "I'm seeing a client now.... I'm afraid you'll have to wait." She made a sour face. "Really!" she said, "I'm awfully busy." The man gave her that look again. He was obviously thinking: who is she kidding? She has nothing to do.

We finished our business, the client and I, in about twenty minutes, as it turned out. When the client left, I called them into my office.

"This is Dr. Ross Tanager," she said. He was a man of about 40, medium height, medium looks, well dressed, neither skinny nor fat, neither tall nor short; wearing a nice gray business suit, and a respectable tie. He had a touch of gray at the temples. This was either as nature planned it, or was done with a little help from manmade sources; it was hard to tell.

Suzie herself was of uncertain age. She was obviously one of those women who spend a lot of time, money, and attention, trying to look young. I'm not sure she succeeded. She was certainly older than Barney. She had orange-red hair, dyed of course, and a rather sharp face. She was not bad-looking. She had piercing green eyes, which clashed (in my opinion) with her dyed red hair. Her eyebrows looked as if they had been drawn with a pencil. She seemed quite elegantly dressed, and she had a certain flair. Celia, my wife, could have told you exactly how much the outfit cost, and whether it was really good or only a cheap imitation.

Her dress was fairly short. Too short, if you ask me, for a woman of her age. And she had a habit of crossing and recrossing her legs, as if she was trying to suggest that she was very seductive, very sensual, with the power to drive men mad. I don't think she was particularly successful. She was about ten years too late, I would guess.

"Ross drove me here," she said. "I don't have a car, these days. I'm thinking of buying a sports car. They're expensive, but so practical, in the city, what with parking and all. Ross is an absolute dear, even though he's so terribly busy. He drives me where I want to go. But all of us these days are so busy."

I mumbled something affirmative.

She said: "This is...a bit embarrassing. But...if you don't mind, I really want to talk to you alone. Ross understands."

"Of course," I said. The doctor excused himself. "I'll be back in...how long, Susan?" She said: "I have some things to do here in town, Ross.... I'll take a cab. I'll see you later, is that alright?"

He nodded. He had a strange expression on his face, which I found hard to read or understand. Was he trying to say something, wordlessly? To her? To me?

At any rate, he left. "Ms. Bell...." I began.

"I'm not Bell," she said. "That's Barney. I'm Susan Brinkley. I got rid of that disgusting name I was born with, just like Barney did. Barney changed his name before I did. To Bell, of course. But I never considered that name for a minute. God forbid I should have a name that would connect me with Barney. It's the last thing in the world I'd ever want."

"Frankly," she went on, "Barney has always been an embarrassment to me. I simply travel in different circles. Barney's taste...well, you can imagine. We're so different. We were always different. Barney...has no appreciation for art, culture, literature. I'm sure you've noticed that. You're a professional man, after all. Barney...has no taste, no real education. I was the intelligent one in the family. If I do say so. If Barney ever read a book in his life, well, it would be news to me. Myself, I love literature. Especially the classics. I find most modern novels vulgar and cheap."

Was I supposed to comment? There was definitely a family connection: like Barney, she loved to hear herself talk.

"I'll be honest with you," she went on. "Barney and I.... How we ever ended up in the same family, I have no idea. He's an absolute fool. He always has been, and he always will be. I'm sorry he's in trouble, and...it's too bad about Blanche; but to be honest, he's utterly worthless, in every way, and that's the plain, unvarnished truth."

That sounded pretty harsh to me. My sympathy with Barney was on the upswing again. His sister was like his late wife. Maybe his whole life, he was under the spell of a certain kind of woman. I wondered what his mother had been like.

She crossed and recrossed her legs again; she tugged at her skirt, and made little finger motions in her hair. She was trying too hard to make an impression: trying to say, I am an exciting, attractive, fascinating woman. But where was this leading?

She continued her monolog. "I always had a finer class of friends. Not the vulgar people Barney had around him. And imagine, he thinks of himself as an actor! An actor! Did he ever read Shakespeare? Or Chekhov? What kind of actor could he possibly be? His taste in movies—well, *Spider-Man*, or those things with nothing but explosions and bodies, and guns, guns, guns.... Has he ever been to an opera? I doubt it. I had friends there, in the San Francisco opera, I used to sit in a box seat, near the Getty's, all the big people. I adored the opera. Barney never had any feeling for the arts. He certainly never had any feeling for *me*. He considered me a snob. Well, alright. I'm an elitist, I admit it."

I tapped on my desk with a pencil.

She said: "I've had bad luck in my life, I can tell you. More than my share of troubles. I married the wrong man, twice in fact. It's the story of my life. In the end, they took all my money. I made some bad investments. Dot.com companies.... I took risks; you have to take risks in life. But now I have nothing left."

"I'm sorry," I said, for want of anything better to say.

"I don't give up," she said. "I have a strong character. I've learned a lot, from Eastern philosophy. I've studied Eastern philosophy, intensely. I do yoga.... And," she added, "I have

Ross. He's fine, he's educated...and he's utterly devoted to me. But Ross is a married man, did you know that? He's separated from his wife. She just wasn't worthy of him. I'm not the only one who makes bad choices; but that goes without saying. Anyway, there's going to be a divorce, but not yet; it's complicated, so many financial details. Ross isn't free, in other words. A year from now, I'm sure, things will be totally different. Ross...you saw him. He's what I've always wanted and needed. The opposite of Barney. Still, because of the divorce, and the complications, I can't be dependent on him, he would give me everything I needed, but not right now, not until this is all cleared up, you realize. We have to be cautious."

I said I understood.

She went on: "As I said, my stocks tanked, you know, when the bubble burst. I listened to the wrong people. Stockbrokers—I have many friends in the business; but I let myself be guided by a broker who gave me truly terrible advice. My portfolio.... well, never mind. I had these severe financial reverses. I had this beautiful apartment, a penthouse, in the City, Pacific Heights.... But I had to give it up. And then I had nowhere to go. I had to ask Barney for help. It was humiliating, utterly humiliating, to be dependent on him, for shelter, for a roof over my head. It cost me a lot to ask Barney for favors. I thought, I'd sooner die. But in the end, I did ask him. Him and Blanche.... She was more sympathetic.... I just needed time, to get my bearings, and...as I said, until Ross could get free...."

"You were living with Barney?"

"Yes," she said. "Well, Blanche made it bearable. Just. He treated me despicably, Barney. My aspirations, they have no meaning to him; my wants, my needs. And he has such a foul mouth.... He made me suffer.... He actually threw me out, did you know that? When we were staying at Travis Hinchcombe's house. He had no right to, it wasn't his house, it was Travis'. But he threw me out anyway. And Blanche, I thought she was on my side, but she went along with it, I don't know why.... I was always friendly with Blanche. I'm going to miss her. Why Barney did this thing, I'll never understand."

"What thing?"

"Killed her. Why he killed her. I never thought he would do a thing like that. Never in a million years. Poor dear Blanche...."

I cleared my throat. "Miss Brinkley...."

"Call me Susan."

"Barney says he's innocent, Susan. He thinks, maybe a burglar...."

She gave a short, unconvincing ha-ha laugh. "Oh, that's nonsense. I wasn't born yesterday. He just made that up, that burglar story. It isn't true. In fact, I *know* it isn't true."

"You *know* it isn't true?"

"Yes."

"You *know* that Barney killed her? How? You weren't there."

"I'm really not at liberty to say. Not to anybody. Not even to his lawyer. I'm certainly not going to help send my brother to the gas chamber, even if he's a worthless bum, which he is; and even if he killed poor Blanche, which he did. But let's not talk about that. That isn't at all why I'm here."

She was another one misinformed about the death penalty in California. No gas chamber. It was lethal injection. Naturally I didn't correct her. "You're here because I called you," I said. "Barney thought...."

"I don't care what Barney thought. I'm here because I want to be here. Because I have a question I hope you can answer. You were acting as my brother's attorney...."

"Yes, I was."

"And...he was making some financial arrangements? A will?"

I said: "These things are confidential, Susan. I'm sure you know that."

She said: "I'm not interested in lawyer slogans. I'm a sophisticated woman. Now that Blanche is dead, I'm his closest relative."

"Well, there's your mother...."

"She hardly knows which end is up. She's hopelessly demented, didn't you know that? Barney put her in some kind of home, in Fresno. They feed her and dress her. She gets some sort of pension, or the state pays for her. I haven't seen her for years. No, there's only me."

"OK, so what's your question?"

"It's a simple question. You might think it is crass, or inappropriate; but I don't care. The question is this: who gets

Blanche's money?"

I said: "Her money? Well, I don't think she has much."

She said: "I heard otherwise. She gets a bundle from an uncle, doesn't she?"

I thought: is this privileged? But whatever ethical qualms I had were overcome by a passionate desire to say something that would get rid of Suzie. "In fact, she doesn't."

She frowned, and said, in a nasty tone, "I believe you're wrong. Frank. I have information...."

I stopped her short. "Her father left money in trust, for her uncle, who is now dead. Under the terms of the trust, the money goes to Blanche, but only if she survived her uncle by six months. She didn't. She's died before the six months were up; and as a result, she loses it all. Every penny of it."

She looked intensely disappointed. "So...where does the money go? To Barney, I suppose?"

"Not at all. It goes, I guess, to her closest blood relative. Her brother, I believe. Possibly her mother, but I doubt that. It's not any of my concern, to be honest; and I haven't seen the actual trust document."

"Didn't she have some money of her own?"

"I suppose. Some. Not much."

"Well, who gets that? Barney?"

"Yes...unless...unless he's the one who killed her."

"Then he loses the money?"

"Exactly."

"And it goes to his next of kin? That would be me. And mother, I suppose."

"You?"

"Well, I'm his sister, he doesn't have children, his wife is dead: who else?"

"I hate to disabuse you, Susan.... But the money would go, I think, to Blanche's heirs, not to Barney's."

"And who is that?"

"I don't know; her brother, probably."

Another disappointment. She was silent for a minute or two, and then she said: "Well, I'd get *his* money, anyway, wouldn't I?"

Was she really this cold-blooded? I said: "But Barney isn't dead. Look: even if he's convicted, it's not going to be a capital case; and even if it was, and he got the death penalty, God forbid, it takes years and years.... So his money isn't an issue; and, to be honest, it's all going to go for lawyer fees. Besides, he has a will.... And he could make out a new will, anytime he felt like it, so I don't think his money is an issue."

This was more bad news. She made a face, like somebody sucking on a lemon. Then she crossed her legs again, and tucked nervously at her skirt. She said: "I suppose I'll just have to soldier on. You must think I'm an awful person...."

"No, no...."

"Yes, you must. An awful person, here she is, talking about money, when her only brother, her closest kin, is in such terrible trouble. I do sympathize with him; it's difficult, but I do. Of course, he did an awful thing. I... I liked Blanche. I really did. But who knows what she did to provoke him? He's not normally a violent person. It must have been...really something unusual. Maybe she was having an affair. Men can become insanely jealous; believe me, I know."

This piqued my curiosity. "You were close to Blanche? *Was* she having an affair? Is there something you know, something she told you? This could be important—it could have a bearing on the situation."

"I'm just speculating," she said. "Blanche was very private. We never discussed sex, or men. But...Blanche...well, she traveled in certain circles, didn't she? These would-be actors and actresses. They have no sense of the proprieties.... Who knows what they do, sexually speaking. They have no loyalty... and the drugs, after all...."

"Drugs? Was Blanche on drugs?"

"Darling, I have no idea. We all experimented, didn't we?"

Well, some of us did. Others didn't, including me and Celia. We experimented with nothing. Once, a long time ago, when I was in high school, I bought a book about different sex positions or the Kama Sutra or some such thing, but I was terrified that somebody might come in the house and see it. I threw it in the garbage. At any rate, I never put its valuable insights to work.

I kept trying with Susan: "Barney says you and Blanche were having heavy conversations, shortly before she died, I mean, a day or two. Could you tell me what the subject matter was? This isn't idle curiosity. Barney thinks, well, it might be useful to him, in his defense."

"What we talked about? Oh.... Gossip. Nothing special."

"Gossip? What about?"

"Oh...people you don't know. Really, it had no relationship."

She was lying. That much was completely obvious.

I said: "Susan, please don't hold anything back. It could be terribly important. You're not telling me anything. You say you know Barney did this thing, but you won't tell me the basis, why you think this. Now you aren't saying what you and Blanche discussed. Barney felt, well, that there was something going on. I don't want to sound overly dramatic, but his life might depend on it."

She said: "Please. Barney isn't going to be on death row, that's ridiculous. It was the heat of passion or whatever you call it. They get a few years in prison, don't they? I mean, the system.... And anyway, I'm not at liberty to say. Even if I told you, it wouldn't help Barney, believe me. If anything, the very opposite."

I kept up my questions for a while; but I could get nothing further out of her. I'm not a terribly intuitive person—Celia says I'm completely tone deaf, when it comes to interpersonal relations, body language, and anything subtle like that. But I had a feeling about Suzie. First, that she was lying. Any fool could see that. She *knew* something. And one of the reasons she came to see me, was to see if *I* knew something. Why?

But I made no progress, and after a while, there was really nothing much more to say. She droned on about this and that, but I more or less tuned out. Finally she swept out of the office. I sat there for a while, rather depressed. I stared out the window. I looked at the clouds in the sky. Then I forced myself to work. I was busy, going over some papers, when the phone rang.

"Mr. May? Ross Tanager here. Are you alone? Has Susan left?"

"Yes, she has."

"Do you have a moment? I'm in my car, in the neighborhood; actually only a block or so away. I'd like to talk to you, if I may."

I didn't have a moment; but I made a moment. Curiosity, they say, killed a cat; in my case, it killed my inclination to get on with my work. But I was anxious to hear what the good doctor had to say.

# 8

Dr. Ross Tanager came rather quickly, sat down briskly; and got right to the point. "You are Barney's lawyer, am I correct?"

"Well, in a sense."

"What do you mean, in a sense?"

"He consulted me. About certain matters," I said. "But now...well, as you know, he's in a lot of trouble; and he's hired a criminal lawyer."

He waved his hand, in a gesture of impatience. "Yes, yes, I know that. But you're his regular lawyer, right?"

"You could say so."

"And he consulted you about his will?"

"Yes, he did."

"Did he discuss...did he make any provision for...a child?"

"A child?"

"A child. A baby."

I was puzzled. "No. What baby?"

"His baby. At least...well, we assume.... Did you know—and did he know—that Blanche was pregnant?"

This was news to me. I was thunderstruck. "Pregnant! You're sure of it."

"Of course. I'm a doctor. This is not a mysterious, rare condition. It doesn't take great diagnostic skill.... Blanche consulted me. She came to me in confidence. I'm not a gynecologist, but I went to medical school, after all. She said she didn't know any doctors, except me. She knew me because of Susan. I'm a rheumatologist but it's easy to find out if somebody is pregnant. I suppose she had a gynecologist, most women do, but she obviously didn't want to go to him. Or her. And, yes, I confirmed that she was pregnant. Not *very* pregnant, a month or so; but definitely pregnant."

I said, rather stupidly: "Wow."

He went on: "I assumed of course that Barney was the

father. She was a married woman after all, and married woman get pregnant. But then, she swore me to the strictest confidence. She said I must tell nobody about this, least of all Barney; and also not to mention a word of it to Susan. Or anybody else, for that matter."

"Did she give an explanation?"

"No. I asked her, but she didn't want to tell me. It was, after all, none of my business. And I kept her secret. Of course, it's not a secret anymore.... The police know all about it, because of the medical examiner, you understand."

My head was spinning. Somehow I found it shocking. I couldn't imagine that Blanche wanted to be a mother. And Barney.... I'm sure he had no idea.... I remembered my conversation with Blanche. She said she was maybe going to have children someday. Someday. She talked as if it wasn't something imminent. Was she lying to me? Or did she intend to get rid of the baby? And she said distinctly, I remember, that she wasn't going to have children with Barney.

I made a mental note to talk to Nolan about this. Did *he* know? He must know, by now. But why was Dr. Tanager telling me these things?

"You can understand," he said, "that I'm very loath to get involved in this...sordid business. Of course, when Barney called me, that night, the night Blanche, uh, died...well, as a doctor, and an acquaintance, I had to come.... And I was, in a way, Blanche's doctor. By default. She didn't need an expert on arthritis, believe me, which is mostly what I do. Frankly, I don't want to go any further. I don't want to be tangled up in this mess. I'm sorry about Blanche. Of course. It's a terrible tragedy. But it's not my affair. I really didn't know her very well."

"I understand."

"There's something else. I need your advice."

"Advice? Of what sort?"

"Shall I go to the police? They haven't questioned me. Except about that night, and there wasn't much I could tell them. When I arrived, Blanche was minutes away from death. I could see that immediately. The paramedics were there, already, but it was hopeless.... The police don't know...that Blanche consulted me. Now the question is, do I have to give my information, would I be violating the law if I just kept these things to myself?"

"Well, what would be the harm in telling them what you know?"

"Frankly, as I said, I hate to get involved. In my profession...my reputation.... And there's Barney. I barely know him, but I don't wish him any harm. My evidence, I'm afraid, is fairly negative."

"Negative? In what way?"

"Our conversation is confidential, I assume?"

"Certainly."

"Well, I don't actually *know* anything. But Blanche wanted to keep the news secret. She didn't want Barney to know about the pregnancy. Maybe it wasn't his child. Maybe she was hiding something? An affair.... But if there was another man, well, that would be a strong motive. They could say, maybe he found out, and...killed her. Some men are terrifically jealous."

"Possibly," I said, "but, after all, maybe it *was* Barney's baby; and suppose she didn't want it, she was going to have an abortion; and she didn't want him to know about *that*."

"But that's not in his favor either, right? Suppose he found out she was pregnant, and maybe it *was* his baby; but she didn't want a child, she didn't want him to know about it, and she wanted to get rid of it, and he didn't.... They quarreled...."

"Who knows?" I said, "Frankly, I'm not an expert on Barney Bell. I met him only once or twice, you have to remember that. To be honest, I can't imagine him with a baby. He doesn't strike me as a daddy."

"You mean, he wouldn't want the child?"

"Right."

"People do funny things," he said. "You'd be surprised. Lots of people have children, and you wonder why on earth. And other people...you'd be amazed; the things I see, in my practice."

I wouldn't have thought that a doctor who mainly deals with arthritis would see a lot of weird and disgusting things, compared to other kinds of doctors. But what did I know?

"Did you know Barney well?" I asked.

"Not well. I agree, I don't think of him as a killer. But, you know, in a fit of rage...."

I shook my head. True, everybody gets mad, I get mad,

Celia gets mad, the kids get mad (all the time); I suppose Barney gets mad. But murderous rage? No, I couldn't see it. I told him, I just couldn't buy the idea.

"Something else," I said. "I don't think Barney knew. About the baby. I'm positive he didn't."

"Oh? On what basis?"

"Just that he never mentioned it. When we talked about a will, and all that, he never said, oh yes, my wife is pregnant. And he's never mentioned it since. I know this isn't really evidence, nothing you could tell a jury, but still...."

He nodded. "You're probably right. But: back to my own problem, what do you think? What should I do?"

"Well," I said, "I don't think you have to volunteer. Of course, if they ask you, you have to tell the truth. And maybe you should discuss the matter with Susan."

"With Susan? What on earth for?" He seemed genuinely startled.

"Well, since you're going to be married...."

He looked at me as if I was some kind of lunatic. "Married? Are you out of your mind? Me marry Susan? You met the woman...."

"Sure, today...."

"Do I have to draw you a picture? Could you possibly imagine, I would marry that woman? Why on earth would I do a crazy thing like that?"

"She said...."

"She said what?"

I started mumbling and stuttering: "I had the impression.... I mean, she told me...you two were, uh, engaged...."

"She's delusional, absolutely delusional."

"But she said...."

"I don't care what she said. Anyway, I'm married."

"I know. She told me that. Married but separated. That's what she said."

He said: "Well, that much is true. I *am* separated. Yes. And we're in the early stages of getting a divorce. And it's not what you might call a friendly divorce. I don't want to go into details. And...you see, my wife has most of the money in the family; she inherited money, from her grandfather, and we have a very expensive house, we have debts.... She's full of resentment."

"Resentment?" Then I was sorry the word came out. I should have known better. I had no license to pry into his affairs. And, anyway, you don't need a reason for resentment. It's amazing, in my experience, how resentment builds up in people. They start out in love, they bill and coo, they kiss at the altar, they make mad love on their honeymoon and all that; and then, not that many years later, there's resentment, exploding like a volcano; and they positively hate each other's guts. Amazing and sad.

"No reason," he said. Of course, he was lying; but why should he take me into his confidence? "She's...just full of resentment. She's trying to ruin me, trying to get everything, all the money. I honestly don't know why she hates me so. I'm telling you this to explain the situation. I'm still married, and there are all these issues, money issues, property issues, and it's ticklish all around. I'm certainly not looking for trouble. And Susan, she's trouble, God knows."

"So...you're not...in a relationship with Suzie?"

"A relationship? God no. She wants to be, I suppose. She tells everybody...that we're an item. Not a word of it is true. If it's not about me she's talking, then it's Travis, it's whoever she feels like.... In my case... she practically threw herself at me, but believe me, I'm not on the market. I met her at a party. At Travis' house. I've known Travis for years. I've been his doctor, sort of. He doesn't really need a doctor. Oh, yes, I treated his father, for arthritis. And his stepmother. I knew her too; I had her as a patient. Fine old woman."

"She was the one who left money to Barney?"

"Yes. She died suddenly, poor woman. Anyway, there was this party, at Travis' house. Suzie, she was there, at the party. I guess she knew about my, uh, marital troubles. She thrives on gossip. And she's always looking for a way to get money, without working of course. And I'm a doctor, medical doctor. In her books that means, I'm a meal ticket. Oh, Travis would be better, he's worth billions; but he wasn't buying her line either. Anyway: no; I'm not involved with her, in any way."

"But...well, you're friends, aren't you? You drove her here?"

"I feel sorry for her, that's all. She has these impossible airs, you'd think she was at least a member of the royal family or something. And meanwhile, she's a failure, she's penniless, she can't get or hold a job. No prospects. No skills, too, unless bullshit counts as a skill. I gave her some money, yes, out of pity. I did befriend her...cautiously. I did it...out of charity. But that's all. If we were having a relationship, why would she be sponging off her brother? No way. They can't stand each other, actually, Susan and Barney; but she had no choice."

"But...she said she'd see you at the house."

"Not my house, I can tell you that. I assume she meant Travis' house. Travis won't kick her out, now that he's back. Why he puts up with her, I don't know; but she's safe there, for the time being. She can pretend to be lord of the manor. She'll try to get money out of Travis. He's a better prospect than I am. Not for a relationship, he's too smart for that. But he's so filthy rich, he can afford to let her siphon off a little. And Barney... from what I hear, he's gone back to his own apartment. He's basically sitting there, waiting for the knock on the door, you know, expecting the police to come get him."

"You were Blanche's regular doctor?"

"Yes and no. She came to see me, as I told you; I wasn't her primary care doctor. I don't think she had a doctor she consulted regularly. I'd be amazed if she had health insurance."

"Why you?"

"I don't really know. Well, I assume, because of Susan. I knew Blanche slightly too, through Travis. Travis can afford dozens of everything, so he has dozens of doctors, I'm sure. But I think he trusts me."

"And...you told her she was pregnant?"

"Yes. I was puzzled at first, why she came to me. Then I understood. I think. The confidentiality. She thought she could trust me."

"When was this?"

"Oh, maybe two weeks ago. She wasn't very pregnant, you understand. Only a few weeks."

"Did you ask her...about...who the father was?"

"Good lord, no. Why should I? It was none of my business. As I told you, I was suspicious, because she said, don't tell Barney, but...well, nothing more than that. I was curious, naturally. But I never asked. And I never found out, of course. So... I still don't know. Maybe nobody does.... Well, somebody does, I guess."

"And, that was the last time you saw Blanche."

"Yes. I did speak to her a couple of times, on the phone. She asked me some questions, about pregnancy, and...she was a little worried, and she wanted to know, how long did I think until it would become obvious.... I don't know where she was, when she made these calls, I suppose when Barney wasn't around."

"She had a cell phone."

"Oh, did she? I guess. Most people do, nowadays."

"You never saw her cell phone?"

He gave me a funny look. I suppose he was wondering, why is this guy asking me about a cell phone. "No.... Was there something special about her cell phone?"

"Not really. Never mind. Go on. She called you."

"Right. She called.... It was pretty strange, it was the day before she died, she asked me, well, first, whether I thought she would look pregnant, if she was on a TV program next month, and I said, probably not. I said, I couldn't promise, women aren't all the same, some of them show right away, some of them never even look pregnant, but in general, no, she'd be OK. Then she said something about Travis' house, I remember, she was staying there, with Barney; she said it was big, and comfortable, and creepy...."

"Creepy?"

"Yes; and I said, really? I never thought so, it's got a really warm style, warm feel to it, comfortable and so on, and she said, well, if you saw somebody skulking around, you'd find it creepy too."

"Skulking around?"

"Her words."

"But she didn't explain?"

"No," he said, "she didn't. I mean, it was a pretty unusual thing to say, and I asked her, Blanche, is something wrong. What do you mean, somebody skulking around. And, well, I had the feeling she was about to tell me, to explain something, but she never did. She hung up the phone, suddenly, you know; she said, I have to go.... It was as if somebody walked into the room, or interrupted her, or she saw something. But of course I don't know what. So that was it. End of the story. The next night she was dead."

We chatted a few minutes more, and then he excused himself. He had patients to see, he said. I sat in my chair thinking. What could Blanche have meant, in that last, strange phone call? She couldn't have meant Barney. Whatever you could say about Barney, he wasn't creepy. Least of all to Blanche. And he didn't "skulk around." Was there somebody else in the house? Or *outside* the house?

After all, what was the case against Barney? Basically, that he was married to Blanche; that they weren't getting along; and that he was the only person in the house at the time Blanche was killed. He had motive and opportunity, and that's important. But if he *wasn't* the only person around...if there really was a prowler, or somebody else....

Yet how could we show this, if it was true? I was deep in these thoughts, spinning around and around in circles, and getting nowhere, when a client came charging in, bringing his problems, his demands, and the reality of the workaday world, and my balloon of imagination sighed and let out all its air.

# 9

I expected the police to move quickly, arrest Barney, and charge him with murder. But for some reason, this wasn't happening; as least not yet. I asked Nolan what was going on, why the delays. Nolan agreed, yes, Barney was probably going to be arrested. "They don't have any other suspect. Not at the moment. They will, though," he said.

"What do you mean by that cryptic statement?" I asked him. This was at lunch, at my favorite restaurant, the Golden Dragon. I was eating with a client, who was chatting away about his impending divorce, and all the problems it would bring, how the money would be arranged, who would get the car, and the golden retriever, and I was listening intently, because this was good potential business. Then out of the corner of my eye, I saw Nolan at another table, alone, wolfing down his food.

I excused myself, said I would just be a minute, went over to Nolan's table, and had the conversation I just mentioned. I said: "Another suspect? What's up, Nolan? Come on, don't play games with me." But he just smiled, and said: "Ah. Just wait and see."

I wanted to probe him some more, but my client was waiting impatiently at the table; and I had to get back to him. I listened to the client with about half of my brain. He went on and on. I muttered some platitudes, paid the bill, walked him to his car, and then excused myself. I went back to the office, and did some work. Then the phone rang. It was Barney. He had been calling me, at least once a day, whining—but who can blame him—and always the same old story: "I'm going bananas, Frank. This is like some sort of frigging nightmare. I can't believe it. They're going to arrest me, I just know it, Frank. They think I killed Blanche. I mean, is that crazy or what? I can't sleep, I can't concentrate, I'm just here waiting, man, it's like I'm on death row."

I tried to be sympathetic. It wasn't easy. He had nothing to distract him. "I'm just sitting here," he said, "and I'm going out of my frigging mind. I keep thinking about it, you know, like turning it over in my mind. I just can't figure out what happened.... I mean, what happened to Blanche. It's got to be some kind of a burglar. Or something. One of those bums you see on the street, you know them, Frank, they let them all out, they used to lock them up, now they're all over the place, they smell bad, they never take a shower. Some of them, they made sausage out of their brains, with all those drugs and booze, these guys could kill somebody, Frank. They hear voices and stuff, you know, they think the CIA put some kind of shit in their food or something. One of those guys, man, he must have come in the house, broke in, and he bashed her head in."

I grunted some sort of agreement. But most homeless people were, as far as I knew, completely harmless. More likely somebody could kill *them*, you know, a thrill killing, or to steal what they carry around with them. And how would some homeless bum get to that elegant neighborhood? How would he break in? It just didn't compute.

A professional burglar? But burglars rarely kill anybody. I read that somewhere. And they prefer empty houses. And apparently, there was no sign of a burglary.

"Frank," he said, "maybe I'm crazy. The whole world is crazy. Crazy things are happening, you know what I mean?"

I could see why he felt that way.

"Crazy stuff. I mean, like I told you, I think I'm losing my mind. There's this cell phone thing. I couldn't find Blanche's cell phone. I said, the guy took her phone. Now they say, she never had one. I said, she did, I seen it, she was using it sometimes; but they say no. They said, they checked with every cell phone company, nobody had a Blanche Baleine as a subscriber, or a Frances Elfenbein. And nobody was billed at my address. Who paid the bills, if there was a phone? I said, how the hell should I know, Blanche paid her own bills, I didn't mix in. But they think I'm lying."

I didn't know what to say.

He went on: "Frank, believe me, she had a cell phone.... I saw it myself; and now it's gone.... I don't know when she got it, not too long ago I think; but like I said, I saw it, with my own two eyes. Frank, why would I lie about a thing like that?"

I had no explanation.

"Another thing. I didn't tell you this. The day Blanche, uh, died: Travis called up. He said he was back in town for a few hours, then heading off somewhere, and how were things going, he wasn't planning to stop by the house, he was at the airport. And I said, OK, yeah, we love being here; it's great, very comfortable; but one thing, I said, I have to tell you, the pool, it's full of algae, it's like disgusting, can you have something done about it? So he said, where's the guy who takes care of it, and I said, what guy? And he says, the guy who takes care of the pool, takes care of the garden, you know, that guy. So I said, who's that? I never seen anybody. So he says, well, I don't know where the hell the guy is, I'm paying him good money, he's supposed to be there every day. But if he's not there tomorrow morning, look in the yellow pages and get a pool service and have them come out, I don't care what it costs."

"And? Did you call the service? Or did the guy show up?"

"No, I didn't call; and no, he didn't show up. I didn't call because that was the night the thing with Blanche happened, and I didn't exactly have the swimming pool on my mind; and then Travis came back, he said he canceled his trip when he heard about the tragedy...and you know, he was upset, I mean, somebody gets murdered in your house, and it's swarming with cops and people, and reporters hanging around and all that.

"He comes in, maybe it's one, two o'clock, I don't remember, and I'm packing, I'm getting out of there, going back to my own place, you know? And Travis, we're talking, and he says, by the way, this isn't a big deal, but are you crazy or something? What about, I ask him. And he says, the pool, you dork, there's no algae, the pool is in perfect condition, what are you trying to do? I said, nothing, why would I lie to you? Yesterday it was all green and yucky; and he just sort of shrugs his shoulder, you know, like I'm completely off my nut. Well, I didn't think much about it, we had a lot to talk about, he was offering to pay for the funeral, and that sort of thing, and I left and went to my apartment. OK: and a few days later he calls me up, on the phone, and he starts chewing my ass out, and he says, I know what you're up to, Barney, all that bullshit about the swimming pool. I said, what bullshit? He said, you know, that stuff about the algae. And he says: now listen here, I'm telling you, this is ridiculous, and I'm not having it. I'm warning you Barney. And I said, I don't know what you're talking about, Travis. And he says: watch it, Barney. You need me. And you know damn well what I mean. Then he hung up on me."

"What *did* he mean?"

"Frank, how the hell would I know? It's like the whole world's gone crazy, you know what I mean? Sometimes I wish I was dead instead of Blanche. Frank, you're my lawyer.... I got nobody to help me. Can you...find out what the guy was talking about? I mean, this business with the swimming pool, it's like he thinks I'm trying to get away with something. I need him, Frank. He's got a billion dollars, he's got powerful friends, and he could break my balls, Frank. I don't want him mad at me...."

"But what do you want me to do, Barney?"

"Talk to him, Frank. Go see him. Find out what's up."

"Talk to Travis? What about, Barney?"

"Find out why he's so frigging mad. Find out what's eating him. You're my lawyer, you can ask questions."

I was torn between curiosity—and, frankly, a little bit excited—and the voice of reason. The voice of reason kept saying: don't get involved. But he *was* my client, wasn't he? To make a long story short, in the end I agreed. Curiosity is one of my weaknesses.

# 10

Travis Hinchcombe (of course) had an unlisted number; but Barney had the number written down, and he gave it to me. I called, dutifully, the very next day. Someone answered who described himself as "Mr. Hinchcombe's assistant," and said his name was Arthur Flansbaum. I asked if I could make an appointment to see Mr. Hinchcombe. He said "in connection with what?" And I said, it was personal.

"Does Mr. Hinchcombe know you? He's a very busy man."

I swallowed hard, and said I was an attorney, that Barney Bell was my client, and that I needed to speak to Mr. Hinchcombe about the unfortunate occurrence at his house. He said he would call me back.

Which, to my surprise, he did; within an hour. He said that Mr. Hinchcombe would like to see me, the following day, at 2:00 in the afternoon, if at all possible. I could tell from the tone of his voice that nothing short of major surgery would be acceptable as an excuse for postponing or rescheduling this meeting. When Travis Hinchcombe calls, there are no options. Or when his assistant calls, who shared in the reflected glory of Travis Hinchcombe and his billion dollars and his condos in Paris, London, and New York, and his vast holdings in publicly traded companies and whatever else Travis Hinchcombe commanded. I said 3 o'clock would be just fine. Would I just come out to the house? I said I would. He replied, in his most bureaucratic voice, that Mr. Hinchcombe will be expecting you, the address is such and such, and he gave me directions.

To tell the truth, I was not at all unhappy about going; I really wanted to see the house. It was a billionaire's house, in the first place; and, more to the point, the house where Blanche was murdered. Partly it was morbid curiosity, the same impulse that makes people slow down on the highway to gawk at an accident, especially if it spatters blood and auto parts all over the place. And partly it was...something else, something I can't quite identify. A feeling of importance, excitement, whatever. My daily life is pretty ordinary.

Don't get me wrong. I love ordinary. Ordinary is seriously underrated. At least the American kind of ordinary. Millions of people would give everything they have for a chance to be ordinary. But as a total diet, 24/7 and 365, it does get weary at times. That's why people go to amusement parks. It's the closest they can get to danger and thrills—and without any risk, which makes it all the better.

I had to juggle my schedule somewhat the next day. I even had to tell a lie: I told a client I had to be in court the next day. That's always a great excuse. It invokes the majesty of the judge and of the law. In fact, I am almost never in court. I get paid indeed to keep people out of court; and that includes myself.

Travis' home was in Atherton. It is a very, very posh and exclusive town. Big homes on big lots. No commercial establishment is allowed to sully the purity of Atherton. The streets are lined with enormous trees, and many of the houses have gates. The whole town breathes a smug air of affluence.

I drove down El Camino Real, the long commercial street that runs all the way up and down the Peninsula. When it enters Atherton, it becomes suddenly all bucolic: no more gas stations and taco joints, at least for the mile or so that belongs to the city of Atherton. I turned right on a narrow, leafy street. The Hinchcombe house was about half a mile in from El Camino. It was surrounded by a high wrought iron fence; there was a rather low and simple gate near the street, also made out of wrought iron. It was unlocked. You drove up a curved driveway. I parked in front of the house, and looked around. It was a two-story house, very large and grand, in a kind of elaborate but fake colonial style.

The grounds were partly wild, partly planted with flowers. I peeked around the edge of the house; in the back, there was a large swimming pool, completely fenced in. At the side of the pool was a kind of garden house or shed. The pool was square and rather large; and the water glistened in the sun. I went back to the front of the house. The doorway was in the middle. To the right, around the corner, I could see into a large living room study, with French doors that opened out onto a tiny terrace; the area just past the terrace was overgrown with tall bushes, which made it difficult to approach the house; a small path through the bushes led through garden beds in a snakelike pattern, and ended up near the entrance to the house.

I went back to the front of the house and rang the doorbell.

The door opened, and a youngish man was standing there. "I'm Frank May," I said.

"Oh, yes, come in. I'm Arthur Flansbaum, Mr. Hinchcombe's assistant."

The assistant was, I would say, in his 30's. He was...how shall I put it? Drab. A pale, nondescript face, glasses, dark hair, a gray suit, blue shirt, and an exceedingly safe necktie.

"I have an appointment," I said.

"Yes. I know. Just follow me."

There was a kind of entrance hall, a stairway leading up to the second floor, and rooms off to each side. I was desperate to get a peek at the murder room, but I wondered if that was on the schedule. Arthur led me into a kind of study, a room with a desk, piled with papers, and bookshelves on all the walls. I noticed a bronze statuette, which was in use as a paper weight. It was a little boy playing a flute or something similar. I wondered if it was an artistic relative of the murder weapon; but I didn't dare ask. The actual murder weapon was no doubt somewhere in police custody.

A man was sitting at the desk. He got up, came over and shook my hand. "Travis Hinchcombe," he said. Arthur discreetly vanished.

Travis was not at all what I expected. But then I don't know what I expected. I had never seen a billionaire before. He was about my age, I would say, a man of medium height, medium weight. He was tanned and healthy looking. He had long ringlets of curly hair tumbling down the back of his head, although he was slightly bald in front. He was wearing very neat, pressed jeans, and a white t-shirt. This surprised me. He obviously cultivated the look of a rich but aging hippie. Or, if not a hippie, a Silicon Valley zillionaire, who made his money by defying the stuffy conventions of Wall Street. A dot-com zillionaire, the kind that built computers in their garage or whatever, and then went public and made more money than the sands of the desert.

Travis, as far as I know, never built a computer in his garage or anywhere else. His money did come from the internet or computers or software or gene-splicing or something equally mysterious and high-tech—I have no idea exactly what—but Travis was no engineer or scientist at all. He was, heaven help us, a lawyer like me. He made his money on some shrewd business moves, of the high-tech type, done at exactly the right time. Travis, people said, had impeccable timing. He knew when to get in and when to get out of the market. Myself, I think it was probably dumb luck. But you can't argue with a billion dollars, which is what Travis was supposed to be worth. Other people said a couple of billion. At that level, does it matter?

He said: "You said this had something to do with Barney. You're his lawyer? I thought Nolan Thom was representing him."

I became to fumble. "Well, yes, but on civil matters...."

"What civil matters?"

"Well, he consulted me, about making out a will. This was before, uh, this unfortunate occurrence...."

"His will? You made out his will? What the hell does that have to do with me? I'm sure he didn't leave me any money."

"Uh, no, of course.... Only...." I gulped and came out with it. "The fact is, Mr. Hinchcombe, Barney asked me to see you. He's, uh, quite unhappy about something you said to him, something that disturbed him."

"You know, he better get used to disturbances. Especially after he gets arrested, which is any day I suppose."

This was not going well. "Mr. Hinchcombe...."

"Travis."

"Travis. You gave him some kind of warning, and, he doesn't know what you mean...the guy is in trouble, we both know that, and...he asked me...if you could explain...." Travis Hinchcombe's face was firm and resolute. He made no effort to conceal his annoyance. "Can you please get to the point?" he said.

"I'm not sure I can," I said. I could see how Travis made money. He bullied people. Or maybe, having made money, he felt entitled to bully people. They would certainly never bully him back.

"Then why are you here?"

I tried to regroup. I repeated, that Barney had sent me, that he wanted to know why Travis was angry, that is, *if* Travis was angry, and what Travis meant by his innuendos.

"Innuendos?"

"Yes...."

"Now you listen," he said. "And you can tell this to Barney Bell, too. I don't deal in innuendos. I say what I think. And what I think is this. Barney knocked off his wife. Right in my house, which I don't appreciate. But OK, OK, that's his business in a way, I don't know why he did it; but he did it. And I'm not going to let him try to pin it on somebody else."

"Somebody else? What are you talking about? Honestly," I said, "I really don't know, and neither does Barney."

He got up from his chair. He stood over me glowering. "Listen," he said. "I'm willing to help Barney. I'll help him with the money, if he needs it. Yeah, I know, he's got some money of his own, but who knows how long it'll last. The way the lawyers charge.... Believe me, I know. He's been crying to me about the money, what it costs, and, shit, if he needs it, I'll give it to him. He's family, in a way. My dad...you know the story. His aunt and my dad were married. OK: the money, that's one thing. But I'm not going to let him squirm out of this trouble with some half-baked story."

"Mr. Hinchcombe, I mean, Travis. Honestly, as I said, I don't have a clue, I have no idea what you're talking about. What story?"

"Well, ask your buddy Nolan, why don't you?"

"Ask him what?"

"How he's trying to get Barney off, by pinning the rap on somebody else. That's pretty miserable, if you ask me. Pretty low down."

"And who's this somebody else? I mean, this is news to me."

"You haven't heard the gardener theory? I said, ask Nolan, he'll fill you in, all the gory details."

I was mystified. "The gardener? What gardener?" Then I remember Barney's tale of woe about the swimming pool. At the time, it just didn't register.

"*My* gardener, Mr. Lawyer. Who else's?"

"But what about this gardener?"

"You really don't know? OK: I had a gardener. Gardener and pool man. The day before Barney killed Blanche, and who knows, maybe he was planning it all along, Barney calls me up and gives me some sort of cock and bull story, about the pool. Which was complete shit, since the pool was in apple pie condition the very next day. I'm not really sure what he had in mind, but it was something to do with the poor jerk I hired to do the garden work, the pool work. Young guy. Well, now nobody can find this guy, he's gone off someplace, for good reason, if you ask me; and Barney and his shyster have decided, this is somebody to blame the murder on. That he, the gardener, killed Blanche, and then ran away. OK, I don't mind Barney trying to wriggle out of this, maybe she had it coming, who knows? But to try to frame this kid...."

"Barney...didn't kill his wife," I said, amazed at my own nerve.

"Yeah, and I'm the Dalai Lama," he said. "Tell me another story. He was alone with her in the house. Or maybe she bashed in her own head."

But I was intrigued now, with this new angle on the case. I tried to get more information: "This gardener...."

But my audience was at an end. "Your time is up, Frank ," he said. "I have other things to do, maybe you have too."

He got up and moved around the desk. His body language plainly said: please leave. I was not inclined to argue. I got up and walked out of the room. In the hall, I met Arthur. "I'll show you out," he said. At the door, I turned and say, "hey, Arthur; could I ask you a question or two?" He looked startled. "I guess," he said.

"Do you work here normally? I mean, in the house?"

He gave me a peculiar look. "Certainly not. Mr. Hinchcombe has an office. In San Francisco. He needed me here today; but it's not where I usually work."

"I see," I said. "So... you wouldn't have a key to this house?"

"Of course not," he said. "Where would you get such an idea?"

"But you could get a key, I suppose, if you needed one?"

"I don't think it's any of your business," he said. His

mouth closed tightly. I asked a few more questions, but he refused to answer. And so I left.

# 11

Two days later, Charley Morgan came to my office. He didn't just barge in; he called and I told him to come on down.

This was Barney's friend, his buddy. He was about Barney's age, I would guess, but a little bit stockier. He had a fashionable amount of brown stubble on his face; and a single earring, in his right ear. He was wearing jeans and a jeans jacket, over a t-shirt. I could be wrong, but he looked a bit unwashed. Barney's buddy seemed every bit as stupid as Barney. He was also in show business, like Barney, but the production end, he said. "You know, I don't have the balls to be an actor," he admitted. "I mean, I did a few gigs, maybe Barney told you about them; and I had a few lines in some shows; but I know I'm not cut out for that life. Me, I like the business end of show business." To me, he looked just as unsuitable for the business end, as Barney was for the acting end. Was he gainfully employed at something? If so, he didn't volunteer the information. For all I know, his day job was repairing yard gnomes.

He certainly wasn't a TV or movie producer. That much I can tell you. Surely producers had more on the ball than Charley Morgan.

"You're Barney's friend," I said. "I'm glad to meet you."

"Yeah. You're his lawyer, right?"

"Sort of. He's got another lawyer too, a criminal lawyer; but you know that."

"Guy in trouble like him, he could use a ton of lawyers."

I nodded in agreement.

"Look," he said, "I can trust you, can't I? I mean, we're on the same side, right? Barney's side?"

I said: "Sure. I'm Barney's lawyer. I have his interests at heart."

"I got to be sure," he said. "Most lawyers—don't take this

wrong, but they're crooks. They're out for themselves, you know?"

"Everybody's out for themselves," I said, "they're no worse than other people."

"I don't mean to be insulting," he said. "But.... I got something here, very confidential, you know; a real secret. So I have to be sure."

"You can be sure," I said.

He reached into the deep pocket of his jeans, and he pulled out an envelope; it looked like an ordinary envelope, not the smallest envelope, letter size, but the next size up. It obviously had some sort of document in it, because it bulged. He handled it as if it was something contagious. "This thing here," he said. "It's from Barney. He gave it to me. To pass it on to you. He wants you to keep it."

"What is it?" I squinted, to get a better look. It was, on the outside, a plain envelope. It was sealed. "What's in the envelope, Charley?"

"It's...a kind of notebook, diary, something like that. Anyway, it was Blanche's. She kept addresses in it, phone numbers, that sort of thing. Also, there was some sheets of paper in it, kind of folded up. I guess it's evidence. That the point. It's probably evidence."

"But where did you get it from?"

"From Barney. Naturally. Who else?"

"And where did *he* get it?"

He was sweating a little bit; nervous. His legs and arms twitched somewhat. He put the envelope on my desk, and stared at it, as if it had the smallpox virus, or something equally lethal, inside. "Charley," I said again, "where did he get it?"

"He....he picked it up out of her purse, you know. The night when she died. She was lying there on the floor, with the blood and all that; he wanted to call the doctor, he didn't have a number. So he opened her purse, he said he knew she had this thing, this little book, and she kept numbers in it, and he took it out of there, and he got the number, the doctor's number, and then he called the doctor, well, you know that."

"But...didn't he put it back?"

"Hey, listen. Was I there? He didn't. He put it in his pocket, and then he took it with him, to his apartment. Maybe he forgot about it, I don't know. Anyway, the next day, he calls me on the phone, and he says, Charley, come on over, this is important. So I come over, and he gives it me, you know, talking in a whisper, and he says, Charley, they're gonna search my place, Charley, I can't keep this thing, you take it. And I said, what the hell am I supposed to do with it? And he says, anything, only don't tear it up, it might be important. He puts it in an envelope, he seals it, he gives it to me...."

"So you took it."

"Yeah. But I didn't want it. I said, Barney, I can't hold on to this. It's evidence. He said, what do you mean, evidence? I said, I don't know. You told me, it came from Blanche's purse. I said, you can't hold on to it, Barney; and neither can I. But he begs me to take it, you know? And I'm, like, hesitating. So he says, OK, I can see your point; so take it, and give it to the lawyer, and he gives me your name and he says, you give it to him, when you get a chance, and Frank, he'll know what to do."

"Me? But what am I supposed to do with it?"

"I don't know. Hold on to it, I guess. Look: he says, Charley, if they find out I'm concealing evidence, or whatever, that's just what they need, the cops, it fits right in with their crazy ideas anyway, which is he killed Blanche. That's nuts, I know it's nuts, Barney wouldn't kill a cockroach, I mean, he's practically like one of those Buddhists, you know, they don't kill things, they don't even step on bugs. But the cops, you know the cops. They get an idea in their thick skulls, you can't get it out with a crowbar. That's the God's truth. So now, I'm giving it to you, lock it up in a vault or something."

I thought: great. Marvelous. Just what I need. Handing me a hot potato. And was this a violation of ethics, if I held on to it.... What was I supposed to do? What was the ethical thing? But Barney was, after all, my client. I thought, maybe I should talk to some expert in legal ethics; I studied legal ethics in school, the most boring subject you can possibly imagine; but now I was faced with a genuine ethical problem. I wish I had studied harder.

We kept on talking, arguing, but it was useless to talk Charley out of his plan. If I refused, I was afraid he would give it to the police. He seemed scared. So I took the thing. I slipped it into the drawer of my desk. Charley looked at me suspiciously. "You're putting it there? Not in a safe or something?"

I assured him, I would put it in a safe. Not that I had a safe in my office. "Trust me," I said. He looked dubious, but what were his options?

"OK, I'll trust you."

He got out of my office as quickly as he could. Now it was my headache. I was dying to look it at, but I had to wait. Or should I look at it at all?

Later that day, I saw a couple of clients, worked a little, doodled a little, stared into space. I called Celia and said I'd be a little late for dinner. "Not too late, I hope," she said. "Maybe half an hour," I said.

I sat there, thinking. Then I opened the drawer, and looked at the envelope. I slit it open with a letter-opener. Obviously Charley had never looked at it. I had to know what was in it, in order to decide what to do, I said to myself. But of course I opened it mainly because of my own damn curiosity.

Inside was a small black notebook, with names and addresses in it; also phone numbers. Nothing remarkable. There were some loose pieces of paper, too, and I took these out carefully and unfolded them. There were three of them.

The first was the draft of a letter. It had no date. It began, "Dear Tony, As you know, I've been on your program a number of times, and I greatly admire your style and your skill. I think you're doing a real service, bringing important problems to the attention of the public. And you give people, real people, an opportunity to tell their stories.

"But of course you also have to make money. You have to attract an audience, and the competition is rough. This means, you have to be constantly thinking, about new ideas for the show, ideas that will grab an audience, and hold them in the palm of your hands.

"I have a number of ideas for themes you can build your show around. For instance, I have a great idea for a show, something quite sensational. 'Men who killed for money.' This sounds impossible—I can hear you saying, yes, that's terrific, but how can we do it? If we use actors instead of real people, that won't work, because people will demand that we get the police involved, and that will expose the fact that not everybody on the program is who they seem. But I have a way of doing this. Let me give you a concrete example. You bring on a woman, and she says that she's suffering from a guilty conscience. She has a terrible secret. There was this old aunt, and her husband—the woman's husband—got poison from someone, and the two of them poisoned her, because they knew she was leaving them her money. Then they had her cremated, so nobody would know. But I, the wife, have proof positive that this happened. I was just an accomplice, he was the main one, he's the really guilty party. Then we bring on the guy, who had no idea his wife was going to say this before an audience of millions.... He would deny it, and you see, there's no real evidence; the woman was cremated, so the police couldn't really get into the act. They would have no basis, only this woman's allegations. But despite this, wouldn't the program really make a splash? Your ratings would go through the roof.

"Do I have a concrete case in mind? Yes, I do. And there would be no risk for you at all. I would like to talk to you, and explain what it is that I mean. And I have another case in mind, too, and I feel that it would be possible to find still others. If you think you would be interested in this proposition, please let me know."

I read this text over and over again. It was obviously meant for Tony Crass, with ideas for his show.

Did she ever send this letter? Apparently not. It seemed to be a draft, something she was thinking of sending. It was sitting inside her notebook. There was no envelope. She never actually mailed it. Why?

And did it really mean what I thought it meant? Was she really accusing Barney of killing his aunt? I remember my first conversation with Barney, he said something about it, but by way of a joke. Or what I thought was a joke. Had Barney seen this letter? I can't imagine he had. He would have destroyed it, wouldn't he?

The idea was simply too grotesque for words. I couldn't imagine Barney killing *one* person, let alone two; no, that was just impossible.

I unfolded the other two pieces of paper. One of them was blank. The other had some rough notes, hardly legible. I could make out only a few words. "Other ideas...programs...the dentist idea...."

I put the pieces of paper back into the notebook. What on earth was I to do with this? Did it have any value? Was it evidence? Was I obstructing justice?

Certainly, if Barney had killed his aunt, or even if Blanche was accusing him of killing his aunt, well, that had relevance to Barney's case. I could imagine what a prosecutor would do with this note. He killed his wife to shut her up. But Barney clearly knew nothing about the note; nobody would be so stupid as to leave such a thing lying around. And it was inconceivable that Blanche had showed it to him.

I put the notebook back into the drawer, locked the drawer —something I rarely do—and took off for home. I tried to put Barney and his troubles out of my mind. Celia had announced dramatic plans for beef stew. Normally, dinner is a makeshift affair, since both of us work. Often, it's Chinese takeout, pizzas, or cheese sandwiches. We've even stooped as low as MacDonald's, or Burger King, or even lower (if that's possible). But Celia had the day off from work—it was teacher advancement day, or pupil advancement, or something like that; she had decided it would be therapeutic to cook a wonderful meal.

She was absolutely right.

# 12

All in all, it was a very pleasant evening. The girls were away, visiting friends. At least that's what they said. Celia and I were alone with the stew. After dinner, I washed the dishes. Celia and I watched some junk on TV. We went to bed early. I read for a while, then got a good night's sleep, long and uninterrupted. Barney Bell and his criminal career, such as it was, were completely out of my mind.

But then came morning. Barney's miseries hit me in the middle of a nice hot shower, and haunted me at breakfast. By the time I was on my way to work, I was churning it over in my mind so obsessively, I nearly ran through a red light.

At the office, I put in a call to Nolan. I didn't reach him of course—sometimes I imagine it would be easier to get hold of the Dalai Lama—but I left a message with his very polite receptionist. A few hours later, he called me back. By then it was mid-afternoon.

"Frank, old boy. What's up?"

"Listen, Nolan. This Barney Bell thing. Can I talk to you about it?"

"Sure. Why not? I didn't know you were...well, working on it."

"Not really. Not like you are," I said. "But anyway. Yesterday, I had a chat with the doctor, you know, Ross Tanager."

"Oh? What about?"

"This and that," I said, "But in between, he told me that the late Blanche Baleine had been pregnant. Did you know that?"

"Sure. Well, not at first," he said. "I found it out recently. Very interesting. What do you make of it?"

"Am I supposed to make something of it? Women get pregnant. That's how the species survives, Nolan. What do *you* make of it? And what does Barney make of it?"

"Ah."

"Could you expand a bit on that 'ah?'" I said.

He laughed. "It meant she was having sex with some-body."

"Hey, Nolan," I said, "I know that. I'm a married man. I know about sex. Did Barney know his wife was pregnant? You'll notice, since you're an expert lawyer, that I didn't say: Did Barney know he was going to be a father."

"I noticed, I noticed," Nolan said. "Frank, between you and me, when I talked to Barney about this news, I got the impression, he was completely in the dark. He was flabbergasted. Kept saying, 'son-of-a-bitch.' Then he said, it was impossible. I said, what do you mean, impossible? You were married, weren't you? You had sex with her, no? Well, not very often, he said. I said, once is enough, Barney. These things happen. Suddenly he got all prudish on me, and didn't want to go into details, as he put it; but I gathered he always used what he called 'protection.' We didn't want kids, he said. Blanche especially."

"She told me that herself," I said. "That's why, well, I'm also surprised."

"But she *was* pregnant. No doubt about that. So Barney says to me, how do I know it's my kid? I said, well, we don't know, do we? Who else's could it be? Was she fooling around? He sort of shrugged his shoulders and said, he didn't know, maybe she was, but she never told him. I asked him: OK, Barney, have you got some suspicions? He said, no.... She had friends, he said, but nobody seemed that kind of friend. The whole thing depressed him, poor guy. Then he said, she didn't tell him a lot of things, or something along those lines."

I was sure that was true. Nolan went on.

"That's the gist of what he said, the poor bastard. Barney, I said, women *never* confide in their husbands, about that sort of business. They never give out a formal announcement-- by the way your best friend is balling me. Then he asked me something about DNA testing, could we figure out if it was his kid, and so on; and I said, I suppose we can. Actually, I have no idea. That's something the police are going to have to decide. If they decide to find out."

"Are you going to ask about it? I mean, ask for tests?"

"I don't think so," he said. "Too risky. Either way. If it's his kid, it really looks bad, killing your pregnant wife, like that guy in Modesto or wherever he was; and if it was somebody else's kid, that's handing them a beautiful motive. I worry about the prosecution. If they start finding lovers and if they can show that Barney knew about these lovers, or suspected something, it's bad for our side. Real bad. They'll argue that he found out his wife was pregnant, and that it's some other guy's baby; then he flips out, and bashes her head in. Not good. So I just think, we'll be as quiet as we can be, never bring up the subject. But the prosecution... I can't control them."

"Can I change the subject?" I said.

"Sure. We're just talking."

"I had a conversation with one Travis Hinchcombe."

"Ah yes."

"He was not exactly friendly."

"Doesn't surprise me."

"In particular," I said, "he was ranting and raving about Barney. Says he likes Barney, which didn't seem to be the case, actually, though he said so, but he said, Barney, he's family in a way, etc., but he's sure Barney killed Blanche, and he's willing to put up money for his defense, he says, but don't give me that innocence crap and so on. OK, a lot of people think Barney's guilty. That's nothing surprising. But then he went on and on about you and Barney trying to pin the rap on somebody else—a gardener or something. What's this all about?"

There was a pause at the other end of the line. Then he said, "OK, if you really want to know...."

"Yes, Nolan, I really want to know."

"OK. It's like this. Barney's my client. They're probably going to arrest him. I had a talk with a friend of mine, guy works for the district attorney, he says it's going to be any day now. I don't know about that. Something seems to be holding them up, he wouldn't tell me what. But it's only a question of time. They want to be sure they've got an iron-clad case. Actually, they don't; not yet. But it's *pretty* tight. Quarreled with his wife; anyway, he was the only one in the house, the burglar idea isn't going anywhere, his fingerprints, etc., etc. So it doesn't look too good. I need an alternative. A theory."

"A theory?"

"I have to be able to give the jury something. Some excuse to acquit him. A story. The prosecution tells a story, I got to tell a different story. They have a story: unhappy marriage. Pregnant with another man. So what's my story? OK: I can always say, prove it, you haven't got enough proof. But it's better to give them an alternative, not just the old 'reasonable doubt' sort of thing."

"So what's your story?"

"I'm getting there. Look: originally, I wanted Barney to agree to cop a plea. I told him, I thought I could get the charges knocked down to manslaughter; and a short sentence, five years, six years the most. Plead guilty, admit you killed her, but you didn't mean it, it was an accident, or you thought it was just a love-tap, or you lost your head. I thought we could do business that way. I mean, it's not that big a case, the prosecution would buy it. I think."

"He turned you down."

"He did. No way, he said. He said, first of all, he didn't do it, he didn't kill her, so why should he say he did? I said, fine, but you know, you could be convicted. And he said to me, can't you get me off? I said I'd try, but I can't give any guarantees. He said, he didn't want to go to prison, he couldn't go to prison, they'd kill him in prison, he knew all about it, he said he's a young white guy, he's very good looking—he really said that—and in prison, the big black guys with tattoos rape all the white guys, maybe not all of them, the ones in the tough white gangs maybe don't get raped, but he wasn't in any of those gangs, so he wouldn't last a month in prison, he might as well be dead, and in the end, he'd be dead, they'd cart him out of San Quentin in a wooden box. That's what he said. He said, he was scared shitless of prison. He said it over and over again."

"And what did you say?"

"I told him it wasn't that bad," Nolan said. "I said, don't believe everything you read in the papers, but he said, no way, I'm not going to prison. You have to get me off. They got O. J. Simpson off. I said, yeah, if you had his money."

"He's *got* money."

"Oh, I know that. He said that. He said, I've got some money, I'm not broke, I inherited money, from my aunt; and anyway (he said) Travis promised to help out, if we ever needed money. He knows I'm expensive.... But anyway, he isn't going to plead. He's got all these ideas about prison. Hey, he could be right, no? People do get raped. Anyway, he's adamant. So I have to have something else, another angle. If I get in front of a jury, and convince them somebody else did it, or even *might* have done it, or *could* have done it, they just might believe me and let Barney go."

I said: "Somebody else? You mean this mysterious gardener?"

He said. "Exactly. I don't know how Travis got wind of it. I think maybe from Barney. The damn fool talks too much. But you know that. Anyway, here's the story: there was a groundskeeper, guy Travis hired to do the garden, do the pool, that sort of thing. Barney said, he never showed up, they never saw him, the whole time he and Blanche were there. Travis says that's a lie. Who knows. Maybe he was hanging around, Barney just didn't notice. Anyway, one thing is clear: he's gone."

"Gone? Where to?"

"Nobody knows."

"And...who is he? Any idea?"

"No idea. It's sort of mysterious. I've hired a private detective, to try to find him. I don't know if I really want to find him. But I figure, if I don't find him, the police will. Funny thing about this guy. We don't have a picture, just a description, young, blondish, a ponytail, medium build.... Nobody even seems to know his name."

"His name? But Travis hired him."

"He did. And, yes, the guy gave him a name. Said his name was Eben Born. Travis says, that wasn't really his name; and Travis said he doesn't know much about him, which is strange. Why did he hire him, in the first place? No ID, no references. No address even. No phone number. Travis insists he has no idea where the man lived. He said, he never asked him for an address. Sounds fishy. A guy like Travis doesn't operate that way. Anyway, this gardener has completely vanished. Not a trace. My theory is going to be: he had a key to the house, he knew Travis was out of town, he broke in, to rob the place, and Blanche took him by surprise. He was familiar with the house, he thought nobody was home, or maybe that they were all asleep on the second floor. So when he came in, wow, there's Blanche. Crisis. He panics, picks up the statuette, and bashes her head in. Then he runs away. He's got to get out of there. It's plausible, isn't it?"

I thought it was marginally plausible. I was uncomfortable with it, but I didn't say so.

"I'm seeing Travis later today," Nolan said. "I'm going to try to find out more about the gardener. I don't expect a friendly reception."

# 13

Nor did Nolan get that friendly reception from Travis, I imagine. In fact, I'm sure of it, because I was on the receiving end of some of the fallout. First thing in the morning, as soon as I got to the office, I had a telephone call, from Arthur Flansbaum. He informed me that Mr. Hinchcombe was on his way to my office, that he, Arthur, was checking to see if I was in—"Yes, I'm in," I said—and that Mr. Hinchcombe wanted to see me, and he expected me to give him a half hour of my time.

"I have clients coming in," I said. It was a lie. But the last thing I needed was to tangle with Travis Hinchcombe.

"Just a moment." I heard him whispering something, no doubt to Travis.

Then he came back: "Mr. Hinchcombe says, cancel them. Your clients. He's in his car, I'm calling from his cell phone. He'll be arriving in fifteen minutes."

He hung up. And, just as he predicted, Travis arrived in fifteen minutes and stormed into my office. Arthur, I suppose, was sitting in the car, patiently waiting below.

Travis was hopping mad. He didn't even bother to sit down. He stood over my desk glowering. "Did you have anything to do with this crazy business? This hocus-pocus, this crusade against my gardener? Were you the one?"

"Me? Mr. Hinchcombe...."

"Cut out the Mr. Hinchcombe. You can call me Travis. Call me anything you like. But don't give me a bunch of bullshit. You were the one, weren't you? You got it from Barney, and you passed it on to the shyster who's trying to get him off. This creep, Nolan, he came to see me yesterday, trying to worm information out of me. But why should I tell him anything? It's none of his frigging business. And you: you listen to me. It's bullshit. I'll say it again. It's just plain bullshit. I think it's disgusting. Despicable. Lower than low."

He pounded his fist on my desk. I felt terrifically un-comfortable. I felt abused, even violated. Nobody, normally, yells at me. Well, my daughters do, but not very often. Where did he get the right to yell at me? I suppose his billion dollars gave him the right. Billionaires can say anything, they can yell at anybody, they can throw their weight around, they don't have to be thoughtful or polite. That's one of the things money buys. I made some feeble protest, claiming I didn't know what he was referring to.

"You know damn well," he said. "You're trying to save Barney's worthless neck, by screwing somebody else. Some-body who had nothing to do with it."

"I respect your judgment," I said, "but how can you be so sure?"

"So sure? About what?"

"Well, to begin with, so sure that Barney killed his wife...."

"Oh give me a break!"

"Or that your gardener had nothing to do with it. Listen: I'm not to blame for this business. I never knew this gardener even existed, not until yesterday that is. I don't know anything about him. But I do know, or I think I know, that Barney never killed his wife. And if he didn't, then who did? You see my point?"

Somehow the storm abated. He sat down in a chair, and for a moment or two, he said nothing. I looked at him. Then he said to me: "Let me tell you something, Frank. This gardener. He never killed Blanche. You know how I know? Instinct."

"Instinct?"

"I'm rich and successful, Frank. You know? I'm proud of my accomplishments. You think it's all luck: it isn't. It's skill. It's having a certain kind of sense. About business, but also about people. I know people. I'm a judge of people. I'm never wrong. Well, almost never. I was wrong about Barney. I always thought he was a stupid, useless twit. A complete loser. I never thought he had the balls to kill somebody. Well, I was wrong about that. Now let me tell you about the gardener."

"OK," I said.

"To begin with," he said, "the minute I saw him, I formed an impression. I *liked* him."

"When was this?"

"How the hell do you expect me to remember? A couple of months ago. I needed somebody, I was using a service, for the pool, and they also did the garden; they came in a truck, three times a week, they horsed around, they were total numbskulls, none of them could speak English, for God's sake. Real creeps. I called the company, and told them I was dispensing with their lousy services. I said to myself, why am I fooling around? Why am I hiring these dingbats, I should have somebody full-time. I can afford it. I put an ad in the paper. You can't believe what showed up, people with pierced tongues, people from countries I never heard of, people who smelled bad, I tell you, the absolute dregs of humanity. Well, I didn't have to see them, most of them; I had Arthur screen them. He got rid of them, except for the one or two who were halfway decent. And then there was this guy, Eben Born."

"Eben Born."

"That's the name he gave me. The minute I laid eyes on him, I knew, this was the right guy. OK, he had a little ponytail, but what the hell? He was clean, he was young, he spoke English. And he wanted the job, badly. He said to me, he'd had a hard life, he'd been in trouble, but now he wanted to turn his life around, he wanted to do honest work, wanted to show what he could do. Something about him *spoke* to me, if you know what I mean. I've always trusted my instincts. They never let me down. He said, I'm looking for a chance. Just give me a chance, he said.

"I kind of understood. Me, I was a real handful when I was an adolescent, I was in every kind of trouble. I drove my parents crazy. You name it, I did it; shoplifting, alcohol, drugs, getting some chick pregnant, kicked out of school, everything. And now look at me. I turned it around. I'm on all the *Fortune* lists. I'm a roaring success, I've got more money than I know what to do with, I have a boat, I have three big cars and a sports car, I've got a flat in New York, I've got a farm in Virginia, I've got it made.

"I wanted to believe in him. I saw *myself*, you know what I'm saying? I said, do you have references? He said, no, I haven't got any references. I don't have anything, he said. He said, I'm at Day One. I'm starting from scratch. Let me work for minimum wage, I need something to eat. I don't even have a place to live, he said, I'm staying in a cheap motel right now, the Cinderella Motel, I think that was the name."

"So you hired him."

"I did. He said, if you don't want to hire me, that's OK, I understand. But I promise you, I swear, you won't regret it, if you give me a chance. There was something solid about him. He was intelligent. My impulses are always on the money. Investment impulses, business impulses, hiring, personnel.... I said, you've got a deal. Now show me. I paid him minimum wage for two weeks, then I saw, he was a good worker, showed up every day, kept his mouth shut, did his job, gardening, cleaning the pool. Everything was done letter perfect. So I said, OK, you've proved yourself. I said, you're worth a decent wage; and I paid it to him. He came every day, worked a full day, kept his mouth shut. He was reliable. And I liked him.

"So you can see: you're not going to tell me, you and that other shyster, that he broke into the house and smashed in Blanche's head. How would he get in the house, in the first place? He didn't have a key. Get that through your head. No key. I never gave him a key. I gave him a job, but I wasn't taking any chances...."

"I thought you said you trusted him."

"I did. I do. But at first, I had to be careful, no? And then, why would he need a key? He worked strictly outdoors, like I told you. Garden. Pool. He kept some stuff in a little shed, with his tools and stuff. I paid him in cash. I never knew where he lived, whether he moved out of the Cinderella Motel or whatever; or what he did when he wasn't working. I never asked, and he never said. I didn't care. He was doing his job. That's it."

"But he's gone."

"Yeah, he's gone. But since *when*? That's a good question. Barney called me up, bitching and moaning about the damn pool, said it was filthy, green algae, blah blah. The day after Blanche died, I went out there, it looked pretty damn clean to me. So Barney was lying, he was trying to set this guy up, you know?"

"I don't think so," I said.

"Oh you don't, do you? Well, I do."

"But it doesn't make sense," I said. "According to you,

Barney was plotting and planning to kill her, all along. So he calls you up and tells you a story about the gardener, but it's before Blanche is dead. That's ridiculous. Even if you think he killed her, you can't possibly believe it was something planned out, you know, deliberate. It had to be spur of the moment. But then, why say that this guy was already gone, why say he was neglecting the pool? That cuts against Barney's theory; if he was already gone, how could he kill Blanche? I mean, it doesn't make sense. Don't you see?"

"Look," he said, "you're talking as if you're dealing with a mastermind. Believe me, there's no mastermind here. You're talking about Barney Bell, a dumb, pitiful schmuck if there ever was one. You think he's logical? Think again."

"But your gardener...this Born guy.... He *did* take off."

"Yeah, he took off alright. But when? And why? Maybe he had an accident, hit by a car or something. How would we know? OK: that's not too likely. So he ran away. Big deal. What does that prove? The guy probably has a criminal record. In fact, I'm sure of it. He's an ex-con, trying to start over. So, he hears somebody was killed at the house. Murdered. He was probably scared shitless. He figured, they're bound to finger me. He says to himself, I'm the obvious candidate, me, with my record. I'm out of here. *Anybody* would run away, under those circumstances... So this is all one huge red herring."

"And Barney?"

"Barney. Barney. He's the one. Isn't it obvious? He was alone in the house with her. They had a fight. Look: I feel for him. She was no bargain. Maybe she had it coming. Drove him over the edge, finally. OK, you're his lawyer. You and that other guy. You're paid to try to get him off...."

What could I say? I tried to explain, first, that I wasn't Barney's lawyer, anyway not *that* kind of lawyer, I had no responsibility for getting him off, and he wasn't paying me for that; also, that Travis wasn't the only person in the world with intuitions; I had my own intuitions, and they told me, Barney never laid a hand on his wife. But nothing I could say was going to convince Travis Hinchcombe. People rarely argue with billionaires; and when they do, they should expect to lose the argument.

I said, "You came back from Paris, the day after Blanche

died? Is that right? You said you saw the pool that day...."

He seemed annoyed. "You quizzing me? Asking questions? What're you driving at? You want an alibi?"

"No, really.... I guess it's none of my business...."

"You're right there. Maybe you already know this, but I wasn't in Paris. That wasn't a total lie. I did go; but I came back after a week. I didn't want anybody to know I was around here. I had some business, in New York, Philadelphia. Arthur knew where I was, but nobody else. And the last few days, I was in Santa Cruz."

"Santa Cruz?"

"I've got a beach house near Santa Cruz. I was there, just relaxing, recharging my batteries."

"You were...alone?"

"What is this? Twenty Questions? No, I wasn't alone. I was with a lady, if you must know. A married woman. And don't ask me to tell you her name. And I did some work, too. Arthur came down once or twice, brought me some papers, things to sign, business stuff."

"And...you had a key to the house?"

"Aha. The key. I get it, now I'm the one that bashed in Blanche's head. I drove up here at night, let myself in with the key, and went back home after I murdered her. Is that your bright idea?"

I was flustered. "No, of course not...."

"I should hope not."

"Don't get me wrong," I said, feebly. "I just don't think Barney killed his wife, and I'm trying to figure out, if anybody else had a key, if they could get in or out. I'm not accusing you of anything, believe me."

"Sounded like you were. Anyway, if you must know, I have an alibi. This woman. For now, I'd rather keep her out of it, if you don't mind. And, Frank, if I were you, I'd stick to my law practice. I'd keep out of things that don't concern you."

I said: "Thanks for the advice."

He said, getting up from the chair, "Yeah? Usually, I charge for my advice."

I said: "So do I."

But he wasn't listening. Our little tête-à-tête was at an end. He got up and swept out of the room.

# 14

I think of myself as patient and mild-mannered. I put up with a lot, especially from clients. I don't often lose my temper. But Travis Hinchcombe really got to me. His total arrogance. Just because he had a lot of money, he felt he could order people around. Were all billionaires like that? Maybe. I don't know any other billionaires. But I imagine, how totally corrosive it must be to a person's personality: all that money and power; and people fawning all over you, night and day. Or maybe it's the arrogant, ruthless people who make the money in the first place. I wouldn't know.

I knew that I shouldn't let irritation get the better of me. I also knew that I should shrug my shoulders, forget all about Barney Bell, and get on with my normal life. Besides, did I really have anything to contribute? My sleuthing skills were, frankly, non-existent. The rational thing was to fold my tent or close the book on Barney Bell. But I just couldn't.

I was intrigued by the gardener. It irked me that Travis assumed I was part of some nefarious plot to frame an innocent gardener. Of course, this was totally unfair. As to me, at any rate. Maybe not as to Nolan.

I was having my mid-morning coffee, sitting in my office; and I sat there, stirring the coffee with a spoon and thinking, thinking, thinking. I thought, maybe *I* can find him. My inner voice said: this is crazy. The police force and all the local detectives can't find him, how can you? He calls himself Eben Born, it's a fake name, and we know nothing else much about him. He's a young man with a ponytail. A needle in a haystack. Where on earth would I look?

I had one clue: the Cinderella Motel. That would be the first place to look. But (I said to myself) the police know that too. It was absurd to think he was still there. Or that I could find out something nobody else had found out.

Still, was there any harm in trying?

I looked in the local phone book, and sure enough, there was a Cinderella Motel. It was just south of Palo Alto, on El Camino Real.

El Camino Real means "the royal road," in Spanish. Everything around here has a Spanish name. You get used to it.

El Camino, as we call it, runs all the way down the Peninsula from San Francisco. Maybe all the way to Los Angeles. I once heard it was the original road the missionaries traveled on, back in the days before California was California. It was a long, tedious journey. It's still pretty tedious, but nowadays the missionaries would at least have their choice between MacDonald's, Taco Bell, or Jack-in-the-Box, not to mention Mr. Chau's fast Chinese food.

After work, I got in my car and drove over to the Cinderella Motel. I won't bore you with the story of my fruitless visit to this dreary place in Mountain View. The employees were very cooperative, very friendly, but they could tell me nothing about a Mr. Eben Born; they said, yes, the police had been there, and gone over their records, and, no, they never had such a person, as far as they knew. I thanked them and left.

I stopped in at a Starbuck's, for coffee and cake, and mulled things over. Starbuck's was just the place for mulling. Of course, mostly it was students, doing their mulling with laptops. But I can mull with the best of them.

Travis had no doubt told the police the same story. But maybe he was lying. He mentioned the Cinderella Motel, but never said he was sure that was the one. When the police drew a blank, did they canvas every motel in the bay area? That seems unlikely. There are an incredible number of motels. This is something I've always wondered at. Who on earth is staying in all of those motels, and why?

I finished my coffee, and drove south to Sunnyvale, to one of those mega-shopping centers, crowned with a Macy's department store. Celia had seen an ad about a terrific sale of men's shoes, and insisted I had to go. I found nothing I really liked. Disgusted, I began driving back home. Just inside the city line in Mountain View, sandwiched between a Dairy Queen and a Mexican restaurant called El Burrito Brujo, I saw a sign advertising the Glass Slipper Motel. An electric light bulb went off in my head.

Cinderella...glass slipper.... Was this Travis' little joke?

El Camino is lined with motels, big ones, little ones, fancy ones, shabby ones. The Glass Slipper was one of many.

I parked my car, and approached the motel office. A big sign out in front said: "Rooms from $49. TV in Every Room." The motel was old and looked forlorn. Everything about it shouted, "cheap." It was a low wooden building, with rooms facing the street, and a stairway (badly in need of paint) that led up to a second floor, where there were more rooms. A few cars were parked in parking slots. Not a single one of them was a Mercedes, a Lexus, or a BMW, the cars of choice in the better precincts of Silicon Valley. All of them looked old and sad. There was also a sprinkling of pickup trucks.

My own car fit right in.

I opened the door to the small room that served as an office. The first thing that caught my attention was a vase of plastic flowers on the counter. A sign announced that no lifeguard was on duty at the dreary little pool.

A young man with an earring was sitting in a chair behind the desk, reading a magazine. He looked to be about twenty or so. He was wearing a t-shirt and chino pants, and had a mop of (dyed) reddish hair, whose color matched his ample display of pimples.

"Yeah?" he said, looking up.

I told him I was a lawyer, representing a client, and investigating a matter which concerned an inheritance. "I'm trying to trace somebody...somebody who was registered here."

"A lawyer? What kind of lawyer?"

"A regular lawyer," I said. I showed him my business card. "So?"

"I'm trying to trace a man named Eben Born. Young man, in his twenties I guess, wore a ponytail."

"Never heard of him."

I noticed that he didn't ask me to spell the name. He just automatically said no.

"Well, I know he was registered here."

"Him and lots of people. So what."

"Can I see the records? I'm an attorney...this is an estate matter," I mumbled, hoping this would sound impressive. Apparently not.

"Hey, listen, mister. The answer is no. What is this, anyway, the third degree? You got a warrant or something? We don't show this stuff to nobody. I don't know you, I don't know what you're doing here, what you want. Maybe you're from a collection agency. The boss doesn't like it, if I answer too many questions. OK?"

He started aggressively reading his magazine. I looked at the cover. It was called *World of Warcraft* or something of the sort; about video games. At least he could read. I kept talking, probing further, but no luck. He claimed they had no records, that no such guy was ever there, or maybe he was (this was after I said how did he know), but there was no way of checking, and it was none of my business, and so on. I felt totally defeated. Actually, I'm the sort of person who gives up easily. I was about to slink out of there, when I had one of my few bright ideas.

"Do you know a....Mr. Hinchcombe? Travis Hinchcombe?"

His eyes lit up. He actually put down the magazine. "Yeah, what about him?"

"He's been here?"

"Not personally. Sent some creep. Arthur something."

"You mean Arthur Flansbaum," I said. "He's Mr. Hinchcombe's secretary. This business, what I'm asking you about, well, it's very important to Mr. Hinchcombe."

"Do you work for him? Hinchcombe? Did you bring me the rest of the money?"

"How much is it?" I asked. "He couldn't remember. He's a busy man."

"Two hundred dollars," he said. "Man, I could use it. Could you...give me some of it, at least? I mean, like a down payment?"

I said: "Sure, no problem. How's fifty?"

He nodded. Reluctantly, I dragged fifty dollars out of my wallet. It was all I had. I held it in front of him. I said: "The rest is coming."

"Better be."

"Anyway...you followed the instructions, did you? The stuff Arthur told you to do?"

"Yeah. Police came around, I told them, no such person."

I said: "Great," and I handed him the fifty.

He said: "Who was this guy anyway? This Eben Born guy. What's the deal with him?"

I said: "Did you get to know him?"

He said: "Sort of. He used to talk to me. About all kinds of stuff. He was pretty cool. He'd been around. So who is he?"

I said: "I can't really tell you. Mr. Hinchcombe doesn't want you to know. Just rest assured it's something important. *Really* important. Meanwhile, we'd like to talk to him."

"Who's the we?"

"Me and Mr. Hinchcombe."

"Well, lots of luck, Mister. He's not here. He checked out in a big hurry, tremendous hurry.... All of a sudden, you know?"

"Exactly when was that?"

He shrugged his shoulders. "Don't have a clue. Don't remember. Not long ago."

"Well, where can I reach him?"

"How the hell should I know? Didn't leave an address. You know what: I think he scooted out of here in the middle of the night. I said: 'checked out,' but he didn't come through the office. Didn't pay his bill, either. I don't know where he went. Or how. Didn't seem to have a car, don't know how he got around. He left his stuff behind. Not that there was much."

"He owes you money?"

"Not anymore.... Listen, it happens all the time, people don't pay their bills, and they get out of here, middle of the night. That's why we ask for a credit card or something. In this case...anyway, he was different. I don't know what the deal was. Maybe Hinchcombe said something, to my boss. I don't know. Next day, after he scooted out of here, this Eben guy, he called on the phone, he talked to the manager, he said, look can you keep my things, store them for me, I had to leave, but don't worry, I know I owe you money, I'm going to pay you. He said, nobody was there when I left, that's why I didn't pay."

"What did he mean by that?"

"I go off duty at 11. There's nobody here after that, they close up the office, we can't afford to have people here all night. Lady comes on, in the morning, 6 o'clock. Sometimes the manager sleeps in back of the office, but sometimes he doesn't. I mean, this isn't the Holiday Inn, there's no room service and stuff."

"And did he actually pay?"

"Every penny. He comes in, the next day, says, he's sorry for the inconvenience, he takes out his wallet, he pays in full, takes some clothes, puts it in a kind of canvas bag; he says, can I leave the suitcase, it's too heavy, I'll come back for it, some-time later; but I don't know when, he says. So the manager goes, sure, OK, just leave it here. I mean, he paid his money, right? We never expected to see a penny. Most of the people, the ones that leave in the middle of the night, we never see them again, and half the time, the credit card they give us is stolen or expired or just plain fake. The world is full of creeps, believe me."

"And...did he pick up the suitcase?"

"Naw. Not a peep from him since then. Maybe he left town."

"Did he pay in cash?"

"Yeah. U.S. dollars."

"No credit card."

"Nope.... I think he had one though. I don't know. Maybe he used a credit card. I wasn't here when he checked in. Maybe Mel knows, he's the manager. He's pretty careful. Must have checked up."

"Can't we find out?"

"No way. Not now, anyway."

"But if I come back, maybe when Mel is here....you'd have a record, wouldn't you? An imprint of the card, if he used one."

"Maybe...but even if he used a card, when he paid the cash, we'd tear up the imprint, see?"

"But you keep records...."

"Mister, I told you, this isn't the Holiday Inn, OK? Give me a break. I'm doing what they paid me to do; now back off, will you?"

I felt frustrated. But I persisted. "I don't suppose you'd let me look at the suitcase. The guy's suitcase."

"No way. Are you kidding? Why should I?"

I had no real answer. "Just tell me, is it locked?"

"No, it's not locked, not that it's any of your business," he said.

I had another of my rare, sudden flashes of insight. If the

suitcase wasn't locked, this guy had surely gone through it already. He wouldn't just let it sit there. This meant he could have taken things out. But of course I had no control over this factor.

I had absolutely no right to look at it myself. The kid's reluctance, though, surely wasn't based on some deep moral principle. He probably had nothing even remotely resembling deep moral principle. His reluctance was probably based on nothing more than sheer laziness.

"I really want to look at that suitcase," I said. "It's... important. It's something that's worth a lot to me, and to Mr. Hinchcombe, too. Uh, what did you say your name was?"

"I didn't say, but it's Tony."

"It's really important," I said, underlining the words. "The suitcase."

"Yeah? How important?"

He caught my drift exactly. "Well, Tony, could we say, $25 important?"

"That's not very important," he said.

"Well, how about $50, Tony. I won't take long; and I promise, I'll put everything back, just like it was."

He hesitated, and shook his head. But it wasn't scruples; it was just that the bribe was too small. We went up to $100, and the deal was done.

Unfortunately, I didn't have $100; I had given him my last $50 already. Nowadays, money is everywhere, though: I suspected there was an ATM machine somewhere close by, so I excused myself, said I'd be right back. There was in fact an ATM machine, next door, in the Mexican Restaurant, where I pressed enough buttons to give me $200. I felt guilty—not about bribing Tony, but about spending money on something which Celia would undoubtedly define as sheer, utter lunacy. And half of it was Celia's money, after all. California is a community property state.

Normally I don't buy a pencil without consulting Celia. But this was different.

I handed over five $20 bills. Tony put the money in his pocket, very nonchalantly, as if it hardly mattered to him. Then he took me into a small room just behind the office. The room was crammed with mops, brooms, cleaning materials. There was also a sofa that had seen better days; the upholstery was ripped and the whole sofa was sagging, a kind of sick, senile sofa, hanging around just waiting to die. A door led to a tiny managerial toilet. And in one corner of the room, there was a small black suitcase. Tony lifted it up and took into another small room, where there was a battered desk, and some files in a rusty metal cabinet. He threw the suitcase down on the desk. "Here it is. Make it quick, though. Don't take anything out of it, you hear? I'm taking a chance here. Sometimes the manager comes in, just to check up, see that I'm on the job. If he saw you, he'd blow a fuse."

"I'll be fast," I said.

What was I looking for? I had no idea, really. Some clue to the man's identity, I suppose. I opened the suitcase. Nothing but rumpled clothes. Jockey shorts, a few shirts, khaki pants, two pair of work shoes in a plastic bag. A windbreaker, and a kind of knitted cap. There was also a small bible, and one other book. This book had a pale blue cover. The title was: "Paths to Enlightenment." The author had some long, unpronounceable name, maybe Sanskrit, not that I can recognize Sanskrit. On the title page, Eben Born had signed his name.

I opened the book at random, and read a few passages. It was full of portentous sentences. One passage, as I recall, went something like this. "Verily, do not rely on the visible world. He who does so has fallen into the trap of the invisible, and the world to him shall be as a swamp of stone. But whoever seeks truly and unselfishly for the things that are blazingly invisible, to him all shall be made supremely visible, and the world will become to him a shining garden of glass."

Heavy.

I leafed through the book. Most of it was pitched at that exalted level. Other passages seemed, well, banal. "Work hard, discipline yourself, be moderate in all things," and so on.

I put the book down. I groped about in the various pockets and compartments of the suitcase, but I found nothing more interesting than pieces of soap and a used train ticket. I was hoping the ticket would be some sort of clue. But it was nothing more exciting than a ticket from San Francisco to Mountain View, on a regular commuter train.

I was about to give up, close the suitcase, and go home

empty-handed, when I lifted up the bible, and looked on the flyleaf to see if there was an inscription or something that might finally tell me something. Nothing there but the name: Eben Born. I turned the Bible over, and as I did so, what seemed like a small piece of paper fluttered out of it. I picked it up and looked at it. When I saw what it was, I shuddered, involuntarily.

It was a photograph of Blanche Baleine.

# 15

"Hey, aren't you done in there?" Tony shouted.

A photograph of Blanche Baleine. There was no question about it. She was standing in some sort of yard or garden, and smiling at the camera. I looked at the other side of the photograph. There was no writing on the other side. I stared at the photograph, again and again. What was this photograph doing in the gardener's suitcase? How did he get it? And why?

"You deaf? I asked you, are you done?"

"I'm done, I'm done, Tony," I said. "Just give me a minute, I've got to put things back the way they were."

"OK; but make it snappy."

I put the photograph in my pocket, and closed the suitcase. I know I had promised not to take anything; but Tony would never know the difference. My stomach was in knots. I felt excited, exhilarated. I was on the right track. This gardener... maybe it had been just a wild idea, on Nolan's part, casting suspicion on this guy, maybe it was nothing but a red herring, as far as Nolan concerned, but in fact, there was something here. This was a lead, a concrete lead.

Maybe the gardener was Blanche's lover. The father of her baby. Who knows?

And then there was Travis. Travis had lied to me. He was hiding something. He knew all along where the gardener was living. He had almost certainly arranged things at the motel. Paid the bills, too, I suppose. Gave the gardener the money, at any rate. Why? Too many coincidences. All of this just had to be connected to Blanche and her untimely death.

I needed time, to think things through. Meanwhile, I brought the suitcase back to Tony.

"Thanks a lot," I said.

"Find what you were looking for?"

I shook my head no. "Not really," I said.

I got into my car and started the motor. Out of the corner of my eye, as I left, I saw Tony yawning. Then he picked up his magazine and began to read it again.

# 16

I was nervous and jittery as I drove home. I felt excited, too. Next move, I had to talk to Travis. I had no reason to expect him to cooperate; but I had to take that chance. I called his home in Atherton, and some sort of maid answered, a woman with a thick accent. "Mr. Hinchcombe, please," I said. "This is important."

"Is not here," she said. "Is gone."

"When will he return?"

"He don't tell me. Maybe late."

The frustration made me irritable. Celia kept asking me, what was the matter. I said, client trouble. What sort of trouble, she asked. I made something up. She listened carefully—she always does—and then gave me a mild lecture, along with some no doubt excellent advice. I nodded my head, and said I'd try. In fact, I had hardly heard a word she was saying.

I had a poor night's sleep that night, tossing and turning, and getting up twice to go to the bathroom. The case was preying on my mind.

In the morning, at a decent hour, I called Travis' house, this time from my office. Arthur Flansbaum answered. "Arthur," I said, "you're there again. Let me talk to your boss."

"He's busy."

"I need to see him."

"I don't think so."

"Look, Arthur," I said. "This is really important. Tell him it's about the gardener. I'll call back in ten minutes."

When I called back, Arthur said, "All right. You can come. He's here right now, and he'll be around for the next few hours. He can give you fifteen minutes."

I cancelled an appointment, using my usual excuse, a courtroom appearance. As I said, it's almost always a lie, but it works like a charm. I drove out to the house in Atherton. I rang the doorbell, and again it was Arthur who let me in. "He's in the study," he said, and led me there. Was this the room Blanche died in? Did that bother Travis? Did he feel it was creepy? I guess not. I looked around for the statuette. Stupid. Of course it wasn't there. It was surely still in police custody. Exhibit A.

As I entered the room, Arthur discreetly shut the door and disappeared. Travis was sitting at the desk when I came in. He got up and walked across the room. I thought he was coming to shake my hand, but instead he sat down in a chair not too far from where I was standing. He was dressed in tennis clothes. His long curly hair looked sweaty. There was no tennis court on his property, but he must belong to some club, I imagined. It's not bad to be a zillionaire. He was scowling, and seemed to be in a bad mood. I wasn't sure whether it was my doing, or whether it was bad tennis or bad something else. A man like Travis likes to win. He waved me to a chair, and said: "OK, get to the point. What's this all about?"

I began by saying that I had gone to the motel, the Glass Slipper Motel. "Why did you do that?" he asked, quite sharply.

I said, "I was following up a lead."

"A lead? What kind of lead?"

I said, "Well, to be honest, you mentioned the motel yourself."

"The hell I did."

"You said Cinderella. It wasn't Cinderella; it was the Glass Slipper, which is close enough. Anyway, I figured it out."

"Sometimes my mouth is too big," he said. "But OK, let's hear the rest of it." I told it to him, in a slightly expurgated version. I never mentioned how I used his name. But I ended up telling him about the picture of Blanche that I found, "among the effects which this gardener left behind. So you see," I said, "it's not pure fantasy."

"*What* isn't pure fantasy?"

"The idea that this guy has something to do with Blanche."

"Oh, really? What the hell do *you* know? And, anyway, who asked you to go to this motel? Who asked you to do any of this? What are you, the FBI?"

What could I say? "I'm looking out for my client's

interests."

He said: "Bullshit. You have some kind of ulterior motive. You're looking out for somebody's interests, that's for sure. Probably your own. Anyway: you had no right to take this photograph. It doesn't belong to you. Do you have it?"

"I do," I said.

"Well, you better give it to me," he said.

"It doesn't belong to you, either," I said, surprised at my own nerve.

"Cut out the crap," he said. "Just hand it over."

"I don't have it with me," I said.

He said nothing. He seemed to be thinking. I screwed up my courage, and said, "Look, Travis, you're trying to protect this guy, this gardener. Last time we talked, you told me a bunch of lies. You know him, you set him up in this motel, you probably know where he is right now. Why would this guy have a picture of Blanche? Who is he? And what's his connection with you? Why don't you tell me the truth, for a change."

He said: "Listen, Mr. Frank. I don't have to answer your questions. You're not the police, you don't have a warrant, a subpoena, you've got nothing. You want my advice? Keep your damn nose out of this."

"I told you, I'm Barney's lawyer," I said.

He sneered at me. "You? You're not anything. Nolan Thom is his lawyer. You're some solo practitioner, some two-bit lawyer who wrote a will for him, something like that. You're out of your league here.... I don't have to talk to you, about anything. If I want to talk to Barney's *real* lawyer, I'll call Nolan."

I swallowed the insults. It's part of my job, swallowing insults, at least insults from clients. I have to humor clients. It's that or starve. I said: "Nolan.... Sure, he's Barney's lawyer. That means he's trying to get the guy off, no? He's trying to pin something on the gardener. And you don't like that...."

"Damn right I don't."

"This picture, it could be evidence."

"Evidence? of what?"

"Evidence.... Let's suppose the gardener was a hit-man. Somebody hired him to get rid of Blanche. Gave him the picture, so he'd know what she looked like."

"Oh, Jesus! You've got a vivid imagination."

"Nolan's is even more vivid. He can ride this hit-man theory for all it's worth."

"And...who hired this so-called hit-man? Is that supposed to be me? You're out of your frigging mind."

He said this with enormous force. He got up and banged his fist on the table. He started pacing around the room. I felt my courage draining away, like water down a bathtub. But I plunged on.

"Of course, I don't think you hired this guy," I said. "But maybe somebody else did.... Or maybe nobody. Nolan...he's just doing his job."

"Telling lies? Is that his job?"

"Well...not lies," I said. "Theories. Look: I'm not a criminal lawyer. I don't do criminal law. I never do. To me, it's poison. But Nolan...well, he's awfully good at it. He makes the jury think, his man is innocent. He tries at least to plant the seeds of doubt. You know, reasonable doubt. Maybe he'll call you to the stand. He'll ask you, where were you that night? The night Blanche died."

"It's none of his goddamn business," Travis said.

"Oh, but it is. You had a key to the house...that's important."

"As a matter of fact, I didn't," Travis said. "I left my keys in the house. I always do. No sense carrying them around with me."

"That's your story. You can't prove it."

He nearly exploded. "What is this? *Law & Order*? I don't have to prove anything!"

"Have you got an alibi? Nolan will ask you."

"Screw Nolan. I was in Santa Cruz.... That's hours away."

"And you were with a woman," I said. "At least that's what you told me."

"Right."

I kept on going: "Then he'd ask, who was the woman?"

Travis paused. He said nothing for a while. He walked around his desk, stared out the window. Then he turned to me and said: "As a matter of fact, if you really want to know, there was no woman. I was there, waiting for her, but she didn't show up. I didn't know why at the time, but now I do."

"What do you mean?"

"Well, if you must know...and I can't for the life of me figure out why I'm telling you this, I was waiting for Blanche."

"Blanche? You were waiting for Blanche?"

"I said so. Are you deaf? Well, not exactly waiting. I called Blanche the day before, told her I was around, I was back in the country, I told her I was going to be in Santa Cruz, I was in a suite at the such and such hotel, and I said, why don't you come down, spend the night with me, we'll have a blast. She laughed and said something about Barney. I said, screw Barney. Dump him. Tell him something, he's too dumb to know if you're lying. So she laughed and she said, she'd think about it. I said, I'll be waiting for you. Just let me know when you're coming."

I have to admit, that shocked me a little. I don't want to sound naive. I know people have affairs. They sleep with this one and that one. Married people, unmarried people, whatever. I read about these people in the newspapers, I see them in the movies, and on TV. To be honest, I too have lust in my heart, from time to time, as President Carter once put it. Or in other parts of the body. But that's as far as it goes. I mean, Celia would positively castrate me if she thought I was sleeping around.

Not that all that many women out there are boiling hot for my body. Especially after I put on those last twenty pounds. And do women consider a receding hairline sexy?

Besides, who has the time?

But Travis.... Zillionaires can have all the women they want. They can be fat, old, and bald; it doesn't matter.

I guess my face gave me away. Travis laughed, and said: "Maybe you didn't know this; but Blanche and I were once a thing. Did you actually know Blanche?"

"I met her."

"She was a terrific woman. One of a kind. Crazy, at times. A bitch, at times. But she was something. When I met her, it was just after my third divorce. Third divorce. God. That was a holy mess, lawsuits, the whole business. She wanted buckets of money, my ex-wife. Stupid bitch. I don't know why I ever married her. I had that in common with Blanche; she married a jerk, herself, in a moment of weakness."

"Barney."

"Of course Barney. Who else? Anyway, Blanche and I, we were together for a while. This was before Barney. Then we broke up. Next she married that idiot. Must have been some sort of rebound. Or sheer perversity. She still loved me, I know it. I mean, we had sex the day after she and Barney came back from their honeymoon. Honeymoon—if you can call it that. They went to Vegas. Anyway, what's a honeymoon these days? It's just a trip somewhere. Nobody's a virgin anymore. Maybe in Alabama, you know, the Baptists or something like that, they still have virgins; but they're extinct in California.

"Blanche and Barney, they were screwing since the day they met. Blanche had a healthy appetite, believe me. I said to Blanche, hey, is this going to make a difference? This marriage thing. She laughed and laughed, and said, let's see. We had sex, I swear, it really was only one day after they came back from Nevada. But I was a good guy, I gave them a nice wedding present, and I lent them my beach house.... I used to get to see her, once in a while, we had a little thing on the side. He never suspected anything. Or maybe he did. Maybe that's why he killed her."

"You're so positive he killed her...."

"Well, who else? There was nobody else in the house. They were fighting like cats and dogs. You know, even a wimp has his limits."

"So you...and Blanche.... And it was still going on...."

"I just told you. Yes. Can't you grasp things the first time around?"

"You...loved her?"

"I didn't say that. The 'l' word; I never use it. *She* loved *me*. I think so, anyway. How did I feel? That's a different story. You know something: I can't love anybody but myself. That what my shrink tells me. He says, Travis, you're incapable of love, it's one of your biggest problems. And even yourself; he says, it's tough for you to feel love, even for yourself. You don't really like yourself. I'm beginning to believe him, that's the funny part." He paused and gave a little hollow laugh. "Maybe my problems with other people, well, they're really problems with myself. Three failed marriages. And God knows how many failed affairs. So, with my shrink, we explore these questions, like, what's wrong with me? What's going on with me? Why can't I have a decent relationship?" He stopped. "You ever been in therapy?" I shook my head no. "You can't believe the shit they tell you. Sometimes I believe it. I really do. Sometimes I don't. I pay this guy $500 an hour, maybe more, he's the most expensive one there is, and this crap is what I'm getting out of it. Sometimes he just looks at me and nods his head. At $500 an hour, you know, those pregnant silences cost me plenty. So why do I go? That's what he asks me, that's what I ask myself. Because maybe he can help me. Get me to like myself. I know, it sounds like bullshit, but who knows?"

"And...Blanche...." I said, feebly.

He said: "I *liked* Blanche. She was something! I've had a lot of women. I've got heaps of money, I've got charisma, women smell it a mile off. They smell both of those things, the money and the charisma. But Blanche...she was... more than just one of the crowd. Don't get me wrong. She didn't mean that much to me. I told you, I didn't love her. Also: I'm not into a deep grief thing, if you know what I mean. I'm sorry she's dead. The shrink talked about it, you know, stages of grief and all that crap; but I'm telling you, it's not that big a deal to me. Maybe it should be."

Did the police think of him as a suspect? Did they know about the affair? No, I decided; they were fixated on Barney. And Travis was too rich and powerful to be a suspect.

I said: "You told the police?"

"Told them what? About my goddamn therapy?"

"No, I mean, about...you and Blanche."

"You think I'm crazy? They didn't ask, and I didn't tell. Oh sure, they wanted to know certain things. Keys. They wanted to know all about the keys. They had keys on the brain. I told them, I wasn't around that night. I was in Santa Cruz. I told them they could check it out. They were all fawning, you know, all kiss-ass, oh that won't be necessary Mr. Hinchcombe. I told them, personally, I didn't have a key, not that night, anyway."

"And Arthur? Did he have a key?"

"Arthur?" he said, his voice dripping with contempt. "Oh sure, Arthur. He came in and bashed in her head, just for fun. Forget Arthur. And no, he didn't have a key."

"The gardener?"

"No key. I told you that. He never came in the house."

"Your housekeeper? The one you fired?"

"Why would she have a key? She never had one to begin with. She didn't even speak English. God, the things you think about."

"You're sure? You didn't leave her a key, when nobody was home?"

"No. I think. Who the hell knows? I don't keep track of every stupid detail. One thing is sure: when she left, if she had a key, she had to give it back. I insist on things like that. Arthur takes care of it."

"So...maybe she gave Arthur the key, and he kept it."

"Oh, come on, forget Arthur. You've met him. Knock it off, it's too ridiculous."

"OK, OK; so you didn't have a key; and Arthur didn't; and the housekeeper didn't and the gardener didn't. Then who did?

"Barney. And Blanche, of course. They both had keys," he said. "When they came and stayed, I gave them keys. And a real estate management company—Atherton Realty; they had a key. How many keys am I supposed to have?"

"So somebody from the real estate management company...is that a possibility? Where are they located?"

He gave me a withering glance of total contempt. "They have an office on El Camino. Come on. What are you saying? Some real estate nerd took the key from the office, and came around, at night, just to make a hole in Blanche's head. You're hallucinating."

"But somebody did...."

He interrupted me. "Somebody did. Right. Barney. Can't you get that through your thick lawyer's head? He killed her. Just do me a favor. Don't go pestering my real estate people, OK? I'm a busy guy. I've got to shower, and go off to a meeting. Here's my advice: stick to whatever it is you do; don't get messed up in this business. Your buddy Nolan, he'll do what he can. You stay out."

Driving back to my office, I asked myself: had I learned anything new? A little. Travis and Blanche. Could he be the father of her child? Was that a motive? Somehow I doubted it. I was following a trail, but was it leading me anywhere? I really didn't know.

# 17

In the late afternoon, I went for a walk, because I felt it was time for some serious introspection. Normally, I prefer drift to introspection. I love to procrastinate. I love to put things off. Not at the office: I can't do that in the office, or I'd lose all my clients. But at home, yes. Like getting somebody to fix the leaky faucet in the bathroom. I'll do it, but mañana.

Fortunately, I have Celia. Celia is a master of creative nagging. She would say, did you call the plumber, about the leaky faucet? Naturally, I hadn't. When *are* you going to call the plumber. Soon, dear, I say. Then she asks me again, a day or so later. And again. Eventually I do call the plumber.

I locked the office, and went off to the Crystal Springs reservoir, a beautiful walk through the woods along the edge of the water. It was quiet—pretty empty at that time of day and that time of year. There were a few mothers with strollers, casual hikers with leather shorts, an occasional biker in orange and purple spandex outfits, and a few grim, determined anorexics, running or walking off the few pitiful remnants of meat on their bones. On weekends, the place is jam-packed; but on this day, cool, breezy, and in the soft, diminishing part of the day, I had long stretches all to myself.

I was asking myself, why was I so hooked on the case of Barney Bell. Why, Frank, I said to myself. Do you even like the guy? Well, in a way I did. And I felt sorry for him. Perhaps because he was such a loser. Because people like Travis Hinchcombe and the late Blanche Baleine had such contempt for him. And because I was so sure that Barney was innocent.

But what could I do about it? The police were investigating, they have staff, they have laboratories, they do fingerprints and hair follicles and DNA and God knows what else. And I have nothing.

Yet somehow I didn't trust the police. Maybe I'm too

liberal. Maybe I've read too many stories about how the police frame people. I didn't really think they were framing Barney. I think the problem was something else. They get an idea in their heads, they decide, this is the guy, he did it, he's guilty; and you can't get them even to *consider* an alternative, no matter what you do. Their collective minds close like a steel trap. And they're cynical and mistrustful. You tell them, this guy didn't do it, he's not the type; and they think, sure, sure. You say, my daughter didn't run away, she's a good girl; my son doesn't take drugs; and again, it's sure, sure. Because all they see are the dregs of humanity. They forget the rest of us aren't dregs. We have our dreggy aspects, but we keep them under control.

I walked two miles in and two miles back, briskly, watching the deer grazing on the hillside. They looked nervous, on edge; they scanned the horizon. I felt like telling them, don't worry. It's not the hunting season. The wolves are extinct around here. Nobody wants to kill Bambi.

I went back to my car. It was starting to get dark. What was I going to do next?

Actually, I had two leads. Or at least two things to follow up. One was the mysterious gardener. I knew now that he had some connection to the case. The picture in his trunk was proof of that. Travis was wrong, dead wrong; or, more likely, Travis was lying through his teeth. Maybe the gardener was the killer, maybe not. But he was *something*, he *knew* something; and he had something to hide.

The other lead was Blanche's notebook, and the Tony Crass show. I decided to tackle this first, and right away. Driving home, I called Barney on my cell phone. He answered the phone, sounding half dead. I said, "Barney, I've got to talk to you. Can you come in and see me? Tomorrow?"

Of course he could. He was unemployed, miserable, and had nothing to do but sit around waiting to be arrested. I said, "How's ten o'clock?"

"Yeah. I'm not exactly booked, you know? I just mope all day. I'm going nuts, Frank. But what's this about?"

"Nothing major, Barney; I just want to clear up a few things. Don't worry about it. Just come see me. It'll do you good to get out of the house."

He showed up ten minutes late. He looked like a wreck. He

needed a shave, he had dark circles under his eyes, he had a kind of nervous tic. Even his little moustache seemed ragged. You had to feel sorry for him. He had the look of a hunted animal. "Man, I'm really hurting," he said. "Can't sleep, can't eat. I watch television, I just fiddle around the house. Nolan.... I don't know. He says, not to worry. Right. *He* doesn't have to worry. They're not going to arrest *his* ass. Me, I'm going to be nailed, Frank. I know it. I'm totally screwed."

I tried to calm him down. I said I sympathized. "I know it's really tough," I said. "But you can do it. I know you can. Hang in there." And I praised Nolan to the skies. He's a great lawyer, I said. "If he says not to worry, then you shouldn't worry."

I don't think I convinced him.

"Barney," I said, "there's one issue I want to discuss. You know I want to help you, don't you?" He nodded. I went on: "The notebook. The one you sent here with Charley Morgan. You read the letter in it, didn't you?"

"Sure...who wouldn't?"

"And that's why you gave it to Charley, and made him promise not to read it; and that's why you gave it to me, right? You didn't want the police to have it."

"God yes. I'm not giving them something else they can stick me with.... Maybe I shouldn't even be talking to you about this. Maybe I should just shut up. Nowadays, they bug lawyer's offices, don't they? The government, you know, CIA, they let the police do any frigging thing they want. Or the FBI, real hard-asses. My house, it's bugged, I'm sure of it. This place too: how do I know?"

"Barney," I said, "the federal government isn't interested in you. The attorney general doesn't care. Not in the slightest. You're not a terrorist. You're not a drug kingpin. You're not some big tax evader. And you aren't named Abdul. You're not even an alien. Get serious. You can say anything you want in here, I'm not wired or whatever they call it."

He seemed to calm down a bit. I offered him some coffee. My coffee maker makes awful coffee; but there are times when you need something really hot to get yourself going, and the taste hardly matters. He said no, then he said yes, then he said maybe, and in the end he wanted some. I made coffee for both of us.

"Let's get down to business," I said. "I've got two issues. First of all: do you know anything about this guy, the one that's missing? The gardener, I mean. The guy who was supposed to clean the pool and fix up the yard and that sort of thing? Is there *anything* you can tell me about him?"

"No, man, nothing; like I told you, I never saw him, never laid eyes on this guy. He's the one that killed Blanche, isn't he? That's what Nolan thinks."

It was very unlikely Nolan thought so, but I didn't say this out loud. What Nolan actually thought—well, I would never presume to plumb those depths.

To Barney, I said: "I don't know. It's possible. We know *you* didn't kill her, right? So it had to be somebody else. He bugged out, the gardener, ran away, nobody knows where, so who knows? It might be him."

He loved the idea. It was a glimmer of hope.

"Barney," I said, "here's another thing. Let's talk about this letter. The one in the notebook. Blanche wrote it, but she never sent it. At least it seems that way. But maybe it's a draft, and she actually sent something like it, to Tony Crass. Do you know anything about this?"

"How would I know? First I heard of this, was when I read that letter. It threw me, man, it bowled me over. What kind of crazy shit, I said to myself. That's Blanche. OK, she's dead now, I have to be respectful; but seriously...."

"The letter," I said, interrupting him, "it talks about a show, men who kill for money, and there's the suggestion in it, well, I hate to even say it out loud, but it's the idea, maybe you killed your aunt Martha."

"Didn't I just say, completely crazy shit? Is the world going nuts, or what? Frank, what are you saying—you actually think I did this? Killed the old lady?"

"No, Barney, of course I don't; it's completely ridiculous. The question is, did Blanche think so? And if so, why?"

"Listen, she could act crazy sometimes. She could get crazy, you know, yell and scream and that stuff. But she wasn't *that* crazy. She knew me, I wouldn't hurt a fly, I don't even like to look at blood, you know, when somebody's bleeding, I'm out of there, I don't like getting injections, that kind of thing, see? This is just nuts. But Blanche.... You know, sometimes I think, did I *know* this broad? I mean, I was married to her, she was Mrs. Barney, but she was...I dunno.... She was somebody I never understood. I mean, I thought I knew her, you think you know somebody, you live in the same house, you sleep in the same bed, but...I mean, this letter...and the pregnancy thing...."

"So you don't know anything about this."

"Man, I already told you."

"Could there be something to it? What did your aunt die of?"

"Hey, she died, that's all. She was old. Real old. She had chicken pox, I told you that; she was real sick. I wasn't there, the old guy, her husband, he was there, I mean, the day she died. They just found her dead."

"Was there a doctor? An autopsy? Something like that?"

"An autopsy? You mean, like on TV, when they cut them up in pieces, and look at their insides and all that stuff—no, why should they do that? I mean, she was an old lady that died, no big deal, we all have to go.... Oh, shit, if they're going to try to pin this thing on me, just because she left me the money.... I swear, I had nothing to do with it."

"She was cremated, right?"

"Right. Her husband, he decided it. It wasn't me."

"So....there's no body to dig up."

"They took her ashes and scattered them someplace, who the hell knows. Maybe he did it. The old guy. Travis' father. What am I saying? *Nobody* did it. She just died."

I said: "OK, OK, I believe you. So Blanche was just making it up. An idea for a program. And then she says something else, about a dentist."

"Yeah, the dentist thing."

"You know about that?"

"Well, sort of. It was a show, an idea for a show, well, more than an idea. She was going to be on it, that show. A thing about dentists. That's been in the works, oh, for a while."

"What about dentists?"

"I don't know exactly. Some sex thing. Do you ever watch it? The Tony Crass show."

I had to confess I didn't.

"It's shit. I know that. But it's popular shit. And a gig's a gig, you know? I heard that this woman, Molly Stover, she's going to take Blanche's part."

"Blanche was going to be on the show?"

"Yeah. She had a part. I don't know exactly what."

"Is there some connection? With Blanche's death? Do you think this show has something to do with that?"

He shrugged his shoulders. "I don't know anything.... I can't see how.... Anyway, it's going to be on next week, Tuesday, 8 o'clock. You can watch it."

"You think I should?"

"Why not, Frank. Do you good."

I promised I would watch it. For clues? It seemed ridiculous. And yet...would it hurt me, once in a while, to keep up with popular culture? I don't see much TV, as I think I said already. I don't watch the reality shows. I saw Judge Judy once, thought it was ridiculous. And the shows about lawyers, there's a million of them, starting way back with *L.A. Law* and *Ally McBeal*. They're completely absurd. Nothing to do with the real live practice. But of course, if they made a TV show out *my* kind of practice, the station would go broke.

The Tony Crass show was notorious. I didn't want Celia to see me watching the program. I had never actually seen it, but I had heard a great deal about it. Secretly, I had always wanted to catch a glimpse of it, but I never had the nerve or the opportunity. Celia's very modern, very understanding. But on a few selected subjects, she can be as hard as a rock. Trash television is definitely one of them. I would watch the program, then, but not at home.

# 18

So I found myself at Barney's apartment, on a Tuesday evening, with a beer in my hand, and Barney sitting next to me. I had invited myself over. I told Celia a little white lie; I said I had business to take care of, and I had to visit a client. Well, it wasn't that much of a lie. Barney was a client, and this was definitely business. Not *paying* business; but that wasn't the point.

Barney lived in Mountain View, California, in one of those stucco apartment complexes that seemed to spring spontaneously from the earth right after the Second World War. It was called Bel-Air Vista Estates. It was a two-story development of cheap apartments, built around a small pond with a fountain in the middle. The stucco was peeling badly; and the fountain was nothing more than a melancholy drip. In general, the place had a sort of mournful air. It had definitely seen better days. I wondered who the other tenants were. Blanche could not have felt satisfied, living here with old Barney, at Bel-Air Vista Estates, Apartment 206-B, Mountain View, California.

Even his city's name did not deliver on its promise, at least not from the vista of Bel-Air Vista Estates.

The inside of the apartment was as depressing as the outside. The furniture was motel-modern. The place looked fairly run-down. Now that Blanche was dead, it definitely lacked the woman's touch. Not that I could see Blanche spending her time mopping and cleaning, or decorating, for that matter. And of course, Barney, in his present state, wasn't much of a house-keeper. I noted, for example, a potted palm that seemed to be at death's door, probably for lack of water. "Water your plants, Barney," I said to him. "Or they'll all die."

"Don't give a damn" was all he said.

He dragged two kitchen chairs into the bedroom. A big TV set dominated the room. The bed was unmade, of course. I wondered when the sheets were last changed. He took a can of beer for himself, and offered another one to me. I took it.

I won't bore you with details about the way the program started. The commercials seemed interminable. The program was apparently taking place before a live audience—a very live audience. Most of the audience seemed quite young, college students I would say, and they all cheered wildly when Tony Crass came on the set and waved to them. He was a man about 40, with curly hair, wearing an open-neck shirt, what looked like chino pants, and carrying a hand-held mike. He had a kind of smirk on his face. When he turned to the audience, they shouted "Tony! Tony! Tony!" as if he was a bullfighter or a rock star.

"The guy makes millions," Barney said. "Show is a frigging gold mine."

Tony announced that the theme of the evening was "dentists who drill their patients." The smirk turned into a leer, and the students screamed with total delight, some of them jumping up and down in their seats.

It was a plain, unadorned set. Tony stood to one side, with his microphone. Center stage were four plain chairs, empty at first. Two beefy guys in t-shirts stood with their arms folded, off to the side of the set. Then the first guest came onto the stage, from the side. This guy, a Chinese American, was slight, very smooth looking, and he wore a business suit and a neat necktie. He was, I'd say, about 35.

Tony Crass said: "You're Dr. Peter Chang, am I right?"

"Yes, I am."

"And you're a dentist?"

"Yes sir, I am."

"How long have you been practicing?"

"Oh, about ten years, I'd say. General practice of dentistry. I have an office in downtown Los Angeles."

"And you're here...because you've gotten sexually involved with your patients, Dr. Chang, is that right?"

"Well, that's not quite right...."

"Oh? In what way?"

"You said patients. There's only one patient, Tony, that I'm involved with; only one. That's Marla Kidwell."

"Marla Kidwell?"

"Yes, Tony, she and I...."

"Well, let's bring her on," Tony said, waving his hand.

A handsome woman, about the same age as Dr. Chang, entered the set. She was wearing a plain skirt and blouse, and her hair looked dyed to me; anyway, it was glossy and very dark. She sat down next to Dr. Chang. They kissed each other lightly on the lips.

"You're Marla Kidwell?"

"Yes, I am."

"And you're having a sexual affair with Dr. Chang, is that correct?"

"Yes, that's correct," she said. "You see, Tony, I fell in love with him, the minute I saw him.... I was referred to him, when my own dentist retired. My dentist was Dr. Winters. Well, he got to a certain age, and he said, Marla, I'm retiring. So I needed a new dentist, I'm very careful about my teeth, I floss every day.... Well, Dr. Winters said, there's a fine new dentist, Dr. Peter Chang, he's Chinese, very competent. I said, OK Dr. Winters, whatever you say. So I went to Peter's office, you know, for my regular checkup. And... I fell in love with him, the minute I saw him. There was something about him.... I can't tell you exactly what, but...the chemistry...."

Tony Crass interrupted her. "Marla, before we get to the chemistry, let's get something straight. You're a married woman, aren't you?"

She looked at him and her eyes seemed to widen. "Yes, I am, but...."

"But what, Marla?"

She paused. Then she said: "My marriage...it's kind of, well, hollow. My husband...he's not a bad man. I'm not saying that. Only that, with him, I'm afraid there just isn't any chemistry."

"The chemistry is all with Dr. Chang?"

"It is," she said. "Love is...something really powerful, Tony. You must know that. You can't fight it. I mean, when I was called into his office, from the reception room, I was sitting there, waiting, reading a magazine, you know? And the nurse said, Dr. Chang will see you now, and...and...there he was... well, it came over me, it was like thunder and lightning, my knees were wobbling, honestly...."

"Thunder and lightning," Tony said, with a little bit of a sneer. But she went right on talking: "He was...so strong, so macho. He examined me, I had a cavity, and...."

"You wanted him to fill your cavity," Tony said, and the audience howled. Marla seemed to pay no attention. She went on talking, in a measured voice: "He said, I'm going to have to drill this...and I said, of course, doctor, whatever you say. My head was whirling. And, well, when he started drilling my teeth, I felt funny all over. I thought, is it the anesthetic, the stuff he injected, but no, I knew, it wasn't that, it was...this feeling, it was like nothing I ever experienced before. I thought I was going to have an orgasm, right then and there."

The audience shrieked with demonic pleasure at this; the kids laughed and made whooping noises, and clapped their hands; and Dr. Peter Chang, who seemed embarrassed, looked down at his feet.

"You thought you were going to have an orgasm?" said Tony, licking his lips. "Wow, that's pretty strong stuff."

She said: "I guess I was gasping for breath, and making funny faces. He stopped and stood there, with the drill in his wonderful hands, those strong hands, and he said, is something the matter, Ms. Kidwell? And I had to tell him, I said, Dr. Chang, or can I call you Peter, I'm so attracted to you, I find you so...strong, so...beautiful. Do you feel you could ever, well, love me? And he said, yes I could, you're an attractive woman, Ms. Kidwell, and then we kissed, oh, so passionately, and the next thing I knew, we were...we were doing it...."

"Doing it? Where?"

"Right there. On that dentist chair, he got on top of me and....we made love. Oh, it was so marvelous, it was like nothing I ever experienced before, there, on the dentist's chair, I can't tell you how I felt, it was awesome...." Dr. Chang was still looking at his shoes, and the kids in the audience were beside themselves, screaming, laughing, making noises that sounded like "woowoowoo," and so on.

Barney said, "Isn't she great? I mean, Blanche would have been pretty good, too, but this kid, she's amazing; Molly Stover. She's a friend of ours."

"You know her?"

"Yeah. Of course."

Meanwhile, the show was going on. Tony Crass said to Marla or Molly or whoever she was: "So. You made love in the dentist chair. And then what?"

"Well, he had to finish the drilling. He's a terrific dentist, very conscientious."

"No, I didn't mean that. I mean, what happened afterwards."

"Well," she said, batting her eyelashes. "Let's put it this way: I found myself frequently going to the dentist....I go as often as I can, and, well, we're having an affair."

"You always have sex in the dentist's chair?"

"No...he's got a kind of sofa...but sometimes, yes, sometimes we do it in the chair, for old time's sake, you know?"

"And your husband?"

"Andrew?"

"Does he know? About your affair?"

"No...he doesn't, Tony." she said, a little sheepishly. "He's got to be told. I know that, Tony. We—Peter and I—we don't want to keep this secret anymore. I hate the lying."

"You want a divorce?"

She hesitated. Then she said: "I just don't know about that, Tony. Andrew—Andrew and I, well, we've been together a lot of years. We were high school sweethearts. We've got kids, two kids.... Benny is six, Alicia's four—and they love their daddy, like most kids do. Andrew is...a nice person. Very nice. I do love him, or I think I love him. But there's no magic in it anymore, as I said. The sex is...boring. We're just going through the motions, you know what I mean? It's all so... flat...."

Tony said: "Flat, huh? Not like the way Dr. Chang can do his drilling, right?" This got another huge roar from the audience.

She said: "Really, Tony. Peter—Dr. Chang—and I, we have something holy, something wonderful together."

Tony said: "But you think it's time for Andrew to know...."

"I do.... The deception...."

"And you, too, Peter?"

He said nothing, but slowly, quietly nodded his head.

"Well, let's bring the husband on. Folks, meet Marla's husband, Andrew Kidwell."

Andrew Kidwell—or whoever he was, because it was clear to me by now that this particular segment was a fake—came storming onto the set. He was a stocky man with a big chin, and he came on with his fists balled and started screaming at his wife, "Bitch, bitch," and trying to punch out poor Dr. Chang. The two beefy men who had been standing around in identical t-shirts and gray pants rushed up to him, grabbed him, and held him back. Husband and wife yelled at each other. Dr. Chang sat there with his head down. "You're disgusting, Andrew," she shouted, "making a scene like this!"

"*You're* making the scene! Carrying on with this creep," he said. He seemed to be struggling to get free from the grip of the two strong men.

"I'm leaving you, Andrew, you're no good, you're rotten in bed, you're not a real man," she said, standing up and pointing her finger at him, and shouting at the top of her voice. There was general pandemonium, in the audience; the two beefy guys more or less pushed Andrew off the set; Tony made a few comments, addressed to the love-birds, words which I didn't quite catch; and then there was a break, with a whole string of commercials.

"What did you think?" Barney asked.

"Unspeakable," I said.

"Pretty gross," Barney said. "But that's what people like. They like gross."

So far, I couldn't see any connection to Blanche or to anything else of relevance. But I kept on watching. When the commercials were over, the cameras came back to the set, which was now empty once more. Dr. Peter Chang, Marla, and Andrew had conveniently disappeared; and it was time for another edifying example of modern dentistry.

Tony came back on, and brought in the next two persons, a patient and a dentist. This time the patient was a young man. He looked a little bit like Barney—slight, dirty blond hair, a small moustache, tiny blue eyes. He was shifty and rat-like in his motions. He had on a short-sleeved shirt, with a tattoo faintly visible just above the elbow. He fidgeted in his chair and seemed ill at ease.

Next to him was the dentist; or what I assumed was the dentist. She was a powerful-looking woman, with bleached blond hair, in her 40's I'd say. She had strong, well-defined features. She sat bolt upright. She was wearing a plain black dress; and over it, a white coat, as if she was on the job, poised to extract somebody's molar.

"These guys might be for real," Barney said.

"Oh? You think?"

"Maybe. Who knows. I don't recognize them."

Tony Crass pointed to the man and said, "This is Joe Tanner. He's 26 years old. Tell us your story, Joe."

Joe had a self-conscious grin on his face. He said, "Well, I had this problem, I had this toothache, you know? And I went to my regular dentist, and he went, wow, boy, you need an extraction Joe, this tooth is rotten, it's got to go, it was one of my wisdom teeth. He doesn't do that kind of work, he said, you know, everybody's a specialist these days. So he sent me to this dental surgeon, that's Dr. Pilbrow here. I was, like, surprised at first. I thought, a chick dentist, that's something you don't see much, right?"

"And?"

"Well, when I saw her, right away I thought, this woman is something else. I was attracted. You know, the white coat, the hands, like she was taking charge of me, you know? I like that kind of a woman. My ex-wife was like that, only she wasn't a dentist, she was a police officer. She was big, like Dr. Pilbrow. Anyway, so I made an appointment, to have the tooth out, and the whole time I kept thinking about her. She was, like, on my mind, you know? And then, well, I was in the chair, and thinking funny thoughts, like, this is some woman, and she said, I'm going to give you anesthesia, for the pain, you know, and she had this long needle, and I had a weird feeling, there's something about needles, maybe I'm a masochist or something; and she stuck the needle into my gums, and that side of my face went numb, but...well, it's embarrassing to say this, but there was some other parts of me, they weren't numb, if you get my point...."

"I get it, Joe," Tony said. The audience got it, too, and the usual whooping and stomping took place. Tony went on: "And what happened then?"

"Well, she noticed, uh, my problem; like how could you not? And she put her hand down there...and...kind of felt things.... But, first she like did her job, I mean, she took out the tooth, and my mouth was all bloody and she rinsed it out, and she said, there's going to be some pain, when the stuff wears off, why don't you lie down for a bit, in this other room here, you're my last patient for the day. So I went in there, and there was a sofa there, and I stretched out, and closed my eyes; and I heard her tell the assistant, you can go now, I don't need you, and then she came in, and took off her white coat, and then her blouse and.... Well, we had sex right then and there."

"You had sex. Wow. How was it."

"Fantastic. We've been dating ever since. I travel a lot, on my job, I'm a salesman, I sell paints, paint supplies, but when I'm back in town, the first thing I do, I call up Dr. Pilbrow."

"And what about you, Dr. Pilbrow? Do you share his feelings?"

"I do," she said, in a low, throaty voice. "Joe is...marvelous. He's everything I want in a man.... I've fallen in love with him."

"You're not married, Joe?" Tony asked.

"No. I'm divorced," he said.

Tony turned and looked straight at the audience. Then he swiveled about, looked at Dr. Pilbrow, and asked: "Doctor, I'd like to ask you something: Is Joe here the only patient you've, uh, had sex with?"

She seemed to hesitate a bit. "That's a little embarrassing.... Actually he's...not the only one, to tell the truth. A lot of attractive men come to my office.... More than my share, I think sometimes. And some of them are...needy. But Joe was, well, different, he wasn't like the rest of them."

"You're married, aren't you, Dr. Pilbrow?"

"I was. Not anymore."

"Well," Tony said, "let's bring in an old acquaintance of yours." From the left side of the stage, a tall, rather slender man, about 40 years old I would say, comes in, with very dark hair, wearing a business suit. He looks vaguely Latin. And Dr. Pilbrow said, in a voice full of horror, "Oh my God, Carlos, what are you doing here?"

"Carlos you said? Who is this guy?" Joe asks, looking startled.

"That's *my* question," Carlos said. "Janice, who is this

man? What's his relationship with you? I thought we were lovers.... I thought you and I were...special...."

Tony said, with a smirk: "We did a little investigation, Dr. Pilbrow. Seems that Carlos here is another one of your patients who had more to do with you than dentistry." Dr. Pilbrow looked stunned. She kept shaking her head and saying, "oh my God."

"Janice, are you sleeping with this squirt?" Carlos said. "You're cheating on me with this worm, this imbecile?"

I thought there was going to be fireworks, but Joe just seemed to squirm and look embarrassed, and Dr. Pilbrow remained speechless.

"Carlos, sit down, tell us your story," Tony said.

"Nothing much to tell. It all started with root canal work.... Frankly, the sex, well, it was Janice who started it...she came on to me.... She used to touch me, when she was working on my mouth, you know, her other hand, well, she did things that were sort of inappropriate. But I didn't mind.... I found her fascinating, strong, attractive...."

"And then?"

"And then, well, one thing led to another. I used to go to her office, come in the back way, after the last patient. We made wild sex. Really wild sex. I thought we had something really beautiful going on. Janice, Janice, how could you do this? I left my wife, I left my children, this was all for you, Janice. I gave everything up, and this is what I get in return."

She said, "Carlos, I'm sorry."

He started sobbing. "Sorry? Sorry? You're sorry? My whole life is in ruins, and you're sorry, that's all you can say.... and how many others are there, Janice? Are you sleeping with every guy on your rolodex? Every guy who comes in for oral surgery? Is that what you're up to, Janice?"

"Carlos, no, I swear it," she said. "It's not so." But she reckoned without Tony Crass. Suddenly yet another patient appeared, an African-American with a goatee, who announced he was Lester Sudge, and he too thought he had something beautiful and exclusive with Dr. Janice Pilbrow. It all began, he said, with an appointment about a cracked incisor. It had to be put out of its misery. Then came the sex.

"Wild sex?" Tony asked him, with a sneer. "With Carlos,

the sex was pretty wild. How about you, Joe?" But Joe just sat there, as if paralyzed. He said nothing. Tony then waved his hand, and yet another male entered, this one very young, maybe 16 or 17, wearing baggy jeans that for some reason failed to fall down, even though they were miles too big for him, a really skinny kid, with a bad complexion, who looked a lot like the kind of kid my daughters sometimes dragged home.

"Here's Dustin," Tony said, and Dustin started blubbering about how he had given up his virginity to Janice, how he thought she loved him, and now he saw, she was nothing but a cheap whore. Then, suddenly, there was shouting and sobbing and recriminations all around; everybody seemed to be talking at once; basically, everybody was dumping on Dr. Janice Pilbrow, they all felt betrayed, men and boy alike, outraged and disgusted; they all announced they were through, through, through; and then they stomped off the stage, to the infinite glee of the audience. Some of the guys in the audience began shouting at Dr. Janice Pilbrow, who was now all alone on the stage with Tony. They were hollering obscenities, or things like: "Hey, Janice, how about me drilling you for a change?" She shook her fist at these people, but said nothing. Tony had a huge grin on his face.

Mercifully, the program was soon over, except for Tony's final homily, which I didn't bother with, and more commercials. I guess Janice Pilbrow was left without her stable of lovers. If she was real, not an actress, but an actual dentist—and Barney thought so—then I wasn't worried. The next round of appointments for defective gums, root canal work, and the like would present her with fresh opportunities.

I have to admit, I enjoyed the program. It was so over the top that I could see why people liked it. Maybe it represented the end of civilization or the decline of the West. But was the Tony Crass show any worse than some of the other manifestations of low culture on all those dozens of channels? I wonder.

Barney squeezed the remote and turned off the set. "Nothing on but junk," he said, as if the Tony Crass show didn't fall into that category. He took another swallow of his beer. I asked him, "Was there some clue there, Barney? Did anything strike you? Any ideas?"

He shook his head sadly. No idea. I pressed him: "Some

kind of riddle, something hidden? You knew her, Barney. Something about drilling? Drilling for oil? Dentists? Who was Blanche's dentist? Is there something we should know about him?"

"Dentist? Hey, Frank, I don't know. Blanche hated dentists. She never went, far as I know. I mean, she was careful, you know, brushed her teeth and stuff, twice a day, you know, and she used those little strings you put in your teeth, dental floss, and she had little sticks, she was always massaging her gums with something, she told me. Gums are important, if you let them go, she said, your teeth can fall out. She had nice teeth, I'll give her that. Some people, you know, they've got these crooked teeth, awful teeth. Or they're all brown. They have to have caps, have to have them whitened, costs an arm and a leg. Not Blanche...."

"No dentist at all?"

"Well, maybe. I don't know. She didn't tell me everything. Boy, did she ever not. *Now* I know that. So, maybe she had a secret dentist, too. But if she did, I don't know who. His name, nothing."

Still, I felt, we must be missing something. There was a point there, I was sure of it. Something easy and obvious. But hard as I tried, I came up blank. Maybe I was just reading too many mysteries; maybe I expected too much, expected hidden clues.

"She was one weird chick, that Blanche," Barney said, shaking his head. "One weird chick. And now she's dead."

I had a sudden thought. I said, "Hey, Barney, do *you* have a dentist? You told me, Blanche didn't go to dentists. But you did, right?"

"Sure. Yeah. I mean, my teeth are pretty rotten. Always have been. It's like cavity city in my mouth. Shit, I even had root canal once. Hurt like hell. Cost a fortune, too, I didn't have dental insurance. Actually, Aunt Martha, she helped me out. I told her about the problem, the teeth, and how I didn't have the money; and she said, Barney, you have to have good teeth. Show business people, they have to have beautiful teeth. She insisted on paying for it. She was hot for my career, Aunt Martha."

"Who was the dentist?"

"Let me see. What was the guy's name? He was an Asian guy. Wong, Wang, something like that. Wang. That's it, Wang. Hamilton Wang, that was his name."

An "Asian guy." Like Dr. Peter Chang, on the program. Did that mean something? "Is his office around here?"

"Yeah. San Carlos. I could look it up."

"You don't have to, Barney. That's OK. Just tell me: where'd you get this dentist? Who referred him to you?"

"Travis. I needed a dentist, I asked Travis. I think Travis uses him. That's why he costs an arm and a leg, he's used to people like Travis. I should have known better. But this tooth, it was hurting me, I mean, it was pounding away inside my head. I took aspirins like they were candy, it was still killing me. And I didn't have a dentist here, since I moved, you know, and no insurance, like I told you...and the money, well, I was embarrassed, but Aunt Martha, she said, money's no object, Barney, so I went, I said, God bless you, Aunt Martha, I'll never forget you, and she said...."

I wasn't listening anymore. Maybe this was a wild goose chase, but I felt I had to follow it up. I sat around with Barney for a while, then I said goodbye and went home. Celia asked me how it went, with the client, and I said, not bad.

# 19

The next day, I called Dr. Hamilton Wang. I got a receptionist of course, but eventually, the doctor himself was on the phone. I told him I was a lawyer, I was representing Barney Bell, and I had also been representing the late Blanche Baleine, and was it possible for me to ask him a few questions.

"Questions? What about?"

"Dr. Wang, I really don't want to do this over the phone.... An estate matter...."

"Estate? Whose estate?"

"The late Ms. Baleine.... She was Barney Bell's wife."

"What does that have to do with me? I don't see the connection."

Of course, there was no connection to see. Nothing I could tell him honestly. I was, as usual, not exactly a brilliant liar. I mumbled something incomprehensible. He asked more questions, and got more mumbo-jumbo out of me. But in the end, perhaps out of curiosity, Dr. Wang agreed to see me. "I get through at six. You can come then," he said. "Before that, I have my patients to see."

I drove to San Carlos, and arrived just before six. Dr. Wang's office was a typical dentist's office. It was in a low-rise complex made up entirely, as far as I could see, of dentists: dentists of all stripes—ordinary dentists, oral surgeons, periodontists, pediatric dentists, the whole dental fraternity, a kind of shopping center of dentists.

I rang the bell and waited. A very businesslike woman, in her 40's I would say, opened the door. She was wearing a white coat. "You must be Mr. May," she said, "I'm Dr. Wang's assistant. He's waiting for you."

I got a sinking feeling in the pit of my stomach just walking in the door. I've never quite gotten over my childhood fear of dentists. It's all I can do to control myself when they start drilling. The noise really gets to me, you know, that buzzing sound.

Dr. Wang was sitting in a kind of office, writing something in a large notebook. He was a man in his 50's, I'd say, his hair elegantly gray, a slender man, very clean looking, very dignified. He was wearing a white coat, of course.

He motioned to me to sit down, in a comfortable leather chair. "Now, what's this all about?" he said.

I had rehearsed this part, more or less. I knew I had to be at least somewhat convincing. It wasn't easy. I couldn't possibly tell him about the Tony Crass show and the dentists who were drilling their patients, and that I was here because there might be some dental connection with the murder of Blanche Baleine. I said: "Doctor, as you know, a woman named Blanche Baleine was found dead a few weeks ago. Her husband, Barney, was a patient of yours...."

"Yes, yes," he said. "And so was she."

"She...Blanche...was your patient?"

"Yes. Is that so surprising?"

In fact, it was. "I....didn't know she went to a dentist."

"Why shouldn't she go? She had teeth, after all. Most people go to dentists. Or should go, I might say."

"Did you see her...often?"

"As a matter of fact, only once or twice. She was a new patient. I assume her husband referred her to me. Or perhaps it was her husband's aunt, Martha Hinchcombe. She was my patient, too."

"Martha was?"

He was clearly annoyed. "Yes, she was. So? I have dozens of patients."

"Have you....told the police? About Blanche? Her being your patient?"

"The police? Why on earth should I," he said. "She came to me, to have her teeth cleaned, which my assistant did; and I examined her. No cavities. I'm very sorry she's dead, but I can't see why I should go to the police with this astounding information. And I still don't know what you're after."

"And...Martha Hinchcombe...."

"She was a very old lady, as you know. She took good care of her teeth, though. A lot of women her age have dentures. She had most of her teeth. She came in regularly, every six months, we did X-rays, and she had her teeth cleaned. Then I examined her. I paid particular attention to her gums. I was a little worried about her gums, but not seriously. Funny thing, she did speak to me, on the phone, shortly before she died."

"Oh, did she?"

"She was quite ill. Chicken pox, I think she said. It's serious in elderly people. She called and said, she had a terrific toothache, but she couldn't come see me until she got better. She said, could I prescribe something, a painkiller. I said, well, your regular doctor can, anything at all would do; but she insisted, and I did give her a prescription. She said somebody would come and pick it up. It was a young man, somebody who worked for her stepson, I think his name was Arthur something. I assume somebody filled the prescription; but in any event, she died the very next day."

I felt like asking him if he found it odd that two of his patients should die, but after all they did die months apart, and Martha had been quite elderly; so I let the subject go. "And... you never saw Blanche, after the checkup, I mean."

"No. Well, she called on the phone.... Actually, it was a little peculiar, I have to admit. She didn't speak to me, I was with a patient. She said it was important, she had to get in touch with me. So, the receptionist said, he can't come to the phone, can he call you back. She said, I'll be moving around, but here's a cell phone number. When I was done with the patient, I...well, I got the message, but I was late for a social engagement, so I asked Libby, that's my receptionist, to call the number, and find out what she wanted. And if it was urgent, Libby could call me on *my* cell phone. In the event, Libby did try, but there was no answer. I called her myself the next morning, but there was no response. No wonder. She was already dead."

"Can you give me the cell phone number? This could be important."

"You think so? Why on earth? But I can't give it to you. It was, you know, just scrawled on a little piece of paper, and it's long since gone into the garbage."

"And...is there anything else you can tell me?"

He gave me a quizzical look. "Anything else? About what?

Isn't it time you told me what this is actually about? All you've done is ask questions."

I didn't quite know what to say. I stuttered out something about the investigation, into Blanche's death, and the estate she left behind. It must have been perfectly obvious to him that I was babbling incoherently. But he also saw, no doubt, that I had no intention of telling him the truth, whatever that was. So he let me go. Basically, I just slid out the door, leaving him puzzled and no doubt annoyed.

Had I learned anything? I thought it was curious that Dr. Wang had treated both Blanche and Aunt Martha; and that Barney had no idea that Blanche was seeing his dentist. Why was it a secret? Maybe *he* was having sex with Blanche—the dentist. I couldn't ask him that, of course. He was a fairly attractive man. Or maybe he was having sex with Libby, his assistant. Was he married? What kind of medicine had he prescribed for Aunt Martha? Maybe he poisoned her. But why would he do that?

I was walking slowly, trying to digest matters, when I heard a voice calling my name. I was just outside the office door. I turned and saw Dr. Wang's assistant. She said: "I'm Libby. I couldn't help overhearing part of your conversation.... You're a detective, aren't you? You're investigating this case?"

"Well, not really...."

She said: "Never mind. I realize you can't admit it. But maybe I have some information.... Dr. Wang doesn't know this, but Ms. Baleine spoke to me.... She had this rather strange conversation with me."

"Strange conversation? When was this?"

"I don't remember exactly. Before one of her visits. She asked me, did I know something about dental ethics. Suppose a dentist slept with a patient, could that get him into real trouble? I assured her Dr. Wang would never do such a thing. And I'm always around, in the office, when patients are here, so frankly it's impossible, I said. Now, in retrospect, I realize that I was terribly, terribly naive. But we'll come back to that. Anyway, she said, I wasn't necessarily thinking of Dr. Wang; but suppose it was some other dentist, and I said, I just don't know. She said, would there be trouble with the dental association, and I told her, I had no idea. That was the gist of the conversation. I thought...maybe it's important...."

"It might be," I said, quite gravely.

She said. "I suspected as much."

I found it exciting that she imagined I was a real-life detective. I was enjoying this, playing the part.

"There's something else," she said. "I hate to tell you this. Dr. Wang has been very good to me, and I respect him very, very much, but...."

"But what?"

"I understand, this is a murder investigation, isn't it?"

I wasn't *exactly* lying. "Yes, Ms. Baleine was murdered, and, yes, there's an investigation."

"They say her husband did it. Out of jealousy."

"I really can't comment on that," I said.

She nodded, as if to say, she understood. Then she went on: "Well, the last time she was here, and I could check the date, I don't know exactly when it was...anyway, she was the last patient. And they were finished with the dental work, whatever it was, and Dr. Wang, he said to me, you can go. And she was still there. I think. So I left, but when I got to my car, I realized I had left my car keys in the office, so I went back, and...I don't think Dr. Wang saw me.... He was in his private study, and, well, I'm embarrassed to say this, but I heard noises...."

"Noises?"

"Well, heavy breathing...you know, noises. I'm...a married woman, and I thought...." Here her voice trailed off.

Dr. Wang? With Blanche? Was this possible? I guess it was. Blanche seemed to like to have sex, and with all sorts of people. I made a grave face, nodded carefully, thanked Libby, told her not to speak of this to anyone else, said she had done a real service, and went out to my car. My head was full of theories. All of them, as it turned out, wrong.

# 20

I don't think my regular clients suffered, during this period, despite my obsession with Barney and Blanche. I have a family to support, and I take that seriously. Still, I have to admit, I would often wake up in the middle of the night, thinking about some aspect of the case. And sometimes, I wouldn't be able to fall asleep again, so I would shuffle into the living room and look at a magazine, trying to bore myself back to sleep. And of course, in the morning, I had trouble waking up. Sometimes I slept right through the alarm clock.

Celia, I thought, simply slept through these episodes in the middle of the night. She seemed so peacefully asleep. But I was wrong, of course. A wife develops a kind of sixth sense, when it comes to husbands. That's why it's hard for some men to have an affair. Wives can practically smell things on your breath. Anyway, after about three bad sleep nights, I found myself at 3 a.m. reading a magazine—I think it was *National Geographic*—in the living room. I was reading a long article about the life and times of the lesser kudu. This is not a subject that normally interests me. Another article was about frozen Peruvian mummies.

I finished the lesser kudu and was in the midst of the mummies when I heard a soft sound. It was Celia, in her nightgown.

"Frank, what's going on?" she said. "You've been getting up a lot lately, in the middle of the night. What's the trouble? There's something on your mind."

"Lots of things on my mind, honey," I said.

"Frank, don't give me generalities. I *know* when there's something wrong. I want to know what's bothering you."

"Oh, some stuff with clients. Technical."

But she wasn't buying that line. In the end, I gave in, and I told her the whole story, from start to finish. I told her about

Barney and Blanche, I told her about the Tony Crass program, and about the gardener. Above all, I said, I was worried about Barney. I thought he was innocent, a poor jerk caught in a web; and it was eating away at me that I wasn't able to help out.

She listened, and didn't interrupt. At the end, as I expected, she gave me good advice. Stay out of it. It's none of your business. "Frank," she said, "don't you ever learn, what am I going to do with you." And so on. The usual litany; but she wasn't totally serious. I could see that she was interested in what I told her. We even began to discuss the case.

"Frank," she said, "you're not a policeman, you're not a detective. Who knows who might want to kill this woman? And, to begin with, suppose a burglar broke in...."

"Celia, there was no burglar."

"Alright. But why are you so sure it wasn't Barney? He's the obvious one."

"I can't believe it," I said. "Honey, if you'd met him.... I know the guy. He's not a killer. Besides, why would he want to kill her?"

"Be sensible," she said. "Men kill their wives all the time, they get mad, jealous.... You read about it in the papers every day."

"Not Barney," I said, stubbornly.

"There's Suzie," she said, "his sister. She hated Blanche; then there's Hinchcombe, maybe she was out for his money, maybe she was playing him for a sucker, they were sleeping together, maybe they had a fight. You just don't know, Frank. That's why it's so crazy for you to get so involved."

"She wanted to be an investigative reporter," I said. "Maybe she was investigating something."

"Honey, you're out of your league," she said. "Suppose she was, well, investigating. She had some idea about, whatever, insider trading, or companies in Bermuda, or some kind of scandal; maybe it was this television business. Maybe she wanted to expose all the fakery, actors pretending to be people on reality shows. We'll never know. And anyway, we're not going to do anything in the middle of the night. Let's go to bed."

"I hear and obey," I said, trying to smile. I followed her into our big, warm bed. The conversation made me feel better, somehow. I fell asleep in an instant. Celia was pressed up against me. I mean, wives are great to sleep with. I'm not talking about sex. Not that sex is a bad idea. But I feel sorry for all those people who sleep alone, without a warm body next to them at night, a cozy body. I don't care if they're having all kinds of wild and crazy sex. There's no substitute for cuddling. Maybe these people use teddy bears, who knows.

In the morning, we were both bone-tired. But we had breakfast together. Celia packed the girls off to school. I was slurping down the last of my coffee. "Honey," she said, "I've been thinking...."

"About this case?"

"Yes. Two comments. First, I think the dentist thing is a blind alley. That's just my feeling. Second, there's two leads that are much more promising...."

"And they are?"

"The baby is one. It isn't his baby. I don't think it is, anyway. Talk to him about it. Where did this baby come from? And the gardener. Don't give up on the gardener."

"I won't," I said; I kissed her, and went out to the car. Celia always made sense. And, despite the preaching, despite her excellent advice, I actually think she wanted me to keep going. And that was exactly what I planned to do.

# 21

In the middle of the morning, during a lull between clients, I called Barney. I was following Celia's advice but I tried to be sly about it. First I asked about Blanche's ambition to be an investigative reporter, did Barney know anything about it? He said no.

"Frank, she never told me nothing. Like, now she's dead, I'm realizing stuff, I mean, like I never knew her. Take this pregnancy thing...."

That was actually what I wanted to pursue. But I was cautious. "She wasn't looking into something, doing research, something like that? Think hard, Barney, it could be important."

"Yeah, why?"

"Motive. She might have found something out. You know, some scandal. She was getting close to something big, maybe. So they hired a hit man...."

"Who? What kind of hit man?"

"I don't know. That's the question. Somebody.... Somebody she was after."

"Hey, I doubt it," he said. "I think it was all bullshit. She was all talk, no action, if you ask me. I mean, what kind of reporter was she? She didn't know shit about journalism, she didn't have any job, with a newspaper, or TV or anything."

"Well, I was just wondering," I said. "I'm looking for a motive."

Barney obviously liked that idea. A motive! Something to pin on somebody else. "Yeah, maybe. I mean, I said, she didn't know shit, but, you're right, did that ever stop her? No, she did what she wanted. So maybe that's it. Maybe that's the thing. Maybe you're right. She had some dirt on somebody. That's maybe why he did it, why he smashed in her head.... Frank... you'll find out, won't you? You'll follow this up, no?"

I reminded him I was not a detective; but I did promise to try.

Suddenly he said, in a frightened voice: "Jesus, Frank: do you think they're bugging my phone? Maybe we shouldn't be talking."

"Barney, I told you before, they're not bugging your phone. Why should they? Anyway, you aren't saying anything incriminating; and you're not going to, right?"

"You're right, you're right. It's just that I'm so damn nervous."

"One other thing, Barney," I said. "This baby business."

"Yeah, what about it?"

"It's awkward, Barney. But you think...I guess you think, it's not your baby."

"Frank, how can I know? But, shit, yes...I think she lied to me, Frank. She never said anything about other guys. Is there some way they can find out? Tests, that sort of thing?"

"I guess so. You know, the DNA."

"Should I ask Nolan, you know, make them do the DNA thing. I mean, it doesn't make any difference, in a way, like she's dead, the baby's dead, it's old news; but if Blanche was fooling around...."

"I'd leave it be, Barney," I said. "You can talk to Nolan if you want to. But my advice is, let it go. It's either your baby or it isn't. If it isn't, they'll say, that's why you killed her. It's not a good thing for you. But...do you have any idea, I mean, whose baby it could be? I know this is kind of ticklish. You say, you didn't know Blanche was fooling around. But if she was, is there somebody you're suspicious of?"

"Frank, how would I know? I haven't got a clue...."

"None at all?"

"Well...maybe.... I always suspected maybe Travis...."

"Anybody else?"

He sighed at the other end of the phone. "Who knows. Could be anybody. God, why did I ever get involved with her. I should have my head examined. She brought me nothing but trouble. Next thing, I'll be sitting on death row."

"You'll get off, Barney," I said, "you're innocent, aren't you?"

"Sure, sure; I know it, and you know it; but what difference does that make? You read the paper, there's all this stuff about innocent guys.... They've got all those guys in jail, guys that did absolutely nothing...the police frame them, it happens all the time...."

I tried to reassure him, I told him, this wasn't some big corrupt city, the police weren't like that, and so on. It wasn't easy to console him. "Frank," he said, "You don't know what I'm going through here. I'm like a prisoner, you know? I'm afraid to go out of my house. I get calls from reporters, I think they hang around the house, this is big news around here...they don't get a murder every day of the week.... And Nolan warned me, he said, well, they might arrest me soon. He said, don't worry. Sure. Don't worry. Why should *he* worry? It isn't his ass on the line."

It was a litany I'd heard from him before. Poor guy. I made encouraging, clucking noises. He went on and on: "I'm all alone here, Frank, nobody comes to see me. You'd think I had AIDS or something, or God knows what, some kind of disease. I thought Charley would come but he didn't. I wanted him to come, you know, play cards, eat a pizza, watch TV. *Anything*. He said he'd come, but he never showed up."

I thought, maybe I could help. I promised to drop in and see Barney. "You've been great, Frank," he said. "I won't forget it."

When I got off the phone, I called up Charley Morgan. It was none of my business, but I felt sorry for Barney.

"Charley, this is Frank."

"Frank who?"

"Frank May. Remember me? Barney's lawyer."

"Yeah, so what?"

"Charley...I want to ask you something. You know Barney pretty well. You knew Blanche, too...."

"Yeah. So?"

"I just got off the phone with Barney. He's in terrible shape, psychologically. You're supposed to be buddies. He says you're avoiding him. He needs some company, Charley, how about it?"

"Hey, what's it to you? I'm busy."

"Busy, Charley? What with?"

"Just busy. Things. Maybe I'll go see him, later on. Hey,

this is a coincidence.... I was thinking of calling you, asking you something. The cops were here the other day," he said.

"Yeah, and?"

"They asked a bunch of questions. A whole lot of questions."

"What about?"

He said: "Never mind. Here's *my* question: This DNA stuff. Can they make you do it? I mean, give them a sample, I don't know, your urine or something, or a fingernail. You know what I mean? Can I just say, no thanks?"

"Why are you asking, Charley?"

"It's this baby thing.... Blanche's baby...."

"Is that what they were asking about?"

"Well...let's say they were...."

"And they think it's *yours*, Charley?"

"Hey, no, don't jump to conclusions. I mean, that chick got around, you know what I mean? She and I...just once...it's not like we were doing it on a regular basis. I had a lot to drink that night. Barney was God knows where. She seemed awfully eager. Normally, I wouldn't do that to a friend, I mean, make out with his wife. Not unless I was drunk."

"You told them that?"

"Told them what?"

"That you and Blanche had sex?"

"They...they knew it. Look: Barney was out of town, there was this party, Blanche was there, and Barney's sister. You know her? A big mouth. And, I said, Blanche was drunk. So was I. It was Barney's apartment. Everybody went home, I stayed. She...the sister, the bitch, she knew I was staying. She must have gabbed to the police."

"So it could be your baby?"

"Hey, it could be anybody's. Do I know what she did in her spare time? Who she ran around with? There was just this once. I mean, it's probably Barney's kid, no? The two of them, they were married, weren't they? That one time, me and Blanche.... she said, it was OK, she was on the pill or whatever. If they take this sample, urine or stuff.... Suppose it *was* my baby, they could think, I had a motive, you know, a reason to kill her.... I swear, I wouldn't lay a finger on her."

I told him not to worry. I told him he was right about

Blanche. She was not exactly a model wife. I was thinking, for example, of Dr. Wang. But when I put down the phone, I wondered: could it *be* Charley? What did I know about him?

But I had reached another dead end. That left two more paths to follow. One was quite promising—the mysterious gardener. As it turned out, I was due to have a break. Oddly enough, it involved Charley again. Another path, more dubious, was Aunt Martha. Could it possibly be true that somebody helped Aunt Martha along, in her journey out of this world? Did Blanche's insinuations have some basis? And was this basis connected to her own death?

I felt I had to get in touch with Travis again. I had no idea what else to do. I felt I was spinning wheels.

It wasn't easy to wangle another session with Travis—it took many phone calls, conversations with Arthur, and complex negotiations. I was finally granted an audience, and I drove out to Travis' house, down the leafy, elegant streets of Atherton. It was the middle of the day. Nobody was around, except a few Mexican gardeners, cleaning up leaves and pruning bushes; and an occasional nanny pushing a stroller down the quiet avenues.

Arthur answered the door. "He's very busy today. Don't waste his time," he said.

I mumbled something. Travis was sitting in his study, dressed in chino pants and a coal-black t-shirt. He was looking at a pile of papers. "I haven't got much time," he said. "What's on your mind?"

I said, rather timidly, "I wonder if you would mind answering some questions."

"Questions? What about?"

"Blanche...."

"Oh, for God's sakes. Blanche again. Can't you leave it alone? What are you doing, playing detective?"

"I'm...following up on some things."

"Yeah? Why? And what things?"

"Blanche...made...some wild accusations."

He said; "Blanche? Last time I checked, she was dead."

I said: "I know that. This was before she died."

"What kind of accusations? Something about me?"

I said, "no, not you."

He said: "Well, then, what do I care? Anyway, if she told

you, was it in your office? She was some kind of client, no? Aren't you supposed to keep your mouth shut?"

I said, "well, she's dead, as you say. She's not a client anymore."

"Alright, what did she say?"

I said: "This is very delicate...."

"Oh, for God's sake, get to the point."

"It wasn't...something she said to me directly...somebody else told me...it was about your stepmother, your father's wife...."

"Martha? I never called her a stepmother. She was an old bag by the time she married my father. Not that I minded her. Don't get me wrong. It was a good deal for him. Her too, I suppose. Anyway, she's dead too, as you well know."

"I do know. Blanche...well, Blanche was hinting around that, uh, that maybe she didn't die a natural death."

"What on earth are you talking about?"

"Well, that maybe somebody...Barney maybe...kind-of helped her along...."

"Helped her along? Do you always talk in riddles? I pity your clients if you do."

"She hinted that Barney killed his aunt."

"Barney killed his aunt?" He sounded totally incredulous.

"Yes. Specifically, poisoned her."

"Poisoned her? Jesus, I never heard such shit. She died in bed. She was a million years old. She was sick. She went to sleep, and she didn't wake up. End of story."

"Well...but, I mean, you can't be sure...if it was poison.... Blanche thought...."

"You're out of your mind. Blanche was too."

"Well, maybe," I said. "But it wasn't just Blanche. Susan...."

"Susan? Another crackpot."

He had gotten up. His face was red, he seemed angry. "You're all stark raving mad. Or you're watching too many movies," he said.

I said: "I just wanted to know...what you thought."

"Well, now you know," he said; and he indicated, with his body language, in no uncertain terms, that this session was at an end.

"So you think it's impossible?" I asked.

"Arthur, show this creep out," he said, raising his voice. Sheepishly, I followed Arthur. When we got to the door, he hesitated, and seemed to clear his throat. "I'd...I'd like to add a word or two," he said.

I stopped and listened.

"I...overheard your conversation," he said. "Mr. Hinch-combe often likes me to, ah, become apprised of such things."

"I see," I said, somewhat frostily.

"About Martha Hinchcombe," he said. "I don't believe, well, that such accusations have any foundation. She was a very sick woman. She also had a toothache, and she spoke to her dentist."

"I know that," I said.

"He prescribed some sort of painkiller, I believe. Mr. Hinchcombe, Mr. Millard Hinchcombe that is, asked me to pick it up at the drugstore. CVS Drugstore, on El Camino. I did pick it up. I brought it to the apartment. She was in bed. I don't know whether she took it or not. As you know, she died that night. The only person there at the time was Mr. Millard Hinchcombe. Barney Bell called his aunt on the phone, and she spoke to him, I believe. But he was not there that day. Not at all. Only one person came to see her, and it wasn't Barney Bell."

"So he couldn't.... I mean, if there was poison...or the painkiller was doctored...."

"It couldn't be him. So you see, the whole thing is absurd. It's a fantasy. Now you understand why Mr. Hinchcombe was so angry. If there was anything to the story, don't you see, suspicion would fall on his own father...and that's ridiculous. Why would he want to poison his wife? They were very happy together."

"Thank you, Arthur," I said, and I turned to go. But then I stopped. "You said she did have one visitor, though, that day. Could I ask you who that was?"

"Certainly," he said. "It was Blanche Baleine. She came and stayed for about an hour. It was somewhat surprising...she rarely visited Mrs. Hinchcombe. But that day she did. Yes, she stayed at least an hour."

"Thank you," I said. I got in my car and drove away.

*If* the old woman was poisoned—and that was an enormous if—the two main suspects had to be Millard, her husband, and Blanche Baleine. Blanche...could Barney have sent her? Absurd. It was totally out of character. Could she have done it on her own? So that the money would go to her husband? Or was it possible that the poison wasn't in the painkiller, or whatever she drank that day? Old ladies are poisoned all the time in mystery stories. In these books, they take some sort of tonic or some other liquid, every day.... Somebody puts the poison in the liquid; but if this was the case, the poison could have been put in the liquid some other time, maybe the day before, or even earlier.

What is a tonic, anyway?

Did I dare talk to Millard Hinchcombe, the widower? Maybe he would have something to say, something that would shed light on this business. I would have to think of some excuse, of course; but I made up my mind to do it, by hook or by crook. And I did.

# 22

It was late the next day that I finally had a chance to call Millard Hinchcombe. I can't spend all my time on Barney's case, or even most of my time. The work goes on. Leases, wills, trusts; my stable of clients.

I introduced myself to Millard over the phone, I said I was representing Barney Bell, not in the criminal matter of course, but with regard to his other matters. I understand, I said, that he, Millard, was the husband of the late Martha Hinchcombe, and that he was what we call an heir-at-law, even though he was not making any claims on the estate. But I wondered if I could see him, ask him a few questions, in regard to the estate.

"I don't understand," he said, "My son is very rich.... Martha didn't leave me money, she didn't have to...so I don't see...."

I didn't let him finish the sentence. "Yes, of course. Just routine. You see, you are, after all, the husband, the widower, and...under California law, you have certain rights.... If I could talk to you, for a few minutes, it won't take long. I can come to your place, if you like; or you could come to my office."

"Where's your office?"

I told him. He said: "I'd rather come to you. Give me an excuse to get out of the house."

We made an arrangement for the next day. He came in a taxi. He was a little old man, with snow white hair, and a tiny white moustache. He was shaped like a dumpling; and I strained to see any signs of resemblance to Travis. Maybe the eyes, the chin. Travis was rather tall; his father was squat and round. Maybe he had shrunk with old age.

I babbled on for a bit, about California probate law, and what the estate process was going to be like, and of course he was not going to have much to do with it, the executor would handle it all, although there was of course perhaps a problem, seeing as how the executor, Barney, was in trouble with the law. Perhaps a new executor might be in order. But not to worry, these things will be worked out. He nodded his head.

Then I said. "This is all rather unpleasant, I'm sure, Mr. Hinchcombe. I mean, here we are talking about estates, and executors; and the sad fact is, you've lost your dear wife."

"Oh, that's kind of you to say," he said. "Yes, yes. It's been so terrible. I can't tell you how upset I am," he said. "Maybe I've lived too long.... I've buried three wives. Three wives. Well, actually, my first wife...we were divorced...that's Travis' mother. But she's dead now. The second one...it doesn't matter. Martha was my third wife. We met at a senior center. She was so alive, so strong.... We were very happy together."

"I'm sure you were," I said.

"People think old people are, I don't know, freaks. Aliens from outer space. But we're human beings. On the inside, we're the same; we don't change, just because we get old. But nobody understands.... My son...he's good to me, he gives me anything I want, I don't have any money problems... but he doesn't take me seriously.... I'm like a child to him, a senile child, not a person. I tell you, it hurts."

"Oh, I know," I said. And I did. Travis treated me that way too, and I was half Millard's age.

"When I married Martha.... He thought I was crazy. Doddering. Getting married at 75, he thought it was ridiculous. You're 75, he said to me. What are you doing? When it comes to women, I think all he thinks about is sex. Martha and I...we had good times. Very good times. She's gone now, and it's terribly lonely. I have family, but still, I'm lonely."

I said, "I'm sorry."

"Her memory," he said, "it's very dear to me. She was a good woman. She was so lively! She had a sense of humor, I can tell you that! We laughed and laughed, some times. Went to shows together. Even went to Las Vegas. We both had money, that helps. Travis...well, you know about him. Anyway, I'm boring you. You think, these old people, they just talk and talk...."

"Your wife died suddenly," I said, trying to be sly.

"I know what you're thinking," he said. "I know what's going on. I've heard these vile, disgusting rumors. You think I don't know? I heard it from Travis. He was very angry. But he shouldn't have told me. It upset me terribly. The idea that somebody killed her.... Mr. May, I was appalled. I didn't close my eyes last night, I just tossed and turned in bed. I was crying, like a baby. Believe me. Why would Blanche say a terrible thing like that? It's a lie, it isn't true.... I was there when she died.... She was sick, very sick.... She had chicken pox, you heard that ...and, well, maybe her heart....You don't believe that terrible story, do you? About the poison?"

"Well...not really...."

"Is the idea, Barney did it? He wasn't even there that day. Anyway, my Martha, she loved Barney. She liked Blanche. Somewhat. Said she was OK. But Barney! Barney was her favorite. He wouldn't have touched her, I know it. He called, he spoke on the phone, but he wasn't there...the day she died. Only Blanche was there.... But I'm not saying Blanche did anything...nobody did anything.... She was old. Sick...." He kept shaking his head. "Why should anybody say such terrible things?"

"Maybe it was a joke," I said, feebly. But then I got up my courage and said: "Could you...tell me something, about...the illness.... You said chicken pox?"

He seemed to be sobbing, and very agitated. He nodded yes. "Poor dear.... But that's not what did it.... She was very sick, and...I think her heart gave out...."

"When she was sick, did she have visitors?"

"Of course she had visitors! People cared. Everybody came. I was afraid they'd tire her out, but Martha, she liked people. Oh yes, she had visitors."

"And...who were they?"

"Barney came. He came twice, I think. Blanche came. My son.... The neighbors. Oh, they loved her, all the neighbors! Widows, nice women, mostly.... She used to play cards, every Tuesday, with the women. Bridge, gin rummy.... They were so nice to me when she died.... Hilda, that's the one who lived next door, she came over every day, made me a casserole, she said, Millard, you know how I loved her, Martha was like a sister to me, if you ever need anything, Millard...."

I cut him off in the middle of the casserole.

"So there were people around...but not that day, the day

she died...."

"No, not that day.... That was very quiet...."

"And...please forgive me for asking, but...well, it's just so I can eliminate this ridiculous idea. Did anybody give her something to drink, that you remember? Tea? Soda? Water?"

"Who remembers such things? That day...of course she drank, you have to have fluids. Take fluids. The doctors said so. A cup of tea.... And Blanche came over, she brought a bottle of wine.... Martha had a glass of wine.... That was the night before she died.... Oh God, you can't mean...you don't think there was something in the wine...."

"No, I didn't mean anything."

"It's not even possible, no," he said, raising his voice.

But was it possible? Here, Aunt Martha, have a little wine. She sips it. Tastes funny, she says, a little bitter. Oh, that's alright. It's a very dry wine. So she drinks it. And then, after she's asleep, it does its dirty work on her. But don't people have symptoms when they're poisoned? Don't they turn blue, or smell like walnuts, or something like that? I have to confess a total ignorance of poisons. Poisons don't come up in my line of work.

Millard, however, had gotten himself into a state. "Oh.... I can't believe it.... Why do people say such things...." He started breathing heavily, and panting; then he seemed to be gasping for breath. I ran down the hall to an office with a water cooler, and got him some water in a paper cup. When I got back with the water, he was on his hands and knees, on the ground, twitching and making funny gurgling noises. I was in a panic. I thought, oh God, he's going to die on me, right in my office. He was stretched out on the floor now.... Was he even conscious? His eyes were closed, and he was making rasping noises. Is that what a death rattle sounds like? I took out the key, opened the desk drawer, and got out the little book—Blanche's book.... I couldn't think of anything else to do.

I found Dr. Tanager's number, and I dialed it frantically. To my relief, he answered himself, not a receptionist, but Dr. Tanager in person. "Yes? This is Dr. Ross Tanager."

"Dr. Tanager, this is Frank May. I have a problem. A man in my office, an old man, I think he's having some sort of heart attack.... It's Millard Hinchcombe.... Can you come here?"

"Frank: calm down. No, I can't come. This is my cell phone. I'm in San Francisco. Don't be frightened. It's Millard, you say? He has a history.... But do call a doctor. You're in San Mateo, right? OK: call Dr. Gus Meadows, he's in the phone book, he's right nearby, he's got an office on Third Street...."

I was sweating bullets. The old man was still lying on the floor, but at least he was breathing, and the rattling noise had stopped. I looked up Dr. Gus Meadows and dialed his number. I got some idiotic voice mail thing, but finally I reached a nurse, after punching several numbers. Meadows was away for the day, is this an emergency, and so on. Damn right, it's an emergency, I said. She recommended the emergency room of some hospital, I forget which one.

Oh Lord, I thought, what now? I had another crazy thought: maybe somebody poisoned *him*? He seemed somewhat better though; he was trying to get up off the floor. His face was pale, ashen. I said, "don't get up, stay there, Mr. Hinchcombe, please don't exert yourself." But he shook his head, and reached out his hand for me to take. I helped him up; and he staggered over to a chair, and sat down heavily.

I said: "Are you alright? I'm trying to get a doctor."

He said, weakly, "no, no doctor...I'm OK.... Just let me sit for a while." I offered him the cup of water, and he drank it. "Let me take you to an emergency room," I said, "they'll look you over." But he absolutely refused. After a while, I decided it was best to let him alone. He did seem to be doing much better.

"Thank you," he said, in a weak voice. "These things happen to me.... I'm not supposed to get stressed.... I have a heart condition.... I take pills...."

I made a sympathetic face.

"You've been very nice to me," he said. "I appreciate it."

"It's the least I could do," I said. "I'm really so sorry I distressed you."

"Oh, that's not your fault," he said. "Anyway, I get these attacks.... It happened, oh, once when I was visiting Travis... visiting his house I mean. He wasn't there. It was summer. Martha was still alive. I think it was a Tuesday, she was playing bridge. I was in the garden, sitting in the sun, reading.... I had a hat on, you know, to protect me, the sun is very strong. Then...I don't even remember what happened, but I passed out, I think, right there on the grass...."

"Oh my."

"There was this nice young man who helped me.... I was lucky. Nobody was home, oh maybe the housekeeper, and that other man, Arthur, but he was inside.... It was the nice man who worked there, the gardener...he helped me up, he was so gentle with me, just like you...."

A bell rang in my head. "The gardener."

"Oh yes, that's what he was. Took care of the garden. And the pool. Travis has such a nice pool. Of course, I don't go in, my swimming days are over...."

"Was his name Eben Born?"

"Whose name?"

"The gardener."

"I never asked him his name. Was that his name?"

"Yes. Did you know: he's missing? Nobody knows where he is."

"How sad."

I was on thin ice, but I went right ahead: "Ran away, apparently. After Blanche was murdered. That's odd, don't you think?"

Millard mopped his face with a handkerchief. "Oh, you can't be suggesting he was the one.... Oh no, that's not possible," he said. "He was such a pleasant person. I saw him, a few times, when I was visiting my son. I used to sit in the garden, it's so nice there. Sometimes I came with Martha, poor soul. After she died, Travis said, dad, you come over, sit in the garden, you like to sit there, you come whenever you feel like it.... I do get lonely...."

"Did you ever talk to him?"

"To Travis? He's my son...."

"No, I mean the gardener."

"Oh...him...yes.... A couple of times. I was sitting there, and he was clipping the bushes. I said, am I in your way? And he said, oh, no, just stay there, enjoy yourself, that's what he said. He was clipping the bushes."

"That's all you said?"

"Oh no. We had a regular conversation. I remember it, now. He had long hair, a ponytail. Usually I don't like that. But with him, I didn't mind. Blond, with blue eyes. He had a very kind, gentle face. Very young man. I said, nice day, isn't it. Such nice sun. Good for the flowers. He said, yes, oh yes. I said, it's a beautiful house, isn't it, my son has wonderful taste. And he said, I guess so, I don't get to see it much, I don't go inside."

"And?"

"I said, that's too bad, why don't you come in with me, we'll have some coffee, and cake if there is any. Usually, there's something, in the fridge. My son...."

"So you went in, the two of you?"

"No, he said, thank you, pops; but I have a lot of work to do, and I don't think your son wants me inside, besides, my shoes are muddy. They *were* muddy, too; he'd been watering. He said, it's nice to have a lot of space, beautiful grounds, like this. I used to live out in the country. Now I'm in a cheap motel, four walls. I like to come here, it's relaxing. Funny, isn't it, he said, that it's relaxing to work. But I like flowers, I like gardens, he said. I said, you don't have a home, a real home, and a garden? You're in a motel?"

I was fascinated, of course. I wanted Millard to go on talking; and he did. "He said, well, I was in a motel, but I can't stay there much longer. I have another place to stay, but there's not much room. Still, I guess I'll go there."

"Did he say where?"

"I think he said, a friend. I'm not sure. He said his friend had a little house, a shack almost, no yard or anything, around here somewhere...his name.... He did mention his name...."

"Can you remember it?"

"No...you know how old people are...the memory goes.... I can't remember names sometimes. It's so frustrating...."

"Try. Try to imagine it."

"I don't know. Dick, Sam, something common.... Maybe Charley. Yes, I think it was Charley."

"Charley?"

"Now that I think about it. Yes. I'm pretty sure. He said Charley."

The world is full of Charleys. That is, even assuming the old man's memory wasn't playing a trick on him. It could be Charley. Or Carlos. Or Larry. Or Buster. And yet...it was a chance, and I felt I had to take it. If the gardener had some sort of connection to Charley Morgan.... Maybe the gardener, after all, *was* the key to this whole business. Maybe the case had nothing to do with fornicating dentists. Or poison in an old lady's wineglass. Maybe it was the mysterious gardener.

I hid from Millard Hinchcombe my growing excitement. He asked me to call him a cab. "Shouldn't you rest a little more, Mr. Hinchcombe? You've had quite an episode here," I said. But he was a tough old bird. "I have to go," he said.

I called the cab, shook his hand, and watched him totter down the hall. I could hardly wait for him to be gone. This was something real, now, something to follow up.... A long shot perhaps, but nothing ventured, nothing gained.

Not that I could follow it up as quickly as I wanted to. I had several clients to attend to. That night, some neighbor had us over for pizza, and we were supposed to watch a basketball game together on TV. I don't even remember what game. My mind was a thousand miles away. I had some free time the next morning, though; a window of opportunity, between ten and noon. I thought about calling Charley on the phone, and making an appointment. But I decided against it. A quick surprise visit was better. Of course, he was probably not at home; but I felt like taking a chance. If he wasn't home, I'd have to use Plan B.

# 23

I had gotten the address from Barney. Charley lived in Redwood City, in a run-down neighborhood near the freeway. It was on a rather sad block, all tiny houses, with tiny driveways and tiny yards. The yards were mostly unkempt and covered with weeds. They were filled with toys, old tires, and debris; in one yard a hideous ceramic gnome leered at passers-by. Most of the people who lived on the block seemed to own rusted-out pickup trucks. In the background, I could hear the roar of the highway.

Charley's house certainly fit the description old Hinchcombe had given, or rather what the gardener said. It was a dilapidated wooden structure, a kind of cottage; originally white, but the paint was peeling. Its small yard was off to the side, overgrown with weeds that choked off the corpses of a few flowering plants. There was a heap of rubble, and a tire with no tread, which seemed to be the neighborhood emblem, in the middle of the yard. I walked up to a small porch. The steps looked as if they were about to collapse, and they squeaked as I went up. I opened a torn screen door, half off its hinges, and rang the doorbell.

It was ten-thirty or so. I had no real expectation that someone would be home. I rang the bell again. No answer. I tried a third time, and was about to leave when the door opened a crack. I said: "Charley?"

"Yeah. Who the hell is it?"

"It's me. Frank May. Could you let me in?"

He opened the door. He was yawning. He had on rumpled blue pajama bottoms. His hair was a mess. His eyes were bloodshot. He needed a shave.

"You were asleep."

"Yeah. Christ, what time is it?"

"It's ten-forty."

Shit," he said. "I'm so hung over. Anyway, come on in."

I followed him into the apartment. It was a dismal place. The shades were drawn, and the place looked incredibly dreary. He led me into a living room filled with battered furniture, couches and chairs that the Salvation Army or Goodwill might very well reject. The air smelled foul. There were newspapers and old envelopes strewn on the floor.

I thought: this guy seriously needs to fire his feng shui consultant.

"Want some coffee?" he asked. "I got to have some myself."

"Rough night?"

"Yeah. Hey, they're all rough."

I followed him into a kitchen which was, if anything, even more of a mess than the living room. The sink was filled with dirty dishes. There was a table in the middle of the room. A slice of ancient pizza, half eaten, turning moldy no doubt, sat on a filthy plate in the middle of the table. In a waste basket, I could see empty beer bottles, cans of soda, and the tell-tale paper buckets and sacks used for Chinese takeout and Kentucky Fried Chicken.

"Place is a mess," he said. "Don't I know it."

I said nothing. I shrugged my shoulders.

He said, "My girlfriend used to keep it pretty clean, you know? She was a stickler, you might say. But since she dumped me, I let it go to hell."

"You live alone?" I asked.

"Yeah. I told you that. She—Mona—she was with me, couple of years, maybe more. Off and on, though, know what I mean? Last Christmas, we had this fight, big fight, she was seeing other guys, right under my nose, so we really had it out. Anyway, she packed up and left. Good riddance, you know?"

"Sorry about that."

"I'm better off. She was driving me nuts. But she kept the place neat, I'll give her that."

"So you're alone."

He was puttering with a coffee pot. It looked rusty to me, but then my standards are extremely middle-class. He gave me a look. "I said I was." But he seemed definitely startled.

"You sure?'

"I said, Hey, what's this all about? What's with the third

degree?"

"Don't you have somebody staying with you?"

"Who, me? Does it look like I'm taking in boarders? Whoa...."

"Charley," I said, "This is serious business. You're not telling me the truth. I think somebody's staying here, with you. I don't mean a girlfriend. A guy. I'm pretty sure of it. Don't lie to me. You could be in big trouble. Potentially."

"Yeah? Who says? What kind of trouble?"

"Big trouble."

"Like what?"

"First of all, you were concealing evidence—remember that. That's not good. It's a crime. Now you're harboring somebody—a man. Somebody the police are looking for."

"You're nuts."

"He calls himself Eben Born," I said, "though I don't think that's really his name. He worked for Travis Hinchcombe, kind of a gardener, maintenance guy, cleaned the pool, that sort of thing. He disappeared, right after Blanche died, or maybe right before; anyway, he's definitely under suspicion."

"What kind of suspicion?"

"Maybe murder. Not sure."

"Hey, man," he said, in a whiny voice, "lay off, will you? I never heard of the guy."

Was he telling the truth? It was possible. There were no obvious signs of anybody else who might be occupying this dung heap. The world is full of people named Charley. All I really I had to go on was an old man's rambling. But I persisted. I said: "I happen to know otherwise."

"You don't know shit. You want to, you can search the place."

"Charley," I said, as if I had a bucketful of proof, "I *know* he's staying here. There's no point telling me a bunch of lies."

"Hey, knock it off. I don't have to answer these questions, OK?"

"Charley, I'm not the police," I said. "I just want to talk to this guy. Why don't you admit he's staying here, and tell me how to get in touch with him."

"I told you, there's nobody here but me," he said.

"Well, *was* he here?"

"I never heard of the guy," he said.

He stopped for a second. He poured a foul looking brown liquid into a cup, and stirred it. He licked his lower lip with his tongue. The coffee was steaming hot. He took a sip or two. His hands were shaking slightly. Maybe he wasn't just hung over; maybe he was scared. Of the police? I was sure he was lying, but what could I do? How could I possibly worm the truth out of this creep? I felt helpless.

"Been nice seeing you," he said. In other words, get out.

"You're making a mistake, Charley," I said.

"You think? Listen, mister, my whole life is a mistake."

I got up and started to go. I slunk away, defeated. I was on the porch, going out the door, when I noticed a car that had driven up, and was about to park right in front of the house. The driver got out. I was amazed to see it was Arthur Flansbaum. He was just as amazed to see me, and he started to back away.

I said: "Arthur, what on earth are you doing here?"

He backed away. "Nothing. What a coincidence. I... have the wrong address."

I said: "You're coming to see Charley?"

He said: "Charley who?"

He was an even worse liar than I am. "Arthur, got a minute? Let's talk," I said, "I have something I want to ask you about."

"Can't. Too busy. Some other time. See you," he said, getting back into the car, and driving off as fast as he could.

What *was* he doing here? Obviously, he had some business with Charley; and ten to one it concerned the mysterious gardener. I felt vindicated. And emboldened. I went back into the house. Charley of course had seen this whole little scene. He was sitting on the sofa, holding his head in his hands.

I said, "Look, Charley, you're lying, *I* know you're lying, *you* know you're lying. That was Arthur Flansbaum, Travis' yes-man, you saw how he skedaddled when he saw me, but of course he came here to see *you*. Or maybe your houseguest."

He said: "Man, my head feels like it's split open. I've got the headache to beat all headaches."

"I'm sorry. You shouldn't drink so much."

"You my mother? I know I shouldn't drink so much. Look: like I told you, I don't have to talk to you."

I said: "OK, then I'm going to the cops. I'm going to tell them about the evidence you hid. You know, that's a federal offense." In fact, it wasn't. But federal offense sounds very impressive.

"You don't scare me."

"I'll turn you in, Charley, I swear."

"Yeah? You will? You're supposed to be on Barney's side. How the hell would it help out Barney, if you told the police...."

"About you?"

"Yeah, about me. Doesn't help him a bit."

"I'm trying to get at the truth," I said. "Barney never killed anybody. So the truth is on his side. That's what I think."

"I don't give a shit what you think. Anyway, the cops have it in for Barney."

I said: "Charley. We're wasting time. Level with me, will you? For God's sake. I know the guy was here. I just know it. He could be an important, uh, witness."

He paused for a while, and licked his lips. He poured himself another cup of coffee-like liquid. Then he said, "OK, he was here."

"That's more like it."

"Yeah. But he's gone. Flew the coop. He's not here anymore."

"Where did he go?"

"How should I know? I'm not his old lady. I was just doing him a favor...you know? Letting him sleep on the couch. OK? Now you know it, so now get out."

"Charley, I've got to know more. How did he get here? Where was he from? He didn't just come to the door, asking if you had a spare couch."

"That's nobody's business.... He was here, I told you. Here and gone. Where from and where to, it's no goddamn business of yours."

"But he's a material witness. Barney's lawyer even thinks he's the killer. This gardener. He ran away after the murder, right? That looks suspicious."

Charley snorted. "He killed Blanche? Bullshit. No way."

"How do you know?"

"Hey, he's not the type, OK? Nice guy. Quiet. Never bothered anything."

"But who *is* he?"

"Maybe he's an old friend of mine."

"Come on, Charley. He's a friend of yours? Where did you meet him?"

"Hey, who remembers? Some place. Maybe we went to school together, or something."

"Charley, be serious. Why were you hiding this guy? Whoever he is. A murder suspect, no less; that doesn't look good."

He sat down on his filthy sofa, and slurped a bit more. He had a crafty look in his bloodshot eyes. He said, "Hey, supposing—just supposing—this guy is here. Was here. You say this lawyer, Nolan, he's trying to get Barney off, trying to pin it on the gardener, right?"

"More or less."

"So where does that leave Barney? This guy is Barney's only hope. Barney's in deep trouble. The police, they have him by the balls.... Here's another fall guy. Guy used to do the garden. Maybe he was some kind of bum. Homeless, sort of. Then he runs away, looks bad, don't it? But only if they don't find him, you know what I mean? If they don't find him, they can blame all this shit on him. Murder, anything you want. You know, tell the jury—look, it could be this guy, this gardener. Reasonable doubt. That's what helps Barney."

I saw his point. "And if they do find him...."

"Well, maybe he has an alibi, you know what I'm saying? Or maybe he's got some other story, he's clean as a whistle. Then where does that leave Barney. In deep shit. He's better off this way, right? I mean, nobody knows where this guy is. So let's keep it that way."

"Right. But the trouble is, I don't think you can get away with it. Assuming he's here, or was here. They'll get him. They're bound to."

"Not if you keep your mouth shut they won't."

"I'll keep my mouth shut, I promise. But...as I said, it's not up to me...the police, they know how to do these things, they'll put out bulletins, pictures, whatever."

"Well, we'll just see about that," he said.

I changed my tack. "Charley, you know this guy. He was

staying here. Tell me about him. Who is he?"

"Young guy. Blondish hair. Ponytail. Calls himself Eben Born."

"And who brought him here?"

"Well, if you got to know, it was Travis. Travis Hinch-combe. The guy with the money. Money talks, you know. He said, put this guy up for a while, and keep your mouth shut. He gave me a wad of cash."

"Did you talk to the guy?"

"Once or twice. He was quiet as a mouse. Read books a lot. He was one of those vegetarians, too. I brought in pizza, with sausage; wouldn't touch the sausage."

"That's all you know?"

"It was none of my business. I did what I was told."

"And where is he now?"

"I don't know. I told you, he cleared out. Packed up his few things, and left, yesterday. Before, he was staying at some motel, and he went back there for his things, and then he came here, seemed a little upset, and said, he had to go, had to get out of here, move on, that sort of thing...."

"And you don't think he...killed Blanche?"

"Him? That's a joke. Well, who knows. You can't trust people. They put on an act, you know? But still.... He was just a guy. Harmless guy, quiet like I said. He was sort of religious. I got that impression. Always reading some book, maybe the Bible, I don't know. Just seemed the type. Reminded me of my cousin Joe. Fooled around for years, drank a lot, did drugs, screwed anything that wasn't nailed down, did a term in prison, and got religion when he was in jail. You can't talk to him now, every other word out of his mouth is Jesus. Well, different strokes for different folks."

I probed some more; but I got no more information. Maybe there was nothing more to get. But I had learned more than I expected. Obviously, this gardener, this young man with the ponytail, had some connection to the case. And Travis was in it, up to his neck; it was Travis who was orchestrating this man's disappearance. Travis was behind all these shenanigans. I couldn't for the life of me imagine what his motive might be. Travis, after all, was firmly convinced of Barney's guilt. Then why shelter this mysterious gardener? Why give Nolan a chance to pin the blame on somebody else?

I had no answers. I could confront Travis, and ask him, of course. But there was absolutely no chance he would tell me what I wanted to know. It's just too hard—no, it's impossible—to manipulate or badger a man who has all that money. The money forms a kind of coat of mail, it's like a suit of armor.

Would I ever get to the bottom of this miserable affair? In my more gloomy moments, I thought the answer was no. I had run out of ideas. But lady luck intervened. Fortune, it seemed, was about to smile at me.

# 24

A day or two went by. I was busy, but nothing happened that you would be interested in. Then, one morning, I got to the office at about 9. It was a nice day, and I felt good about the world—I'm not sure why. Maybe it was the doughnut I had for breakfast.

As I approached my office, I noticed somebody in the hall, near the door, waiting for me. It was a young man, with blond hair, tied in a ponytail. He was clean-shaven, and neatly dressed in jeans and a white t-shirt. His round, open face reminded me of somebody else, but I couldn't place who it was.

"Mr. May?"

"Yes, that's me."

"I wonder if...if I could talk to you. In private."

"Come on in," I said.

"I won't take up too much of your time," he said.

He was soft-spoken, polite. I opened the door, and we went into my office. "Sit down," I said.

He wasted no time coming to the point. "You're Barney's lawyer, aren't you?"

"Yes and no. I'm not representing him in this murder case, but I did do some legal work for him, on something else."

"I know that. There's another lawyer, Nolan Thom, and I know he's in charge of the murder case. But I don't want to talk to him. I want to talk to you."

My heart was pounding. I now realized who was sitting in front of me. This was the man all of us were looking for. The description, everything about him, fit: the ponytail, the eyes, the manner. This had to be the mysterious gardener. "You want to talk to me? Sure; but what about?"

"About...that night. The night Frances died. I mean Blanche. And I want to talk to you because...because you've been looking for me. I know that too. And I want to explain to you, well, certain things."

"You're Eben Born," I said.

"Yes," he said. "I was Travis' gardener. You've been look-ing for me. Well, here I am. I need to clear things up. I don't like hiding. And I want to help Barney out. But you understand, I can't go to his lawyer, this guy Thom. He's spreading the idea I'm the killer here...."

"How did you know that?"

He didn't respond. But I knew the answer: Travis. He said: "And that's a complication. That's why I need to talk to you, get your advice."

I looked at him closely. He seemed...earnest, sincere. And gentle. There was a quality about him. Something quiet, serene; yet somehow wounded. I can't explain it. I thought: half the city was looking for him, including me; and he shows up on my very doorstep.

My visit to Charley Morgan no doubt set some sort of process in motion. No doubt, too, Arthur Flansbaum told Travis he had seen me, and the news quickly got to young Eben Born. And here he was.

I said: "Well, if I can help in any way.... But first, can I ask you: is your name really Eben Born?"

He said: "In a way. But that's not my real name, the name I was born with."

"And what was that?"

"Max Elfenbein. Blanche Baleine was my sister."

A big fat light bulb went off over my head. This was Blanche's long lost brother. *He* was the mysterious gardener. I must have shown on my face how surprised and puzzled I was. Why was Blanche's brother working for Travis, cleaning his pool, clipping his hedges? What was this all about?

He said, "I know, it's surprising.... You're wondering why...well, why I was there and...and...the rest of it. It's a long story. I'll make it as short as I can. When I was a kid, an adolescent, I was all messed up. My folks got divorced; I don't know, maybe that had something to do with it. I was a real handful. Out of control, totally. I did all sorts of crazy things, drugs, liquor, girls, shoplifting, carrying on. My father, he sort of wrote me off, he called me a no-good bum. My mom, she was upset, worried, but what could she do? I was going noplace fast,

I dropped out of school, I was hanging out with bad kids, wild kids, druggies, people like me, total no-goods. But I guess I wasn't completely gone, I mean, it bothered me, what I was doing, I felt like I was sliding down into some kind of dark hole, and I couldn't keep it from happening.... I used to wake up sometimes, you know, with a terrific hangover, after some crazy night, doing crazy things; and to be honest I hated myself, I thought, Max, what are you doing to yourself? But I didn't stop...."

"Go on," I said.

"Then there was a kind of turning point," he said. "You'll think I'm out of my mind, but this is the truth, this is how it actually happened. I was on a train, commuter train, coming home late at night.... I was dead drunk, I could hardly move.... My usual state.... And I saw this ad, I guess it was an ad, for this group, this guru, about his ashram, you know, a big ad above the window of that commuter train. The words...they were about meditation, karma, who knows, spiritual stuff, I don't remember the text, did I even read the text? But his picture was there. The guru. And I looked at the picture, and there was something about the eyes.... I thought they were moving, they were looking at me. Sure, I was drunk, I was seeing things, but I swear that's how I felt.... The eyes were watching me.... The guru was there, he was on the ad, he was looking directly at me, and he was telling me: Max, you're lost, you're spiritually dead, and I can help you. I was getting, you know? a message....

"I went the very next day. I went to see him, and I was trembling. He had a white beard, I thought he was ageless, something like a God.... Seeing the eyes in person, I mean, it was even more dramatic. He said something weird, like he'd been waiting for me, and I believed it. Probably it was bullshit, but I believed it. Then he mumbled something in Sanskrit or whatever, and he waved a purple feather over me, and he touched me, he touched me on the cheek and the chin, and the shoulder. And I felt, like, an electric charge was going through my body. I was hooked, you know what I mean? Today, I have more perspective, I'm not so gullible, but at the time.... I was just a lost soul, looking for something. You know what I mean, Mr. May?"

"Call me Frank," I said.

"Did you ever have that feeling, Frank?"

"Not really, to be perfectly honest," I said. I didn't want to say this, but I'm basically immune to mystics, psychics, and gurus. No crystals, no ashrams, no tarot cards. I have no idea what sign I was born under, or whether my birth year was the year of the rat or the dog or the hippopotamus. Maybe I'm just mentally lazy. These spiritual people are all so *intense.* Somehow, I just haven't got the energy.

He went on: "Anyway, I was ready. Ready for a change. I wanted to make over my life. So I told him, I wanted to be with him; and I joined his ashram. He said to me, your spirit is new, it's been reborn. He even gave me a new name. Your name is Eben Born, he said. Eben, he said, means 'just now' in German. So you're just now born, you're new-born, you're born again. I thought, wow, that's who I am. I'm not Max Elfenbein. I'm not this drunken asshole, this piece of driftwood, this jerk, this scumbag. I'm Eben Born. I have a new life. So I spent the day chanting and peeling potatoes and living in some tiny room, and listening in the evening to the guru, talking about all sorts of things, which I never understood, but they seemed so terrifically deep. They made my head whirl.

"The guru, he was in charge of everything. He decided everything. Told me what to do. Told the rest of us. There were about a hundred of us. Men and women. We wore white linen clothes. There was money, from somewhere. I think some of the others had been rich, they gave him their money. Anyway, I was enthralled; and the hard work, the potatoes, all of that, well, somehow it was therapeutic. Then the guru said to me, you are a man, you need a wife, for your soul and your body. He said he had a wife for me. Well, to tell you the truth, I don't know about the soul, but I did have a body, and the idea of a wife appealed to me. I hadn't had any sex since I joined the place. Anyway, if the guru said so, I had to obey. I was like a little child. I never saw her before we got married. I mean, I suppose I had seen her, but I didn't know which one of the women would be my bride, there were about thirty of them that were possible. One of them was so pretty, I used to dream about her; and I hoped she was the one...."

"And was she?"

"No, she wasn't. Came the day; my bride was in a heavy veil, he put his hands over us, and he conducted some sort of ceremony, all mumbo-jumbo, with incense and more of the purple feathers. Thank God I wasn't allergic to feathers. It was a nice scene, actually, everybody there, all dressed in white. He said, you will sleep in white robes tonight, but you won't touch her or look at her. In the morning, you will sit in the lotus position, and she will be naked, and she will sit on your lap, and you will enter her yoni. Yoni, that's what he said. That's some sort of Sanskrit word, it means vagina."

He paused, and then went on: "So I did it, everything, just like he told me. The whole thing, including the yoni business. He told us what to do. How often to have sex, and what positions, and everything. How to live. We didn't have to decide anything, he did everything for us, everything but breathe.

"Anyway, after a while, I began to have some doubts. I was working so hard, peeling potatoes, digging ditches, at night I was so tired, I would fall asleep during the spiritual sessions, and there were times I couldn't even bring myself to have sex, even though it was on the schedule. And I didn't really like her, my wife or whatever she was. She was skinny as a rail, and she had funny fingernails, and a nervous twitch, and she used to pick at scabs on her skin.... To be honest, Frank, she was just plain ugly. And I had nothing to say to her. She was pretty dumb, or maybe her brains had been pickled on drugs before she got into the ashram. I just don't know. I didn't even know her name, just some phony name she had, like me....

"But I went along. I had these nagging doubts, but I told myself, I wasn't deeply spiritual enough, I had to work on the spiritual thing. Until the day I discovered I wasn't the only one entering her yoni. I got sick at work, maybe it was sheer exhaustion, and I felt, I can't go on, I have to rest, I was digging a ditch, and so I came back to this sort of dormitory where we had a room, and there she was, with him, the guru, on the bed, having sex. White beard and all; you have to hand it to him, he was really flying, if you know what I mean."

I wasn't sure I did. But I just nodded, so he'd go on.

"And I said, what the hell are you doing, that's my wife, you assigned her to me; and he wasn't even ashamed. He was bold as brass. He said, I'm her spiritual husband, I'm the spiritual husband of all the women in this compound; and we're having a spiritual union. I thought, spiritual union, my ass, you're in her yoni, you're screwing her; you're screwing all the women here, you just take a woman when you feel like it; and the rest of us men, we're supposed to be chaste and moderate, and you tell us what kind of sex to have and when and we just follow you like sheep.

"I felt like a fool. It was like my eyes were finally opened. I wasn't buying his line anymore. I left the next day.... I just packed up and left. The way I figured it, I wasn't really married. All that hocus pocus, and so on, but it wasn't a real marriage. And as soon as I was out of there, I felt terrific, I felt free, like a great load had been lifted off my back." He paused. Then he said, "But I was broke. Completely broke. I had a duffel bag, a suitcase, some clothes; but no money, nothing. The guru never paid us. People paid *him*. My family, such as it was, had no idea where I was, what I had done, whether I was dead or alive. I was starting over. And here's the funny part: you know, that place, that ashram, it wasn't all phony baloney. This guru, he was robbing us, exploiting us; but he was giving us something too. I think in a way he was just what I needed. He cleaned out my mind and my body. Got rid of the poison. All that chanting, all that potato-peeling. It actually did me some good. I thought: I've been through a stage, I'm a new person, I really am Eben Born; now I have to make a life for myself. So I borrowed a few dollars from one of the other guys at the ashram, and I came back here; and I wanted to get some work...."

I nodded: yes.

"But I had nothing, no reference, no ID. I went to see Travis. I knew about him from Blanche. I told him my story; and I said, I didn't want to go back to what I was before, I want to work. I wanted honest work, and I didn't want to see anybody from my old life, least of all my family. Not yet, anyway. And he said, OK, sure, I'll give you work. The one thing I learned, at the ashram, aside from how to peel potatoes, was garden work. We had a vegetable garden, all organic of course, and a little flower garden; and I liked that work. So that's what I did, for Travis—I did the garden; and I did the pool too. I learned to do the pool. It wasn't a big deal. Anyway, I worked hard at these jobs. I was good, I was conscientious. And

I was happy. Oh yes, I was staying at this motel, but you know that; and I was trying to save some money, to live someplace better....

"But then Travis told me, Blanche and Barney were going to house sit. He knew I'd want to know that. I said, I'm not ready, for that, I can't face them yet. He said, maybe this is the time, you're a new person, you should talk to your sister. Then he went away. But I just couldn't go through with it, seeing them.... So I made myself scarce.... I just stayed away....in my motel room.... I'm sorry now, because Blanche is dead, and I never had a chance to show her how much I'd changed. I was afraid she'd laugh at me. She wasn't always, well, very understanding. So I just cowered in my motel room, listening to the radio, and reading my Bible; and some other books, books about spirituality. I still believe in some of it.

"But I didn't want to let the job go, I thought Travis would be back soon, and he'd fire me if I wasn't doing the job. I have to admit, I let things go.... A garden can go bad very quickly, and a pool, too, you know, it gets algae.... I began to think, this isn't right, I'm trying to prove to myself, and to Travis, that I'm a good worker, a dependable worker, and here I'm letting the weeds grow, and the pool, it must be disgusting. So I made up my mind, to come by at night, and at least clean the pool. I came with a flashlight. Frank, I was there. The night Blanche died. I was outside, cleaning the pool, and...inside...oh God, it's so ironic."

I was genuinely startled. "You were there? Did you...see anything? Hear anything?"

He said: "Yes and no. That's why I decided to come here, talk to you. I can't go to Barney's lawyer, that Nolan guy. He'll jump all over me. He wants my balls, you know? You see my problem."

"You were...outside, working?"

"Yeah. I never went in the house. Never. I never even had a key. But I was there, outside. If I tell them, who's going to believe me? I'm an obvious suspect.... A guy with a past, unstable, you know, drugs and things, then he joins a cult; must have had some grudge against his sister. Well, maybe the police don't want to pin it on me, they're fixated on Barney; but Nolan, he'll do anything he can. I don't blame him. It's his job.

But...I can't expose myself...."

He went on: "I want to help though. I want to help Barney, if it's possible. I talked to Charley, I trust Charley on this, he says Barney never did this thing. Anyway, what I saw, maybe it's useful. I want you to decide."

"What did you see?"

"Maybe it's important, maybe not. Look: I don't think Barney killed my sister. I don't even know the guy, actually. But I heard about him. Travis talked to me about him. I know he has his faults. They weren't getting along. My sister...she was tough. I'm not going to judge her. She could be hard, cynical. She was probably too much for Barney. They never should have got together. She belittled him, she despised him, she made fun of him, that's what Travis told me, Charley told me, too. But he wouldn't kill her; never. From what Charley told me, Barney, he's just not a violent guy. How do I know that? I just know it. I have a feeling. Maybe it was the ashram. I have intuitions.... Some people have violence in them, some people don't...it's a kind of inner thing....

"And I know *I* didn't kill her. My own sister. I loved her, despite everything. That's one thing the guru taught me. The power of love. Blanche never had that power, the power of love. That's one reason I didn't want to show myself, didn't want to meet her, I was waiting... I don't know for what.... I waited until it was too late. But I'm talking honestly. Blanche...she wasn't a loving person. Never to me. Or to her husband. Me, I learned to give love, you know? Even at a distance, I felt full of love for Blanche. And for Barney, even though he was a stranger to me. I felt a kinship. And I felt love for my mother. I learned to have feelings about my mother."

"But look, Mr. Elfenbein...."

"Call me Max. Or Eben. Whatever you want."

"OK...uh, Max. *Somebody* killed her. Not Barney. Not you; but then who? Did you *see* somebody? You were there."

"Well, yes and no, like I said. I was there. I was by the pool, you remember? I couldn't really see the front of the house. The pool is in back. I was working, cleaning the pool, it wasn't easy, I didn't want to turn on any lights, so I was using this flashlight...the pool is fenced in, you know, on three sides; and between the pool and the house, there's a row of bushes.... You can see the back door of the house. There's a front door, and a back door; those are the only two ways to get in and out...."

"Well, the windows."

"They're usually locked. Well, maybe. I don't know. Anyway, I was out there, in the back, doing my thing as best I could. Then, I don't know exactly what time it was, maybe midnight, I saw a woman. She came around to the back, back of the house. She knocked on the door.... I crouched down, so nobody could see, I turned the flashlight off...."

"A woman? Did you recognize her?"

"No, I didn't. Anyway, I couldn't see her face, and it was dark.... She knocked again, and a light turned on, and somebody opened the door. A woman, it was. She was facing me, I could see her plainly, it was my sister, it was Blanche. I could see because she was standing in the light. I couldn't hear what they were saying, but she, Blanche, shook her head, like she was saying no to something; and then she more or less slammed the door in this woman's face. I crouched down, until the woman went away, and then somebody, Blanche I guess, turned off the light. I started working again, cleaning the pool.

"Then...later on...I don't know the time, but it was later, I heard a scream, a terrible scream, and then, suddenly I heard a noise, in the bushes, as if somebody had thrown something in there. I was just about done, and I had turned off the flashlight, and I was kind of feeling my way, in the dark, anyway, there was moonlight that night. I didn't want anybody to see me, of course. I opened the pool gate, very quietly, and I groped in the bushes; but it was hard to see. Then I saw a kind of glint of metal; in the moonlight, like I said, no clouds. It was a cell phone, lying on the ground."

"A cell phone?"

"Yes."

"Barney said Blanche had a cell phone. He said it was missing. The police said he was lying, she never had a cell phone. Anyway, did you see how it got there?"

"Somebody threw it, I don't know who. I didn't see anybody. You could, I guess, throw it out the window. Of the house. But that would have to be Barney, no?"

"I don't know," I said. "I guess. Anyway, did you pick it up?"

"No, I just left it there. It puzzled me. I was worried, about the scream. I started slowly groping my way toward the front of the house, I had a bicycle hidden in the bushes, and I was going to go back to my motel. But right then, oh, maybe five minutes later, there was a big hullaballoo, and all the lights in the house were turned on, and I heard a siren or something like that, and I crept up to the house, and peeked around it, and I saw an ambulance come roaring up to the driveway, and I figured, something's going on, I better get out of here. So I waited a bit, hiding in the bushes, and then I got my bicycle, and quietly went back to where I came from. I was nervous, I admit it, I knew I had to get away, I knew my sister was in the house, and I couldn't wait to find out, why was an ambulance there. When I found out, that she was dead.... I was crushed.... You can imagine how I felt. My only sister...and I never got to talk to her. Never told her I loved her."

I should have said something sympathetic; but I was fixated on something else. "Wait a minute," I said. "You were all this time, in the back, at the pool, right? You could see the back door. And nobody came in or went out?"

"No."

"You're positive?"

"I'm positive."

"How can you be so sure? It was dark, and you were working; couldn't somebody slip by, say, come out of the house, and you wouldn't see or hear?"

"Maybe.... But I don't think so. There's a gravel path; it makes a crunching noise. I think I would have noticed. No, nobody went in, nobody came out."

"But, Eben, I mean Max, this is bad for Barney. It isn't good news. We know nobody came in the front door, it was locked. Anyway, we think so. So, if nobody came in, or went out, of the back door...."

"Then....?"

"Well, it doesn't look good, for Barney."

"But the police aren't going to know it. I'm not going to tell them. First, because of Barney. But also because of me. If they found out I was there...or that Nolan guy, if he found out. I told you, he'd hang me for sure. It would fit right into his theory."

I thought: yes, Nolan would pounce on him like a spider on

a fly. He had to. It was his duty, as Barney's lawyer. But some-how I was sure Max was telling the truth. And why would he kill his own sister?

Nolan could find a reason. Make up a reason. Family hatred. Or, better, money.

"The money," I said out loud.

He seemed startled. "What money?"

"You're Blanche's brother.... She was slated to inherit a lot of money, from your uncle. But she had to outlive him by six months. She didn't. A million dollars. I think you're next in line, I'm not sure; but I think so. People kill for a lot less money."

His eyes opened wide. "But I didn't even know about this money. I swear it. I haven't exactly been in touch, remember? And...God, the idea, that I would kill my own sister, for money.... Nobody could believe that. Anyway, money doesn't mean a thing to me. That's another thing I got from the guru; and it's still with me. If that money came my way, I'd just give it to some kind of charity. The Dalai Lama, or Greenpeace, or Doctors Without Borders. Something like that."

"But the police," I said, "might not believe you, Max. Frankly, they're a cynical bunch."

"I know that. That's why I better still lay low," he said.

"At Charley Morgan's?"

"Not anymore. Yeah, I was there. Travis arranged it. I owe Travis a lot. He's not as bad as you think. I know, he's rich, he's arrogant; but he's been very, very good to me."

"He knew who you were?"

"Of course. He knew it from the very beginning. I *told* him. I wasn't going to pretend. I told him, also, as I said, that I wasn't ready to go back to the family. I said I wanted work; and he said, OK, I'll help you out. He needed somebody, as it turned out; so maybe it was fate. Karma. I do believe in that. And I worked hard, too; I did a good job. Maybe I'll stick to gardening. Maybe that's my calling. Living things. Plants. Flowers. Work-ing the earth. I think there's something spiritual about that. Making things grow."

So Travis knew all along. All that stuff about trusting his instinct when he hired his gardener, and so on—pure baloney. He had lied about everything.

"You'll...keep on working for Travis?" I asked.

"Well...I can't do that now. Not while the whole world is looking for me. I can't trust anybody, except maybe Travis."

"You can trust me," I said.

"I do trust you," he said. "But only up to a point."

"What point is that?"

"Well, I haven't told you where I'm living, have I? It's not Charley's place anymore." He laughed. "Place was a pigsty. I was just itching to clean it up, he was personally a mess too, drinking and smoking and just sitting there while his life went down the drain. I wanted to help him, but it was no use, I could see that. Even before you came, I got out of there. I know you were asking about me, at the motel. I didn't know, though, why you were looking for me."

"Because of Barney," I said. "To help him out."

"I believe you."

"OK, Max," I said. "But how long can you keep on hiding? It can't be much of a life."

"I'm used to not much of a life. And I'll keep it going, well, as long as it takes."

"As long as what takes."

"Until...I don't know. I'll leave that up to Travis."

"And you don't mind that Travis thinks Barney killed your sister. He's absolutely convinced of it."

"I know that. He's a cynical guy. I like him, but he's a cynical guy. I wish I could make him change his way of life, or his frame of mind. Make him believe in people. But never mind. He's good to me. He knows what Nolan has in mind, but he thinks, as long as I'm hidden, Nolan won't be peddling his theory to a jury, or anybody else. And Travis is also trying to protect me from the police, from newspaper reporters."

"But what about Barney?"

"Barney never touched Blanche. I just know it. But I can't argue with Travis. His mind is made up. If I could help Barney, I would. But I don't see how, except by letting them screw me, accuse me of something I didn't do. I'm not suicidal. I want Travis to hire a detective, find out what really happened. But for now...."

"For now, what?"

"For now, I'm crawling back into my hole. I can meditate

there. You can meditate anywhere. You know what? I'm serene. I take life as it comes. That's another gift of the guru."

He did look serene. Maybe these gurus know something. They sit in the lotus position, and they close their eyes and levitate or whatever they do. Was it something wrong with *me*, that I could never get into that sort of thing? Mind over matter, or deep spiritual stuff, or reincarnation, or karma, or auras. Law school never taught any of these things, in between torts and civil procedure; and somehow I never picked up on them any time since.

I watched Max as he left. He even walked with a kind of smooth, catlike grace. I looked out the window. He got into a big, black car, on the passenger side. Ten to one the car was registered in the name of Travis Hinchcombe.

# 25

Basically, I believed Max's story. Celia would say, I'm gullible. I know people tell terrible lies, but somehow they don't tell them to me. At least that's what I think.

Whether or not I believed him, there were things I had to follow up. He had seen a woman, at the back door, someone who came that very night, the night Blanche died, a woman who came, rang the bell, talked to Blanche, tried to get in. Max never saw her face. He didn't know who she was. But I had a good guess. A very good guess. And I also felt, somehow, a surge of confidence. The picture was filling in. The mystery of the gardener—that was totally cleared up. The cell phone. Barney was right: there *was* a cell phone. Somebody threw it out the window; but who? Of course, it could have been Barney. And where was the cell phone now? Obviously, somebody had retrieved it. Barney? No, not Barney. He would have said so. Somebody else?

The woman at the door. I plunged ahead. The woman at the door must be Susan Brinkley. I had to get in touch with her. I decided the best way to reach her was through Travis Hinch-combe. Trying to call Travis was a bit like trying to call the Pope, as I think I said already. I called his office, and I did manage to get Arthur Flansbaum. After we exchanged hellos, I asked him, maliciously, what he was doing that day outside of Charley Morgan's house. I enjoyed hearing him stammer and mumble some inane excuse.

After this brief episode, I came to the point. I was trying to reach Susan Brinkley. Was she by any chance staying at Travis' house?

"Mr. Hinchcombe often has house guests," he said. "It's a big house."

"I know that. I've been there. Is Susan currently one of those house guests?"

He hemmed and hawed; but eventually he said, "I believe she is."

At dinner time, I called Hinchcombe's house. Somebody with a foreign accent answered, no doubt a new housekeeper, and I asked whether I could speak to Ms. Susan Brinkley.

"One moment, please." Soon after, I heard Susan's husky, affected voice.

I said: "Susan, this is Frank. Frank May. I have to talk to you. It's serious. When can I see you?"

"I don't know.... I'm going to the symphony tonight...and first there's cocktails; Travis is having some people over...."

Lying was a way of life with Susan. Who knows if any of this, about the symphony, or the cocktails, or the people who were coming over, was true. It didn't matter. I was busy that evening myself. She agreed to meet me for breakfast the next morning, at a coffee shop on University Avenue, in Palo Alto. We fixed on 8 o'clock. She grumbled about how early that was, but eventually she agreed. "I do hate to get up early; and then, I'll have to have a cab...."

"Susan, be there. Please."

I came on time to the coffee shop, and slipped into a booth, which I hoped would afford us a little privacy. The place was pretty empty at that hour, except for the usual graduate students, wearing thick glasses, pale and earnest, sipping their espresso or their herbal tea. They were either deeply immersed in thick books which they underlined with a yellow felt-tipped pen, or else they banged away at a laptop computer. Susan, of course, was late.

That didn't surprise me. I had a cup of coffee and a pastry, and I waited patiently. About 25 minutes later, she burst in, in a whirl of chiffon scarves. She started to tell me all about the cocktail party, about all the important people who were there, and what the food was like, but I had no time or tolerance for that sort of thing, and I cut her off. I'm sure she was prepared to tell me about the symphony, and how she shared a box with Very Important People, but life is too short for such indulgences.

"Susan," I said, "I have to get to work. I'm going to come to the point. I have something important to talk to you about."

She gave me what she must have considered a coquettish

glance. "Really, Frank. Something important. Then I must have my orange juice and a cup of black coffee. Very strong coffee. I simply can't function without coffee and orange juice. Certainly not at this ungodly hour. And certainly not if we're going to be so serious."

I signaled to a young guy in a t-shirt, who seemed to be a waiter, and he came over. "Orange juice," I said. And she added: "Coffee. Black. And very strong." When the coffee and juice were delivered, I said, "OK, Susan, you've got your coffee and orange juice. Here's the thing. The night Blanche died, I have it on excellent authority that you were there, at the house."

"Honestly...."

"Wait: before you start denying or whatever, just hear me out. You came to the house, around midnight. You went to the back of the house, you knocked on the door, or rang the bell, doesn't matter which. Blanche came to the door, but she didn't let you in. I want to know what you were doing there."

"This is absurd," she said. "You're making this up."

"No. I'm not making it up. I have a source."

"A source? What an idea. Somebody must have a vivid imagination."

"Susan, I told you, I just don't have time for this. You were there. Don't lie to me. It's terribly important. Your brother, your only brother, is accused of murder...."

"Don't you think I know that?"

"I know you do. Look, everything that happened that night is important. You were there, Susan. Maybe you saw something, heard something. Susan, I need the truth."

"You say somebody saw me? Ridiculous. Who could that be?"

"I can't say."

She said: "Did Barney see me? Because nobody else was around. Nobody."

"It wasn't Barney. Susan, don't ask me again. I'm not going to answer. The bad news is, we know you were there that night; the good news is, you wanted to get in the house, you rang the bell, Blanche came to the door, you talked to her about something, but in the end, Blanche didn't let you in."

"Why is that good news?"

"Good news for you, Susan. I mean, if Blanche had let you in, I think the police might forget about Barney and switch their attention to you."

"Oh, that's completely absurd. Why would I want to do something to Blanche? Really, Frank. It's too ridiculous."

"It *is* ridiculous. Look, I'm not accusing you of anything. I just want you to know, we have a witness. We know you were there. I haven't told anybody. I have no intention of telling anybody, including the police. But I really need an explanation."

"I don't see why I have to explain *anything*. To you."

"Of course you don't. You have a right to remain silent, as they say on TV. Susan: I don't want to threaten you, or coax you, or anything. But I could go to the police. You might think I'm bluffing, but I'm not. And I *do* have a witness."

She stopped and thought about it. She drank a ceremonious sip from her glass of orange juice. Then she stirred the glass with a spoon. Finally, she said: "Alright, yes. I was there. I didn't think it mattered. She didn't let me in, as you said yourself."

"Why were you there? What were you talking about?"

"Well, really...you know, Barney and I had...a rift; and he forced me to leave. He was dreadful to me. I thought Blanche, if I could speak to her, might be more accommodating. I rang the doorbell, in the back..."

"Why the back?"

"I thought I saw a light. The front, well, it was all dark...."

"OK. And?"

"I rang the doorbell, there's a doorbell in back. She answered. She came to the door. I knew she would."

"How did you know?"

"Well...I didn't really. It was a 50-50 chance, wasn't it? It could have been Barney, that's what I didn't want. Anyway, there was Blanche. But she was acting...strange. Distant. Downright unfriendly. She said: 'What do you want?' In a nasty tone of voice. I was shocked. Blanche and I, we always got along. So I said, Blanche, Barney was absolutely horrid to me, you know that; but I've been in touch with Travis, and it's his house after all, and he insists that I have a perfect right to be here, as much as you and Barney."

"And what did she say?"

"She said I was lying; that Travis never said any such thing, and I knew it, and she was busy, and please get out."

"And *were* you lying?"

"As a matter of fact, I was. I hadn't been in touch with Travis at all."

She sipped languidly at her orange juice, and obsessively poked at her hair. I couldn't read her face. It was mask-like, impervious.

Then I said: "What did you do then? After she said, you couldn't come in."

She said: "Well, for a while, I just stood there. Her behavior was *peculiar*, really. I thought, is there some reason she's acting this way?"

"Did you think she was busy with somebody? Did you think maybe somebody else was there? Did you see somebody? Or any sign that somebody was there?"

"No; I didn't *see* anybody. But, yes, I thought somebody was there. The somebody was Barney. And he was, wasn't he? Of course, now I understand, why she acted the way she did."

"And why was that?"

"Well, you know yourself. They were having a ghastly fight, the two of them. He *admits* it, doesn't it? He threw something at her, or she threw something at him, I can't remember which; but I must have come along right in the middle of their squabble."

"I don't think so," I said. "According to Barney...."

"Oh, please! According to Barney! Why should he tell you the truth? The trouble he's in...."

I interrupted her. "So then you left."

"No, not immediately. I stood there, for a while. I didn't know what to do. You see, I had nowhere to go, not really. I couldn't go to Ross' house, I know he'd be an angel about it, Ross is so sweet; but I just couldn't do that, it wouldn't look right, and with the divorce and all.... You understand. I was in a quandary. Most of my things were still in the house. I hated the idea of going to a motel, they're so depressing. And I didn't have money, at the moment, for anything decent.... And no current credit card; well, that's a long story. So I just stood there, like a fool. Then I went to the front gate of the house. And I stood there for a while.... Waiting...."

"Waiting? For what?"

"I honestly don't know. I was just thinking. I was there, oh, maybe half an hour, I really couldn't say. And then I heard this horrible scream, from the house, and I was frightened. A terrible scream. A woman's scream. I thought, should I do something? Then lights went on. I thought, something horrible has happened, but of course I didn't know what. I was going to go back to the house, but I was too scared; and I thought, they'll wonder, what am I doing here? My car was parked a block away, I did that on purpose, I didn't want Barney to see me drive up.... I just stood there, there was noise in the house, lights, and...then...an ambulance came...and I felt, I shouldn't be here, there's trouble; I waited a few minutes, and then I went quietly to my car, and drove off.... I was dying of curiosity, I didn't sleep at all that night.... And in the morning, I called Barney, and he told me the terrible news."

"Wait a minute," I said. "Blanche was alive when you saw her, right?"

"Of course she was alive. I was talking to her."

"And you stood there for a while. Then you went to the front gate."

"I told you I did."

"I've been to the house. You could see the front door, couldn't you?"

"Yes, of course I could."

"And you stood there, and then you heard a scream...and you were still there when the ambulance came...."

"Yes, what's the matter with you? I told you all this."

"And the scream: that was Blanche. It had to be."

"I suppose. Yes. It must have been Blanche. It's so horrible to think about. Barney...or whoever.... Oh, it's too painful.... Imagine, at that very moment, she was dying, poor thing.... But I didn't realize it, at the time."

"What bothers me," I said, "is that nobody went in or out of the front door, and you were there all the time, right?"

"Yes. I said so."

"This is bad news for Barney."

"Bad news? For Barney? Why is that?"

"Because...if nobody came in...and if he was alone in the house...."

"Well, I suppose he was alone," she said. "But there could have been a prowler, somebody who came through the back door. I suppose that's possible."

"I can't explain," I said, "but it really isn't possible. We happen to know, nobody went in or out the back door either."

She stopped and digested this news. She said: "I suppose I shouldn't be surprised. Frankly, all along, I don't see how it could be anybody but Barney." She seemed quite calm at the notion. Then she said: "Imagine the rage he must have had, stored up inside of him. My own brother."

"Susan," I said, "you've known him all your life. I only met him once or twice. But I just can't imagine him killing somebody. I really can't. And I don't see any motive. OK, they had fights; everybody has fights. What does he gain by killing her?"

She put down her orange juice. "Gain is not the issue," she said. "Mind you, I'm telling *you* these things. I wouldn't breathe a word to the police. After all, blood is thicker than water. I haven't said boo, not to anybody, not Ross, not Travis, no one. It was a conversation I had, with Blanche. Very strange conversation."

"When was this?"

"Oh, a few days before she died. She said, what if I told you, Barney killed your aunt, what would you say?"

"And what *did* you say?"

"I said: Blanche, you must be absolutely stark raving mad. She was an old woman, she was sick, she died. You know those things happen."

"And then what did she say?"

"Well, she laughed. She said, suppose I said, somebody poisoned her, let's say it was Barney, or whoever. And then they had her cremated, so nobody could tell. And I said, Blanche you don't honestly think this happened, do you? And she said, well, stranger things have happened, and she laughed again."

"And then?"

"I said, I'm going to forget you ever said this. I believe it's some sort of macabre joke; and I don't like jokes. And she laughed again. And that was the end of it."

"So what are you saying?"

She sipped slowly and dramatically from her coffee. "I'm saying, suppose she was...serious. About Barney and our aunt. He had a motive, didn't he? She left him a lot of money. Not a penny to me, of course. She disliked me, I disliked her. Barney played up to her, pretended he cared. Never mind; that was Barney all over. *So* hypocritical. As if he cared! Suppose he just got tired of waiting, waiting for her to die and...well, he speeded up the process. And suppose Blanche knew what he did, maybe she was even an accomplice. Suppose she had proof. Well, Barney would have to eliminate her, wouldn't he?"

I said: "Susan, this is totally ridiculous. You're reading too many mystery novels."

"I never read mystery novels," she said. "I haven't time for such trash. I've always preferred the classics. I'm mad about Dostoyevsky. So don't talk to me about mystery novels. I'm not imagining things. Blanche really told me that story; and it does give him a motive now, doesn't it?"

"Well, Dostoyevsky is full of murders," I said, "think of *Crime and Punishment*. Shakespeare, too, for that matter. They're all dead at the end.... And Macbeth, he's a murderer, isn't he?"

"Really, I don't see the point, Frank."

"No point. I just can't bring myself to believe that Barney killed his wife; and the notion that he went around killing other people too, that's just too much. His aunt—I can't see it. How did he do it anyway?"

"Who knows? Some kind of poison."

"That idea is weird. Barney, poisoning an old lady? He wasn't even around that day."

"You don't have to be around. You put it in the medicine or whatever."

"Susan, that's rubbish."

I guess I didn't realize I was raising my voice. One of the nearby graduate students stared at me, his fingers poised over his laptop. Susan seemed to back off a little. She said: "Well, I didn't say I actually *believed* it. I just said it was possible. Barney...."

"Barney what? It seems totally out of character."

"Out of character? How would you know. In fact," she said, "he always had this...this kind of suppressed rage."

"Pretty well suppressed, I imagine."

"Oh, but isn't that the worst kind? When it comes out, it's like an explosion."

"Poisoning your aunt isn't what I'd call an explosion. It's the opposite. Deliberate, planned, cold-blooded. I don't buy this suppressed rage idea."

"Well, really," she said, her voice dripping with sarcasm. "So now you're an expert on rage, and its psychological manifestations. Is that on the bar examination? Really, Frank. I think I know Barney better than you do. Oh, yes, he seems like a wimp. But...as a matter of fact, if you do depth psychology— and I've had my share, I've been analyzed.... I've been in therapy, my therapist was the best there is.... All the famous people go to him. The Getty family. Artists. Actors. I spoke to my therapist many times about Barney. Yes, Frank, I think I'm more of an expert on Barney, and his psyche, than you could possibly hope to be."

"And?"

"And just this: at some level, yes, under that mild facade, well...."

She made a gesture, and never finished the sentence. She was trying to convey the idea that Barney was a seething mass of hidden pathology. Under the mild facade. My own view was that under the mild facade was more mild facade. Susan herself was all facade. I'd hate to say what type; or what there was underneath.

She went on: "You think he isn't capable of this kind of act? I think he is. You can reach a point where killing somebody, well, it's just like swatting a fly. You don't think of Barney as cold and ruthless. But he has this streak of...sadism. Downright sadism. I ought to know...what he's done to me...."

"What has he done to you?"

"Really, in a sense, he robbed me. Took everything away. Poisoned an old lady's mind. I'm referring, of course, to my aunt. Originally, she was going to leave me a lot of money. I have that on very good authority. Then, after he kissed up to her, she changed her mind. Not that I wasn't good to that dreadful old woman. I went to see her every Christmas. But it was useless. Barney, he had her wrapped around his little finger. God knows how and why. And then, you see, his situation, it had become so precarious...."

"Precarious?"

"She could change her will again, couldn't she? She was bound to see through him, don't you think? I mean, he probably couldn't stand her. She was a disgusting old woman. So you see, there *was* a motive. For killing her. Maybe he knew something, about her plans. The will, I mean."

"Come on. You're not serious."

"Oh, but I am. And, Frank, I think Blanche knew it. As I said, maybe she was his accomplice. That's why he had to kill Blanche, too."

"But.... Blanche didn't *actually* say that Barney killed his aunt."

"Not in so many words."

"And don't you yourself think it's too far-fetched?"

"You're entitled to your opinion," she said, somewhat frostily. "Anyway, I have to go now, I have a majorly busy day ahead of me. Many things to take care of. Oh, don't worry, I'm not going to talk. It's our little secret, about Barney and his aunt. I know what I said is safe with you, confidentiality and all that; and it's perfectly safe with me. I won't tell anyone, certainly not the police. Awful as he is, he's my brother; and that means something. To me, if not to him."

She got up, and swept out of the room. She made no attempt to pay the bill. I expected as much. Susan went through life figuring out ways to avoid paying bills. In any event, the bill came to less than ten dollars.

I sat there for a few minutes, thinking. I ordered another coffee, and sipped it slowly. I thought about what Susan had said. If she was telling the truth, and Max was telling the truth, then nobody went in or out of the house, either the front door or the back door. That was troubling. I tried to think about alternatives. The windows? It seemed unlikely. Did somebody just slip by Max, or Susan? This was possible. But somehow I doubted it.

That left only Barney...or? I had a dim thought, somewhere at the back of my mind...something vague and unformed. I tried to bring it to the surface, but I didn't succeed. Not then, at any rate.

The death of Aunt Martha...that was troubling too. Could there be anything to all these rumors? This also didn't seem possible.

Susan...how unhappy she must be, underneath that veneer of baloney and snobbery. I have a sister, Harriet. She lives in Des Moines, Iowa, with her husband, who has some kind of sales job, and two children who seem much better behaved than my own. She's a decent, hard-working woman. She never forgets my birthday, or our anniversary, or the birthdays of our kids. Her husband is overweight, and prone to depression, but basically OK. I felt like calling Harriet on the phone and telling her how lucky I felt, to have her for a sister.

I finished my coffee, paid the bill, and went back to work.

# 26

Soon afterwards, the other shoe dropped, as the expression goes. I got a call from Nolan.

The police had arrested Barney, and charged him with the murder of his wife, Frances Elfenbein, a.k.a. Blanche Baleine.

"No big surprise," he said. "I was wondering what took them so long. I guess what clinched it was the baby business."

"The baby business?"

"Blanche's baby. It wasn't his. They did DNA tests. Not his child."

"Whose was it?"

"No idea. But the police think, wow, there's the motive right there. That's what the fight was about, the night she died. She was playing around. Had a boyfriend; and he got her pregnant. Barney found out, and went ballistic. Oldest motive in the books."

"Poor Barney," I said.

"Tough case," said Nolan.

"Nolan, I'm sure he didn't do it. Aren't you?"

"You know we never talk about that. You should know better than to ask. I'm going to try to help him. Hey, who knows? There's a thousand possibilities. Maybe it was an accident."

"You don't believe that."

"Or maybe it was the gardener. I'm still quite keen on the gardener, too. But Frank, I heard a rumor."

"What kind of a rumor?"

"I heard that you're snooping around, looking for this guy. That you have information you're not telling me. Maybe you even found him already."

"Well, yes, I've been looking."

"And...did you find him?"

I told an outright lie, which bothered me: "No, I haven't," I said. "I haven't found him." Well, it wasn't a *total* lie. He found me. And it was quite true; even if I had in fact found him, now he was lost again.

"Are you telling me the truth, Frank?" Nolan asked.

I said: "Too many questions, Nolan. Let me ask you one. Do you *want* me to find him? Do you want *anybody* to find him? He might kill your theory.... I mean, suppose he has an iron-clad alibi? You're much better off, and Barney's better off too I guess, if nobody ever finds him. Not now, anyway."

"Then why are you looking, Frank?"

I had no answer. I hung up the phone and stared into space.

Something was nagging at me, in the back of my mind. An idea. And later that day, it suddenly crystallized. Suddenly I felt: I can actually solve this case.

# 27

It's amazing how, for a peace-loving, ordinary guy—which is how I define myself—a lawyer in private practice, a married man with children, it's amazing how often I get involved in murder cases. Dead bodies just seem to follow me around; I don't know why. Bad luck, I suppose. I'm not a fan of criminal justice, and the less I have to do with it the better. But it has a lot to do with me.

When these matters come to an end—and they do come to an end—I write them up, just for fun. I don't usually claim credit for solving them. That's not because of modesty, but because in fact I *don't* solve them. Somebody else solves them, or the killer confesses, or something happens that exposes the truth. I mean, I'm an intelligent person, I got through law school and passed the bar, but I'm certainly not Sherlock Holmes or Miss Marple or whoever. I just don't have the knack.

But this time, strangely enough, it *was* me. I was the guy who cracked the case; I put two and two together, and saw the answer. And I did it without forensic science and fingerprint analysis or autopsy reports. I did it without analyzing hairs or fibers. In fact, I did it like Hercule Poirot, with the little gray cells. I did it with a flash of insight.

It doesn't happen every day.

It came on me suddenly, the flash of insight, that is. I was having lunch, by myself. As often, I was wolfing down a Chinese meal. Maybe it was the MSG that inspired me, that tingling in the cheek bones; maybe it was the struggle with chopsticks, maybe it was the taste of hot and sour soup. But suddenly, in the midst of lemon chicken, fried, caloric, but devilishly good, at that point, suddenly, almost without my knowing it, I grasped an essential point. And everything seemed, all at once, to fall into place.

It's not that I'm a genius. It's not that I outwitted the

combined forces of Scotland Yard and the local constabulary. Yet I did think of something the police never thought of. And why did they fail? Because they were fixated on Barney. Once they were convinced that Barney killed his wife, what was the point of considering alternatives? Obviously, no point at all. It would be a sheer waste of time. They started from the assumption that Barney was lying, that he had an argument with his wife, got mad, got very mad; so mad, in fact, that he picked up a bronze statuette, and smashed in her head.

But I started from the opposite premise. I began with the assumption that Barney was innocent. I had no proof. Circumstances pointed to Barney. But I felt I knew Barney. It's true, you never really know *anybody*. You see some mousy guy, he wears thick glasses, he's got a necktie on, he's a certified public accountant, and it turns out later he has a collection of whips and chains in his house, a regular torture chamber; and he's actually a serial killer. People can fool you. I know that. But you have to play the probabilities. Yes, there are CPA's who do satanic rituals and sacrifice chickens or deflower virgins; but *most* CPA's don't do that. With the majority of people, I feel, you can rely on appearances. What you see is what you get.

So in this case, I was smarter than the police. They've got all this experience, they've got labs, they have fingerprints and DNA and God knows what else. And I'm just a rank, bumbling amateur. But in this case, I knew more than they did. First of all, I had Max's story, and Susan's story; and they didn't. But more important, they started from the wrong premise. And they didn't have intuitions. They had experience, but no intuitions. Their experience told them that people were basically scum, capable of any kind of viciousness. They'd seen dozens of guys like Barney, or they thought they had. People who worked themselves into a murderous rage, and got rid of their wife, or their wife's lover, or whatever. But Barney told me he was innocent, and strange as it may seem, I believed him.

But if it wasn't Barney, if he was innocent, if his story was true, then who else could it be? There had to be someone else in the house, or somebody somehow got into the house. How? With a key? No, nobody had a key. Well, Travis did. But he wasn't around; and, no, it couldn't be Travis. Why couldn't it be Travis? It just couldn't. I didn't like Travis, but still, he wasn't a killer either. And why kill Blanche anyway?

Obviously, if nobody had a key, then what else? The windows? I just couldn't imagine somebody climbing in the window. Besides, wouldn't that person be visible? To Max? Or to Susan? Well, maybe it was Max then, Max went into the house. Or Susan. But I ruled them out too. Don't ask me why. Intuition.

So what are we left with? Blanche must have let somebody in. Barney was asleep, upstairs in the house. Suzie came to the back door. Blanche sent her away. But maybe somebody else had come earlier, somebody she didn't send away. Maybe that person was there already, when Susan came knocking on the door. Maybe that's why she didn't let Susan in. And then....

But if there was somebody in the house, then what happened to this person? Max said nobody came out the back door. Susan swears nobody came out the front door. Suppose they were telling the truth. Where did that leave me? With an insoluble problem.

It was at that point that the inspiration struck me. The lemon chicken inspiration. I was trembling with excitement. I paid the bill, never touched the fortune cookie, canceled an appointment, and drove as fast as I could out to Travis' house. I walked around the house. I looked at the French doors, the windows, the entrances, just to make sure I wasn't making a mistake. I convinced myself that nobody could have climbed in the windows. At least not without being seen.

Fortunately, nobody saw me skulking around the house. Apparently there was nobody home.

I drove back to the office. I sat at my desk, thinking and thinking. I was positive now I was right. If Blanche let somebody in, then he, or she, was still in the house when Barney rushed downstairs and found her body. Was that possible?

Yes it was.

That was the lemon chicken insight. There *was* somebody there. And I knew who it had to be. Or thought I did.

I got on the phone and tried to reach Barney at the jailhouse. It took some doing, details I won't bore you with. Eventually I got him.

"Barney, it's Frank...."

"Frank. Hey, I'm dying here...."

"Listen, Barney," I said. "I've got to ask you a couple of questions. Just answer them. Trust me."

"OK, OK...."

"The night Blanche died. You heard a scream, right? You got out of bed and rushed downstairs? How long was all that? Between the scream, and the time you found Blanche's body?"

"How long? Dunno. Couple of minutes, Frank. When I fall asleep, man, I sleep real sound. I mean, I'm a great sleeper. But that scream.... You know, you're asleep, it takes you a couple of seconds, you think it's a dream maybe.... Then, I kind of realized...hey, that's really a scream, it's Blanche, she's screaming. Anyway, I ran downstairs, I was pretty quick. I think."

"And did you hear anything else? A door slamming, for example?"

"No.... What do you mean?"

"I mean, suppose somebody did that thing to Blanche, and then ran out the door, would you hear it? The door?"

"I don't know. Maybe. I think so."

"But you didn't hear anything."

"I told you, no. Didn't hear anything, see anything...just Blanche, lying there, man, it was awful.... The blood...."

"You're sure? You'd swear to it? Nobody slammed a door?"

"I dunno. I don't think so. I don't remember hearing anything.... Is this important, Frank? If Nolan wants me to swear, I didn't hear a door, I'll swear it. I wasn't thinking a lot, you know what I mean?"

"Thanks, Barney," I said.

"Hey, Frank, what's this all about?"

"Don't ask questions, Barney. Just trust me. I think.... I think it's going to be OK. Just cross your fingers."

"OK? What kind of OK? I'm in the goddamn jail, Frank."

"We're going to get you out, Barney. Scout's honor. Hang in there," I said.

I wouldn't blame you if you thought this little conversation was no help at all to Barney. Nobody went out the back. Nobody went out the front. No door slamming. No window climbing. We're back to Barney again. The police must be right. But in fact what Barney told me *was* a help. It filled in a blank. Naturally, it wasn't proof. But it strengthened my idea. It made me more sure than ever, I was right. Somebody else was there, and bashed in Blanche's head with a bronze statuette. And that person was *still* in the house when Barney came rushing downstairs. Hiding in another room. And I knew who.

# 28

Of course, I didn't go about unmasking the killer the way they do it in the detective stories. I didn't call everybody together in a room, and reveal the secret, first teasing everybody with hints and red herrings, and then pulling the big surprise, at which point he or she jumps up and runs away or commits suicide, or whatever. I didn't set a fancy trap. I had no desire to stage a show. After all I had no *proof* of anything. I just had a theory; but a theory that made sense. And I knew the police would pay no attention to me, if I gave them the theory.

I did what had to be done. I called Nolan; I couldn't reach him. I had to spend an anxious evening, and I hardly slept that night. But in the morning, I got hold of him finally, and I said I had something important, that I had to see him; and I said it was urgent. He suggested lunch. I'm always in favor of lunch. We went to our usual Chinese restaurant. Chinese restaurants are crucial to this story, I guess. And we had a nice lunch, and I told him everything, all my suspicions, and why I suspected what I did. I had to confess that I had talked to Eben Born or Max or whatever we chose to call him; and I told him what Eben Born had told me, and what Susan had said; and I told him about the cell phone.

And Nolan listened, listened carefully; and he was impressed, he really was. Nolan is a really smart guy. And he too had lemon chicken; maybe that was what did it.

He saw immediately that I was on to something. He was so impressed, that he stopped eating for a while (but only for a while). In fact, we both had dessert. We walked to an ice cream parlor, and we had a double scoop of ice cream each. Mine had nuts and sprinkles on top; and we were talking all the while. Nolan kept nodding his head, and saying, "by God, I think you're right." He believed me! He had to, because what I said made perfect sense. And he sensed victory—victory for his client. In a case which (by his own admission) would have been awfully tough to win. And Nolan, unlike me, knew exactly what to do. He had friends among the police and the detectives, people who were working on this very case. He called them immediately—that very afternoon in fact.

At first they were skeptical, which doesn't surprise me. But not too skeptical. They thought the idea was at least worth investigating. They promised to look into it.

At that point, they did some *real* detective work. Once they had a name and a theory, they started gathering evidence.

Very soon, they had enough. Once they were on this trail, it was surprisingly easy to find incriminating facts. So much so, that the end came quickly. They got an arrest warrant, and went to the house of Dr. Ross Tanager. They gave him his Miranda warning. They charged him with the deliberate, premeditated murder of Frances Elfenbein, a.k.a. Blanche Baleine.

And Barney went free.

# 29

How did I do it? How did I figure things out? It was the cell phone that gave me the idea. If somebody was already in the house, who could this be? Then I remembered the cell phone. Cell phones have this wonderful feature, you don't know where the person is, when you get them on the phone. Call somebody at home, on a regular phone, and they're either there or not there. Call somebody's cell phone, and if they answer, they could be anywhere. On the road. In a store. In the bathtub. Wherever.

Ross was in the house all the time. When Barney called him, he was already there. He answered the cell phone; he was maybe 25 feet away. But Barney couldn't know that. Maybe Ross already knew, or thought he knew, that this would give him, in a sense, a kind of alibi—if he answered, and pretended to be somewhere else.

It was easy to reconstruct what happened that night. Blanche and Barney had their big fight. She went downstairs, Barney went to sleep. She called Ross on his cell phone. Blanche and Ross in fact were lovers. But he was getting a divorce; there were ticklish questions of money; he was accusing his wife of infidelity, and could hardly admit his own affair. They kept things pretty quiet. He gave her a cell phone so that they could talk to each other, privately, secretly.

That night, she was upset, fed up with Barney, fed up with the lies and the cheating. It wasn't a question of morals; she wanted a new life. She demanded that Ross come right over. She wanted to talk. She was pregnant. It was his child. That much of course he knew. He wanted her to get rid of it; she wasn't about to agree, at least not right away. It was a kind of blackmail item for her. Anyway, Ross came over; she opened the door and let him in. They started talking. Maybe Suzie arrived around that time, and came to the back door—of course,

Blanche had to get rid of her. Then she and Ross had it out. She told him she was sick and tired of Barney. She talked about the pregnancy, and about their whole situation. She accused him of having sexual relations with some of his women patients. Maybe she threatened to reveal things to the world, or the medical board, or whatever. Maybe she said something about her plans to build a program around his exploits, on the Tony Crass show. The cover story for now was that the story was about "dentists" but they could shift to doctors, she said. Maybe she got hysterical. They quarreled, he lost his temper. Maybe he felt his life draining away, maybe he felt trapped... angry... upset.... You know the rest.

The police charged him with first-degree murder. I don't think that will stick. I don't think he meant to kill Blanche. It wasn't a planned sort of thing. Maybe he had a blinding flash of rage. Maybe he was horrified when he realized, by God, she's in terrible shape, maybe she'll die. Probably he heard Barney running down the stairs. He hid somewhere in the house, maybe in a closet. He was scared, desperate. Then Barney called, and he heard the sound on his cell phone, in his closet, or wherever he was. If he was lucky, his phone was set only to vibrate, and Barney did not hear it ring. Was he thinking clearly? Was he thinking, this phone call, this could be my chance?

He heard Barney's anguished phone call. He said, hold on, he would come. He waited till the ambulance came. Then, when everybody was in the room with Blanche, and there was turmoil, he just appeared. Maybe he went to the front door, opened, it and closed it again, as if he had just come in. I don't think so. Or maybe they left the door open. Or maybe he went out through the French doors in the living room, hid in the bushes, and then went around the side of the house, and when he saw the ambulance arrive, he came running up. Maybe the door wasn't locked at that point. I don't know. More likely, he just stayed in the house, and appeared, as if out of nowhere. It doesn't matter.

Susan never saw him arrive. He was already there when she appeared at first. And Max, who was in the back, never saw him come in either. They saw and heard the ambulances, but not the arrival of Dr. Ross Tanager.

Between the time Blanche screamed, and when Barney

came down the stairs, Ross had only a short time—ten, twenty seconds, maybe a minute. But it was enough. He had two things to do. First, quick as could be, he wiped his prints off the bronze statuette. And he took Blanche's cell phone. First chance he had, he threw the cell phone into the bushes. This was a panic reaction. Later, he retrieved it, and I guess, dumped it somewhere. Threw it in the bay or whatever. Of course, once the police suspected Ross, once they were on his trail, it was easy to get all this information—about the cell phone he gave Blanche; about the calls they made to each other; and calls that were obviously Blanche's, made with one of the phones. About a phone under his name that stopped all activity when Blanche was killed. Everything really did fall into place.

That was the point: once they knew where to look, and who to look for, the whole thing was simple as pie. Soon there was an iron-clad case against Ross Tanager. Nolan was my main source of information. He followed the case eagerly. He said, the police found people who saw Ross in his car, driving toward Travis' house. They were even able to identify him (they said). Some people saw his car parked two blocks away from the house, the night of the murder. One guy even wrote down the driver's license. It's not a neighborhood where strange cars appear. The guy forgot all about the incident, until the police arrested Ross, and there was an item in the paper. Then he suddenly remembered. So the noose was pretty tight around Ross' neck. There was other stuff too. As I said, once you knew it was him, it wasn't that big a job to nail him. He was far from a professional killer. He had been lucky—up to a point. But then his luck ran out.

What happened afterwards? Ross never went to trial, as it happened. He copped a plea. After some negotiation, he pleaded guilty to voluntary manslaughter. First degree murder would have been a tough sell. There was no real evidence to support that, no evidence of premeditation. It had all the look of a sudden, impulsive crime. The deal was probably best for both sides.

Nolan, of course, did not represent Ross Tanager. Ross hired a very good lawyer, Myrna Degler, a woman with a great reputation in criminal defense work. She's tough and savvy. I've heard good things about her. She worked as a prosecutor, in Santa Clara County, for many years; then she opened an office in Cupertino. She was the one, I suppose, who talked Ross into copping a plea.

Barney gave Nolan a nice, hefty sum, for services rendered. He also paid me a fee, and a rather generous one. I don't like to harp on it, or to belabor the point; but after all, I was the one who saved his neck. He was grateful, I've got to give him credit for that. But afterwards, I kind of lost sight of him. I honestly don't know what became of him. I think he moved out of the area. I'm pretty sure he went to L.A., looking for the big break. What happened then, I'm not sure. He's certainly not a famous movie or television star. That much is obvious. Maybe he did another dog food commercial. I wouldn't know.

There's one loose end in this case; and I don't think it'll ever be cleared up. That's the matter of Aunt Martha. Was there anything to Blanche's accusations? Did somebody poison Aunt Martha? Could this possibly be true?

At the time, we thought she was accusing Barney. That's what Susan understood. But of course, that was a ridiculous idea. I'm pretty sure she wasn't thinking of Barney at all. It was Ross Tanager she had in mind. But still, was there anything to it? Did he really do something to Aunt Martha? If so, why? What possible motive could he have? None at all for himself. But Blanche.... Maybe Blanche wanted to get rid of Aunt Martha, and she figured, he's a doctor, he'll know how to do it. Barney stood to get quite a bit of money from Aunt Martha. And then she would get the money from Barney. And ultimately, it might possibly line the pockets of Dr. Ross Tanager.

Or maybe not. It seemed far-fetched to me. Maybe this was all sheer fantasy. It's possible Aunt Martha simply died a natural death. It's even probable. Maybe they just talked about killing her; maybe it was just a kind of script, something that they never carried out. Anyway, Blanche is dead, and Ross Tanager is on his way to prison, if he isn't there already. And nobody has raised the subject of Aunt Martha; and no doubt they never will.

I must say, I'm rather proud of myself. Proud of what I did. Proud of saving Barney Bell from the tattooed guys in prison. Proud of solving the case, like a real detective, or like a detective in books, Hercule Poirot or Perry Mason. Maybe more like Perry Mason. After all, he was a lawyer like me.

So.... This story had a happy ending. The bad guy got caught, the good guy got out of his cell, still in one piece. Nobody raped Barney, or sliced him to pieces like a sausage with a home-made knife. He got out, none the worse for wear, and went back to his normal life. Barney left the jail, and Ross Tanager replaced him.

And I too went back to my normal life, my clients, my family, my work. Back to my routine. Writing wills, helping guys who own small businesses, that kind of thing. I come home in the evening. Celia tells me the events of the day. I talk to the girls. Sometimes they listen. My mother-in-law calls long-distance and talks about her arthritis. I call my sister Harriet—the one in Des Moines—more often than before. There are problems with the roof, the plumbing, the car. It's the usual humdrum life.

Humdrum is not what people aspire to. But it's better than most of the alternatives.

## About the author

**Lawrence Friedman** is a professor of law at Stanford University. He teaches courses in American legal history and law and society. He is the author of *A History of American Law*, *Crime and Punishment in American History*, and *Total Justice*, among other works. He recently published *Dead Hands: A Social History of Wills, Trusts, and Inheritances*, a subject which is the backbone of Frank May's (fictional) practice.

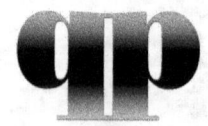

Visit us at *qpbooks.com*.

www.ingramcontent.com/pod-product-compliance
Lightning Source LLC
Chambersburg PA
CBHW071151260626
47162CB00003B/1000